The War Violin

A World War II Novel

Rae Weiser

La La Land Press

Please be advised:

This story contains war-related themes, including violence and trauma, as well as racism and racial slurs that could trigger certain audiences.

Bibliography

Charles Dickens, A Tale of Two Cities, (1859) London: Chapman & Hall (pp. 19 – 22) Public domain reprint of lines from first chapter of this novel.

Desert Sun Newspaper article (pp. 237)

For book club or speaking engagement author visits in person or virtual, please contact information@lalalandpress.com

To receive special offers, bonus content, and information on new releases and other great reads, visit us online at www.lalalandpress.com

Published by La La Land Press
www.lalalandpress.com

Cataloging-in-Publication Data is on file with the Library of Congress.

ISBN 979-8-218-41472-6

For all the brave ones...

In August of 1944, 100 WWII Italian Prisoners of War who had sworn allegiance to the Allies and joined the Italian Service Unit (ISU), were brought to Palm Springs, California, to work at Torney General military hospital to help with a labor shortage due to the war.

Local women volunteered at the military hospital as Gray Ladies which was an American Red Cross program. These women helped the injured soldiers by reading to them, writing letters back home for them and lifting their spirits with companionship.

Part One

Epoch

Chapter One

The convoy of army-green vehicles rolled across the Coachella Valley floor like a caterpillar, flexing together as the road curved.

The invasion of foreigners infiltrating Palm Springs went unnoticed by most villagers even though the blazing August sun spotlighted their approach. The mission was the delivery of one hundred Italian prisoners of war to Torney General Hospital. The men, dressed in light blue jumpsuits with a bold white PW on their back, sat inside the army transports waiting out the hot drive to their next temporary American home. Captured in the North African Campaign, the Italian Service Unit 1967th had initially been lodged at the Camp Haan Prisoner of War Camp a couple of hours away near a city called Riverside.

"Give me those," Frances said to Mary, reaching for the binoculars.

"No." Mary pulled them back. "I long to see their handsome faces ever so." She affected a Scarlett O'Hara drawl and fanned her face, tilting her head back, her Lucky Strike floating on the corner of her mouth as she talked like a boat floating on waves, her right eye squinting like a pirate from the smoke passing up.

Frances and Mary watched the trucks approach from seventy feet up, smoking Lucky Strikes inside a Spanish Revival bell tower, leaning over the railing like laundry on a clothing line, wilted with sweat from the steamy-hot day. Once the landmark for the El Mirador Resort, a getaway for Hollywood elite bordered by the rugged Mount San Jacinto and desert landscape, it now was home to Torney General Hospital. The US Army purchased the financially strapped hotel in 1942, acquiring the main building, an Olympic-sized swimming pool and Palm Springs' first golf course, all sitting on 139 acres. Now the place was a 1600 bed military hospital for wounded soldiers from the Pacific Theater, especially those suffering from rheumatic fever. The dry, hot climate accelerated recuperation. It was an expansive military city of temporary tents.

Frances laughed, as she always did when Mary was around, because she was so overt and over-the-top and Frances was neither. "Handsome?" she said. "They could have hooks for teeth, buggy eyes and fins for ears." Frances made her eyes big, put her hands up beside her face to mimic fins moving forward and back.

"That's what I expect, tall, dark and handsome men coming to my rescue." Mary handed the binoculars over.

"My father says having them here is offensive. Complained at dinner last night that he didn't think it was right that they're getting paid eighty cents a day for work people here should get. Been going on for weeks about it." She said it much nicer than her father had. *Goddamn guinea traitors comin' here. Slap in the face of every soldier at Torney having those dagoes around.* She kept his comments to herself. Airing dirty laundry outside her house just wasn't done. It could ruin her parent's reputation in town.

Mary said, "Italy's not the enemy anymore."

"So, they say. He hasn't forgiven them."

"Well, I might marry one."

"You going husband hunting in the POWs?"

"Yep. Looking for a husband. Someone who can take me away from this desert. One of these POWs might take me back to Italy." Mary went on, "I don't have a handsome guy coming back from the war I'm betrothed to. I'm on the market. I'm available and I think I might be good in bed?"

Frances giggled, "In bed!"

"Don't know yet," Mary answered, "but I'm hoping I am."

"They do say Italian's are romantic."

"I'm not waiting for a handsome soldier to come back to me like your Nicholas."

"And he will come back." Frances added. This was something she said every time someone brought up Nicholas, triggering the spinning wheel of options to set off in her head.

Frances tried not to think of the possibility that Nicholas wouldn't come back or if he did, that he'd come back with injuries like the men she cared for at the hospital. Her mind kept the possibilities only to perfect scenarios. He would return. He'd be fine. He'd marry her, and buy her a house. Father her children. She'd bring him a cocktail when he returned home from work as her mother did for her father. The plan for her life that she'd charted in her diary would happen, she decided. Hoped.

"But one night with one of them. I wouldn't say no."

"Frances!"

"What? I'm not saying lose my virginity, but I nearly gave that to Nicholas the night before he deployed, but there's a lot I could still do —before locking it all down forever." She took her hand and gestured to her body.

"You'd never, though." Mary added.

"No. Never." Frances answered. *I would,* she thought.

Frances leaned over the hot railing. She looked across the valley at the convoy approaching and glanced back at Mont San Jacinto to the west. The majestic mountain range she never tired of seeing as it was picture perfect, like God created it to be worshiped as art. She wiped her forehead with a handkerchief pulled from the pocket of her uniform and lifted the seersucker fabric of her dress up and down to get air between it and her skin. She could feel drops of sweat rolling across her body under the fabric like little balls of rain beneath her uniform. The material was lightweight, luckily, but in the desert heat, still too much clothing. She raised her hair and wiped the back of her neck and around her collarbone.

"Damn hot today."

Mary looked up, pulling her eyes away from the binoculars, at the enormous bell mounted above. "That bell falls, we're doomed."

"You know they brought that bell over from Italy."

"How appropriate."

"Today especially."

"They're getting close."

"Enemy's closing in."

"Ready your weapon." Mary answered sarcastically.

Frances put out her cigarette on the cement, then wiped the ash clean with the bottom of her sandal and put the cigarette butt in her pocket.

The trucks turned onto Indian Canyon Drive. Other workers from the hospital came out to stare at the POWs. A military plane flew overhead toward the Army airfield, as they did all day, every day, delivering supplies and equipment. Bringing in wounded men. The place was always this active, so even though the trucks were moving near, it felt like a normal day at Torney. Except this time the hustling involved captured men from another country, young Italians who now supported the allies.

"I'm nervous." Frances bit her bottom lip, a behavior she did when she was stressed.

"Me too." Mary said, but she didn't seem scared.

"Never had any Italians in Palm Springs before—that weren't American, I mean."

"Definitely no war prisoners."

"World's gone crazy and gettin' crazier still."

Palm Springs was just another small town before the war.

Sparsely populated, had a quaint story. Then the war happened, changing all that. End of an era. Now Frances read novels to men from states she'd never been to, waited for her fiancé to return from another country she'd only heard about.

Mary lowered the binoculars. The trucks were so close they weren't needed. They rolled by on the road below the tower like a military parade. The chatter of the men inside could be heard just slightly above the engines, the sound of tires rolling over the road, the exhaust leaving a trail of dirty combusted air. The prisoners could be seen through the open canopy in the rear as they moved on to a farther edge of the hospital grounds known as the training center barracks. Some of the prisoners looked up at the girls which made Frances feel awkward, as if they knew she was there to watch them and it made her feel bad about herself. One, two, three, four, five, six, seven, eight, trucks loaded with men, following the lead and rear jeeps that secured the front and rear of the convoy, the soldiers holding their weapons in the passenger seat as if they expected an attack to happen, as if Mussolini and his men were hiding behind the desert cactus ready to engage.

"Never thought these foreigners would be here." Mary fanned her face, as if she could faint. "Handsome."

"They looked scared."

"They did."

"Must be weird being here. Can you imagine being taken like that, away from everything you know? Suddenly in another country?"

Mary looked through the binoculars. "They stopped at the training center. You ever been on that side of the grounds?" She handed them to Frances.

"No. Never. It's always been vacant since I started here."

"Makes sense that's where they'd put them. Easy to hide 'em."

Frances looked, adjusting the focus. "Not getting out. Must be hot in there," she mumbled as she waited for the POWs to be let out of the trucks. American soldiers stood guard, some went inside the barracks, some circled the trucks, going in and out of the building preparing for the movement of the men.

Frances handed the binoculars to Mary. "*Real* hot. Why can't they get out if they're not dangerous?"

"Because they are. It's a lie. That's what my dad says."

"Frances, your dad! He's not always right."

"*We* know that, but he doesn't. My father's *never* been wrong about anything," she added sarcastically.

"People don't like know-it-alls," Mary added, with a deserved biased tone. He'd blamed her for the night she and Frances got drunk in high school and stayed out till four a.m.

"Whole town loves my dad, though."

"Because he owns the paper. They're afraid he'll write something bad about them."

A military jeep pulled up in front of the hospital which being a hotel before, had an oval shaped driveway with an awning, the kind of drive-up that gave an impression. An officer stepped out and went inside the hospital. These jeeps were used all around the facility, going from one end of the grounds to the other and were occasionally used to get to the nearby military airstrip.

"Come on," Mary grabbed Frances' arm.

"Where are we going?" she asked as she followed her rushing down the staircase, their closed-toe sandals clopping on the wood, making them sound like mini-Clydesdales.

"What the heck?"

"Trust me..." Mary pulled her so quickly that Frances slipped. "Oh, geez!" Mary said as she helped her up, then pulled her across the plaza to the Jeep.

"Get in," Mary said as she hopped in the driver's seat and turned on the engine.

Stunned, Frances froze in place. "We're gonna get in trouble," Frances whispered, not to alarm the military personnel returning inside the hospital after watching the parade of POW carrying transports drive by.

"When has that stopped me? Now get in!" Mary barked back in a stern whisper.

Frances ran around to the other side and hopped in the passenger seat, barely getting her butt sat or her feet up off the ground before Mary took off, spinning a fast U-turn and heading out on the road the convoy traveled to the barracks. Mary worked the clutch and stick shift like a trucker who'd been driving for decades. The wind whipped their hair around, smacking into their faces.

"We're gonna get in so much trouble!" Frances screamed.

"We can make up a good reason."

"For stealing an officer's Jeep?"

"Borrowing. It's not his. Belongs to the Army. We'll bring it back."

"Gotta come up with something other than chasing after hot Italian guys."

"Yeah!" Mary laughed.

"They're gonna see us," Frances warned as they approached the end of the road, not far from the barracks.

Mary assessed the area, eyes darting here and there fast, making a split-second decision to turn the jeep off the road.

"Mary! What the hell!" Frances said as she was whipped to the side and almost fell out of the jeep.

Mary laughed. "Hang on," she screamed as she hit a ditch, which got them flying up off their seats, landing just after the ditch to face a large rock that Mary had to veer the opposite direction to miss. She spun the jeep back around towards a line of oleander bushes that were growing wild in the field beside the barracks. Bushy and tall, they were the perfect coverage.

Mary hopped out of the jeep, engine still running.

"Mar... " Frances said loudly again.

"Be quiet!" Mary cut her off with a stern whisper, then gestured for her to follow.

The girls crouched low between two oleander bushes to see the convoy up close, only a few hundred feet away.

Mary looked inside the binoculars she'd put around her neck when she started tugging Frances' arm.

"They're just sitting' in there. Baking."

Frances looked the at the American soldiers discussing something off to the side.

"Why don't they get them out already?"

"Not a bad looking one in the mix," Mary said as she scanned the scene through the binoculars.

"Give me the binoculars."

"They're coming out."

Frances pulled the binoculars from Mary's hands and looked through the lenses at the men as they jumped down from the trucks wearing their blue jumpsuits. "PW, like a scarlet letter," she commented, "and young."

"Our age, I'd imagine, twenty, twenty-one, 'round there."

"They're lining 'em up like cattle."

"Give me those," Mary took the binoculars back from Frances. "Oh, I'm gonna faint. I've just fell in love ten times."

"Can't fall in love with the enemy."

"*Were* the enemy! Were."

"Only because Italy's afraid of the Germans and since they're prisoners, they say they like America now to get good treatment. Any one of them would take out Nicholas if they met on the battlefield."

Frances looked again. The men were starting to move into the barracks. She noticed their thick dark hair and strong facial features that were so different from Nicholas who was blonde, fair skinned, thin features—slender nose, narrow lips, light eyes. These men looked sturdy. Nicholas, even though a Marine, had a sort of feathery feel to him, as if he could blow away in a strong wind.

"Seeing them makes me miss Nicholas. You think he's fine? Do you think he'll come through?" She gave the binoculars back to Mary, "I can't watch this. It's making me sad."

"Frances don't get all sour. Nick'll be fine. He'll come back good."

"Hope so."

"We should go back. We're gonna get in trouble for stealing, I mean borrowing the jeep."

Frances took the binoculars once again and got one last look. The trucks were empty and the POWs had disappeared inside, while the American soldiers milled about, lighting cigarettes, some signing paperwork for the handoff from Camp Haan to Torney General. "Hidden away. Gone like ghosts."

"Wonder if we'll ever see 'em again?"

"Might. My dad said they're doing ground's keep. You might run into one when they're working outside."

"I heard they're doin' laundry."

"That too and kitchen work. Whatever labor is needed, I guess," Frances wiped her neck with her handkerchief then looked in the binoculars again. "I like being a spy. Could be a war spy," she added which sent them into a laugh.

"Whose there!" A soldier yelled, on alert for any local angry over the POWs coming there wanting to try something. It was reported in the Sun Times that the Army wouldn't put up with protestors or problems.

Mary looked in the binoculars. "Damn it! They're coming over here!"

Frances looked. Two Army men with their guns drawn, elbows up, approached quickly across the field, knees bent as their legs moved quickly over the terrain, focused.

"Oh crap!" Frances said to Mary and they both ran to the jeep. "We're in trouble now!"

"Whose there? Come out?" The soldiers yelled as they approached.

Mary looked at Frances. "Go!"

They tore off to the Jeep. Mary stumbled. Frances grabbed her arm and pulled her up.

"I'm driving." Frances yelled.

"I'm driving." Mary answered.

"You're an awful driver!"

"Am not!"

The girls both fought to get into the driver's seat. Frances pushed Mary aside. "Out of my way."

Mary folded and got in the passenger side. "They better not shoot at us!"

"Hold on!"

Frances hit the clutch and brake, shifted into reverse, slammed on the gas and backed up fast. The back tires dug in deep, spitting up rocks from the desert gravel and a plume of dusk covered the jeep as they pushed back twenty feet into it. Frances slammed on the breaks, put the jeep in first gear and slammed her foot on the pedal, fishtailing the back end of the vehicle, then they pushed towards the paved road, kicking up dust with the tires behind them.

"They think we're some nut trying to do something?" Mary kept looking back to see if they were being chased. "No one's coming," she reported.

Frances looked in the rear-view mirror. "Yet," she shouted over the engine and the chaotic wind. "But we stole this jeep."

"Borrowed!" Mary answered.

"Stole." Frances yelled back.

"Might not notice if it's back before he returns. Park in the same spot and we're all clear!"

They came up to another car on the road. Frances veered to the left, passing the sedan.

Frances pressed down harder on the gas. "Come on, baby. Come on!" She spoke to the vehicle as she shifted to second, third and fourth. Their speed kicked up to 60 miles per hour.

"You trying to dump me?" Mary yelled as she grabbed hold of the dashboard so she didn't fall out.

"Maybe. This is all your fault!"

"Just go faster," Mary added. "We'll get away with it. Faster!" Mary hollered as she stood up, her face higher than the windshield, getting a view of the front of the hospital.

"Can you see anything? Anyone there....?"

"It's clear so far," Mary confirmed.

"It won't go any faster! Gas pedal's all the way down!"

The jeep hit a rock on the pavement. The vehicle swerved. Mary sat back down and braced herself. Frances got the jeep steady after side-to-side swerving that crossed both lanes and neared flipping over.

"That was scary." Frances yelled.

Mary stood up again to get a view of the hospital. "Just drive. I can see its clear. He's not out there looking for his car..." Mary looked behind them, "and the Army's not following behind us."

Frances downshifted to slow down, making the corner turn into the circular driveway in front of the hospital, and skidded to a stop in the same spot they hijacked it from, cutting the engine and both slipping out of the vehicle nearly at the same time.

The lobby doors opened and the officer came out of the hospital, passing them as they walked away from it.

"Ladies," he greeted them as he passed, looking curious as to what was so funny when their reaction was busting up.

"Officer," they replied as they rushed to a bench under the building awning beside the El Mirador bell tower.

"You are the worst friend." Frances tells her.

"I'm the best friend you'll ever have. I keep you from getting bored to death in this desert."

"You're so crazy."

"I know."

"You think they'd of captured us and turned us in?"

"No, they'd just let us go. A couple of bored desert girls checking out the new guys in town. It's not like we're a crazy guy wanting revenge by doing something crazy."

"Probably," Frances added.

"That was crazy."

"We'd better get back."

"We're not on the clock. They don't pay us, Frances, we're Gray

Ladies. Free labor for the Red Cross. We're not even getting eighty cents a day like those POWs."

"But I left Oklahoma in the sun and he never asks anyone for help to move him," she said, knowing she didn't want anyone to move him. "He's my special patient. I get jealous if I see him with other Gray Ladies."

"Because Oklahoma's in love with you."

"I know." Frances answered and this wasn't in any egotistical way. All the men had some form of crush on the women who cared for them as it was an intimate relationship that blurred lines. War, with its displacement and disruption and uncertainty did that to everyone's relationships, even those not in the service.

Frances wiped the back of her neck with a white handkerchief and accidentally dropped it. It landed on top of a cactus next to the bench.

"You surrender? To a cactus?" Mary deadpanned.

"Why not?" Frances picked up her handkerchief from the cactus arm, careful not to get pricked. "I feel like an old lady already and I'm only twenty. Should just surrender already."

"It's the heat."

"And stress."

"The war."

"Guess." Frances stood tall and raised her arms over her head and stretched again." This heat. August is just dreadful."

"And it's only ten a.m."

"Unbearable," Mary added, then gave a look like a cat that just caught a mouse. "I wasn't gonna show you because I know you'll yell at me."

"What now?"

"You promise not to yell at me?"

"No. I don't."

Mary opened her bag and flashed the inside quickly. "My dad got another girly magazine and I'm sneaking it to my guys."

Frances could see the magazine cover quickly: *Beauty Parade* with a buxom lady in her underwear and shirt, leaning over to show her long legs, looking back with a surprised expression on her face. Frances' eyes widened, "Let me see?"

Mary pulled the magazine out from her bag. "Don't let anyone see it," Mary scolded.

Some military personnel walked by. Frances covered the magazine with her bag. After they passed, Frances flipped through. Mesmerized. Jealous. Mortified.

"Oh, they're huge," Frances said as she stopped flipping, landing on one woman with large breasts. She looked down at her own, in comparison.

"Her back must hurt," Mary added.

"Gotta get back to Oklahoma." Frances stood up as Mary placed the magazine in her bag and they headed towards the lobby doors of the main building. "You should put it back."

"He'll think my mom found it again and threw it away."

"What if Edith finds out you brought it in? She'll kick you out of the Gray Ladies."

"She won't. My guys would never give me up."

"I'm the library liaison and I know nothing. Can you imagine if my mother finds out that I knew smut magazines were being smuggled into Torney?

"You know nothing."

"I know *nothing*!" Frances warned.

Chapter Two

The women headed into the lobby of the once famous hotel where notorious people like Einstein, Chaplin, and Pickford used to come to relax. Inside now, it was a makeshift Army hospital, created out of the bones of the beautiful building it had once been. Tall ceilings, expensive wallpaper, high-end light fixtures and parquet wood floors framed the Army hospital, now filled with medical personnel and equipment lining the halls between the rooms filled with injured or sick soldiers. The contents of sheets and blankets and equipment made the inside of the majestic frame not so good looking anymore. Ugly now with medical waste in trashcans, gauze no longer white, dirty linens taken off a patient's bed in bins to be taken to the laundry, the wood floors shiny wax finish scratched and worn away. A hospital now, the hotel was used for a system of helping sick and wounded soldiers, and in the process things were dirtied, then had to be cleaned, over and over. The cycle repeated to save a life, repair a body part, to fix the wrongs of war in its walls now serving importance over façade, meaning over frivolity, becoming beautiful ugliness.

"So long," Mary said. She turned down a different hall.

"So long, rebel. I know *nothing...*" Frances called out as she headed to a door that led to the garden.

"NOTHING," Mary yelled as she went in another direction.

Frances headed out to the garden where she left Oklahoma. She always put him near other guys, but he was quiet and didn't talk much to anyone except her. He liked reading and he liked her reading to him, that was his favorite pastime as he waited to get better so he could go home. She found him exactly where she'd left him, which caused her to give him a disappointed look and say:

"You're beginning to turn red."

"Like a cherry," Oklahoma said in his Midwest drawl. His real name was Henry Smith, but he wouldn't let her call him by his name.

"I told you to ask someone to get you out of the sun after twenty minutes if I wasn't back."

"But I knew you'd come back."

Oklahoma was in a wheelchair, his transport now, too weak to move himself. Shrapnel in his leg, which turned into an infection that caused doctors to amputate it to save his life. Doctors told him he was lucky and quite the fighter and since he was a sweet farming kid from Oklahoma, all he said back was thank you. He never complained. He didn't have emotional fits of sorrow over losing the leg, which he'd earned the right to do. Instead, he was gracious and appreciative that he didn't lose his life and Frances could never understand how he kept it up. She knew she'd never be able to bravely handle something that grave. Maybe what the guys saw overseas was so bad losing a leg didn't compare.

"Catch sight of 'em?"

"Fast."

"Y'ain't worried are ya?"

"No." She dismissed like *How dare he?!* but what she really felt was *How dare he be so right?* "Really, Oklahoma, too much sun for you. Inside?" she pleaded in a superior, yet affectionate way.

"Nah, staying out. Sick o' those walls."

"You're difficult."

"Yes, ma'am."

Reluctant, she moved him under the shade of a cluster of desert willow trees. It was not her favorite spot as leaves tended to float down into her hair and get stuck in her curls. She'd find them when she washed her hair. This was a spot used often when the midday sun hit. It gave a good amount of shade but disappeared within hours. This small window of protection from the elements was appreciated, however, as the sun was always angry in mid-August.

Frances sat down in one of the lounge chairs already under the tree next to him.

"Gimme the book."

He handed her the book sitting on his lap. Frances opened it where the leaf was they'd been using as a bookmark.

"Don't wanna read anymore today." Oklahoma said.

Frances closed the book. "What should we talk about?" She'd been trained to keep conversations with soldiers' light, always. Keeping their spirits up was the main goal.

"Got a smoke?"

Frances pulled a pack out of her apron and handed him one and a light.

If she didn't have a smoke, someone else nearby had a smoke, was smoking a smoke, or thinking about the smoke they just finished. The outdoors of the hospital was used more for smoking than conversation or reading. A nice dose of fresh air helped the men. Watching a bird, or the steel birds that flew overhead, or the surrounding scenery, the picturesque desert scene where the only battle happening was the one in their mind.

"Would I be your favorite Gray Lady without them?"

"You still would," he said in his mid-western drawl as he lit the cigarette. "In the field, didn't have to ask for sticks. C-Rats had 'em."

"C-Rats?"

"C-Rations. Cigs, canned meat, biscuits, fruit bar, coffee. Oh and gum. Gotta 'get gum for passing time. Can get boring when you dug in for weeks. Kind'a like here"

"Ah, think that means you want me to find 'ya some gum," Frances let out with a laugh.

Another cargo plane flew over towards the landing strip. "They keep flying 'em in. More messed up soldiers."

"War's not over. Most flights are for supplies I'm told." Frances added. They both fell silent. "You seem down? I think we should read. Take your mind off your worries." Francis picked up the book and opened the paperback wide, the spine cracked from use.

"Let's start from the start," said Oklahoma.

"But we're on page 12."

"Wasn't listenin'." He laughed.

"Will you be listening *this* time?"

Oklahoma took a drag and shifted in his wheelchair. "Pain's worse today. Hard to listen."

"Want me to fetch a nurse?"

"Nah. Here, give me that." He gestured for the book. She handed it to him. "Maybe doing the reading will occupy my mind so I don't feel it. I'm gonna start from the start. Now pay attention."

Frances smiled. "Mr. Oklahoma, I'm not the one who had a hard time listening." He smiled. She'd succeeded in bringing up his spirits and that made her happy. It's what she did best at Torney and second best was organizing the reading library. "All right, wise guy. Go on."

He looked down at the page. "*It was the best of times, it was the worst of times, it was the age of wisdom, it was the age of foolishness, it was the epotch of belief, it was the epotch of incredulity.*" He looked up.

"Epoch," she corrected.

"Weird word." He said it twice, pronouncing a short and long vowel. "Eh-pock. Eepock. Which way you think is right?"

"First, I think."

"What does it mean?"

She considered, "I... I don't know."

"Ah. Me neither."

"Has to do with time."

She got up.

"I'll have to get to the dictionary and report back. Go on." She gestured to the book and him.

"*It was the season of light. It was the season of darkness.*" He put the book down. "I 'preciate your time, Miss Pretty Frances. You make my days here so much better."

"Just Frances, Henry."

"Oklahoma." He corrected her. "Don't wanna hear you calling me by my name or I'll get too close to ya and I might just fall in love with ya, if I haven't already."

"Oklahoma." She said sweetly and placed a hand on his arm.

He handed her the book. "Your voice sounds prettier than mine."

She took the book, opened it.

"Second thought, ya got any *Freddy the Pig* books in that library you're in charge of?"

"No. You want to read *Freddy the Pig?* Those are kid's books."

"He's funny. I like that pig. My momma got me a Freddy the Pig book and read it to me all the time when I was little. Charles Dickens, he's a literary big shot, ya know, but he's serious. I don't wanna read serious stories with words I don't know. Better to laugh, I'm thinkin'."

"I'll go to the library then and I'll have a *Freddy the Pig* book tomorrow. And if they don't have the one, I'll run to Oklahoma and find your mom and get your childhood copy. How's that sound?"

"Fair 'nough."

"Then it's a plan," she added, just to be sweet.

"Yep. You know, I think I *will* go in. Hotter than a house on fire." His voice sounded weak.

"Good. You're getting your senses back." Frances said and rolled him out of the grass and onto the sidewalk that led them out of the garden toward the main building.

"Gotta give blood anyway today," she said. "Best to get it over with sooner than later."

"Awful."

"Last time I fainted."

Oklahoma laughed. "Did not."

"I did. They unhooked me, I stood up and bam, right back down again. It wouldn't have been so bad if I hadn't fallen so that my dress uniform was half over my head." She was giggling and got him to giggle too so she didn't care if she was telling him something embarrassing.

"Now that's the Oklahoma I know. Don't you stop smiling or I'll have to keep telling you ridiculous stories about myself and get completely embarrassed."

"Can ya skip it?"

"Can't. Looks bad, being a Gray Lady with the Red Cross and not giving blood. Miss Nancy just got written up in the *Desert Sun*. She's given 14 pints in the last year. People would think I don't care about the boys in service."

"Figure so. Guess you better."

She pushed his wheelchair, so they turned left down a long hall and halfway down, left again into his room where there were two beds, one unused. "No roommate yet?"

"Not this week so far."

His roommate, who was from Montana, got to go home a few days before. She knew it made Oklahoma jealous.

"For the best." She pushed his wheelchair up to his bed and lowered the side rail. "No one here to bug you." He shifted in the chair, preparing to raise himself up and over onto the bed, but winced. "Let me help… "

"No," he said with a bit of a sharp tongue. "I'm sorry."

"No need to apologize. You're in a lot of pain."

"It's that I don't want help getting' in and outta bed. I can do this at least…." He said, then stopped, as his voice cracked a tiny bit and that wasn't what he wanted.

Frances usually stepped away when the patients got emotional, but this time she just turned around and cleaned up a side table that had a tissue on it that needed to be thrown away. When she turned back around, Oklahoma was getting into his bed, on his own, as he wanted.

"Any particular Freddy the Pig?"

"Don't know what they got. There's a bunch of 'em."

"I'll make sure whatever they got I'll get for you." She said this as she headed out the door.

"Don't be a chicken, Miss Frances."

"I won't," she said and laughed.

"Be brave, Miss Frances. Above all else, be brave."

This struck her oddly. "I'm just giving blood, not fighting the axis of evil."

Frances left his room and headed to the donation center shaking her head, upset.

"That was a stupid thing to say. Not fighting the axis of evil. What is wrong with me?" she whispered to herself. *The country is fighting the axis of evil and American men are dying. So insensitive for me to say.*

Frances walked out of the main hospital building, her hands shaking. *You gotta donate blood,* she reminded herself, as the debate started in her brain, her mind trying to find a way out of having a needle puncture her skin and hang out in her vein for a good 15 minutes. Torture and terrifying was how she described it.

The blood donation tent was nearly a quarter mile distant and as she walked there, she thought about the POWs who were not too far away. This made her heart pound. They were hidden away. She'd probably never see them again and as soon as the war ended, they'd be sent back. But that day they were nearby and this excited her.

Daydreaming about them was harmless fun, she reminded herself. Anything that helped get through the day and helped to cope with the hellish war. The wounded men she'd been reading to and spending time with were so traumatized, blank stares behind the laughter—if they even laughed. They knew what life was like outside the desert valley where she'd spent every one of her waking days.

They knew of the war in ways she couldn't imagine or ever experience and she'd come to understand she didn't want to.

Frances entered the blood drive tent and was met with Carla's smiling face, a Red Cross nurse she'd never seen outside the blood donation tent.

"There she is," Carla said as she lifted a clip board with a consent form. "Making you lay down for 20 minutes after you give."

Frances opened her mouth to protest as she took the clip board and signed.

"Ah, no negotiation," Carla interrupted, "and the banana and orange juice are mandatory."

"Jeez. Like I joined the military."

Frances placed the clipboard on the desk and took the banana and juice and followed Carla to a cot where she took her shoes off and lay back.

"Go fast."

Carla had already pushed Frances' sleeve up and wiped clean a spot with a rubbing alcohol cotton pad.

"Look away."

"I'm already looking away."

"One, two, three."

Frances winced as the needle was inserted.

"Never gonna like that."

"This ain't nothing compared to having kids."

"Why do you always say that to me?"

"Because this ain't nothing compared to having kids."

Frances giggled.

"And it makes you smile. Less tension is better for blood flow."

Carla taped the needle and tube down on her arm and adjusted the blood bag as red flowed into it from Frances body.

"You remember Angela? Used to volunteer here?"

"Yes."

"Whole family got put in Manzanar."

Frances turned to Carla, concerned.

"She had a kid, right?"

"Yeah. Daughter. Only four."

"Maybe she won't remember it when she's older."

"Everyone here liked her, now talk about her like she was a spy."

"Why?" said Frances.

"Because she's a Jap. 'Cause of Pearl Harbor."

"She's an American. Lived in Palms Springs for decades."

"Don't matter to anyone anymore. World's shifty."

"It's awful."

"It's how it is."

Carla sat down next to the cot, picked up a Red Cross pamphlet to read as a distraction, the idea of an internment camp in America had a cloud of sadness that swooped in when spoken about.

"Not too much longer," said Carla, nodding to the blood bag.

Not soon enough, thought Frances, still thinking about Manzanar.

Her father had run many articles in his newspaper about that camp and others in the US and often talked with dinner guests about the merits of the camps. Gotta be careful with the Japs, he'd said more times than she could count after Pearl Harbor, but he wasn't the only one. This sentiment seemed felt by everyone she knew. And now they thought Angela was a spy? World had gone off a cliff, thinking that. Sweetest lady.

Frances bit her bottom lip. "Almost done?"

"Almost."

"Feeling claustrophobic being hooked up to this tube."

"Alright." Carla stood, took the tape off the tube, pulled the needle out of her arm and bandaged the spot.

"Finally." She went to sit up. Carla pushed her shoulder back down.

"Stay down and take a bite of that banana." Carla cleaned up, labeling and placing the donated blood in a cooler while Frances peeled her banana and took a bite. "You survived."

"Can I sit up? I ate the banana."

"Slowly. Then stay there for a moment. Don't stand up yet. Drink your juice."

"You see the POWs come in?"

"Can't stand that they're here. Ain't right."

Frances stood. She didn't want to stay and hear it from Carla. She complained endlessly and was known for it, so much so that people avoided her. "Feel fine," she told Carla, not wanting to be locked into her talking on and on about the POWs. "See ya next month."

Frances rubbed her arm where the needle went in as she walked back to the main hospital building the same way she came, stopping once to steady herself as the blood donation had made her faint, but recovered quickly, passing military personnel, nurses, doctors. The grounds were bustling with people everywhere doing this or that, a temporary city that would all disappear—poof—like magic – when the war ended just like it appeared when the military took over the hotel.

She entered a room just off the main lobby. A large and full bookcase lined the back wall. Here was the library she oversaw for Torney. Once a reading room for guests who visited the hotel, now a reading room for the injured men from the Pacific Theater. She scanned for a book, landing on a large Merriam-Webster dictionary. She held the heavy hardcover in her left hand and flipped pages with her right, starting with the E section, then scanned the pages, flipped to EP, then ran her finger down the words, finally stopping...

Epoch:

1 a: an event or a time marked by an event that begins a new period or development.

b: a memorable event or date

Chapter Three

As she drove out of the Vista Las Palmas Estates, their wealthy neighborhood where elite conclaves happen in the form of dinner parties hosted by women pushing to capture local fame, she thought about Nicholas as she drove past his house. He proposed the night before he left in the front yard and she said yes because he was leaving. She loved him. Or thought she loved him—she wasn't sure exactly. He was so sweet though, almost too sweet some days because it made her feel like the mean one in the relationship. He was a marine stationed somewhere in the Solomon Islands. She hadn't gotten a letter from him in over two months and in the last one it seemed he was understandably tired of the war. She wrote back that she was waiting for him and it wouldn't be long until they could be together. All the usual sayings to cheer him up. She included a picture of them taken a few days before he left in the village, one of their last nights out at the movies. That night she could tell he was scared, but he acted brave about leaving to Marine boot camp and she didn't ask him about being scared because... why waste time together?

When she made it to the hospital, she put the books in the return book box back on the shelfs, checking for defects which would certainly get her a side eye look from Phyllis, the librarian at the town library, when she returned them. She organized her books by last name of the author in alphabetical order. She'd debated the best way to organize the library, but this was how Phyllis suggested she go about it versus the book title. She checked the books in on a ledger sheet attached to a clipboard kept on the main shelf above the M section. The return book basket was empty now.

It was a quiet day at Torney—not exactly silent, just less loud than normal. Frances breathed in deep, paused for a moment. She was having a hard day, the kind that felt like she was carrying some undefined sorrow, but needed to shake it off before she visited Oklahoma. She didn't want to be all sour when she walked in his room. She was having relationship issues. Odd, since her relationship was a memory from over two years ago. She and Nicholas had now spent more time apart as a couple than they had together.

She gathered a smile onto her face and headed out down the main corridor, becoming one of many women who filled the halls in a uniform, bustling about. Frances liked this part of working at Torney. Up and down the halls with other people tasked with working for the war effort as she made her way to Room 54.

"Oklahoma, how 'ya doing today?" Frances said loudly and lively as she stepped into his room to which Oklahoma gestured for her to speak softer and pointed to the man behind the drape, but she didn't realize what he was trying to get her to understand.. "Did you read anymore of *Freddy the Detective?*"

On his side table sat a copy of the book his mother read to him when he was only in single digit ages. Frances got the one copy from the library after waiting weeks for it to be returned. It was lime green and had the most fun looking pig on the cover, standing upright on his two back legs, wearing a plaid red cape and a tweed flat cap, and holding a magnifying glass.

"Roommate. Sleeping." He said softly as he gestured for her to quiet down by placing his index finger in front of his lips.

This was new. She thought it might be good for him. "You have someone to talk to." She whispered as she pushed his wheelchair to the edge of his bed and locked the wheels. "This is good."

"Whisper, Miss Frances," he said as he raised up and got in his wheelchair. She didn't offer to help because she knew he didn't it and even if he needed help, he wouldn't accept it from her. Oklahoma was stubborn. Frances often thought: *If only his body were as strong as his pride*—but it wasn't. He'd been repeatedly fighting to maintain weight and was becoming weaker with each passing day. This worried her. Worried him too. He often complained that to live through being in the Army only to come back home and die would be humiliating. To which she'd tell him to knock it off. He was being ridiculous. He'd tell her she was being bossy again.

She unlocked the wheels, pushed him toward the hallway. *Rolling on*, she thought. Rolling on into this next day again, like all the other days, no change, not improvements for Oklahoma's health. She stopped, wanting to hug him, just coming to her then that she should like it'd been what she needed to deliver to him. She walked in front of him.

"'Ya not takin' me? Change your mind? Got summem better to do?"

She reached down and hugged him tightly, no words answering him leaving her lips, just the embrace of her arms around his shoulders, pulling him forward to reach behind his back, her head leaned on his shoulder and she could smell the lye soap used to clean his hair. He took one hand and patted her on the back, his hand timid to touch her, the woman he'd beg to marry him if he'd ever get out of this blasted place. She pulled back, stood upright and he could see the tears in her eyes then that she pushed off her cheeks with her index finger as fast as they rose, then fell down her cheeks. He reached out with each hand and held one of hers in between them, hugging both sides of it between both of his palms, letting go when she let the moment go, smiled, then went back behind him to push him forward until she saw on the patient's board, POW Alessandro Reggio. She stopped, alarmed. "Oklahoma?" She whispered loudly and pointed to the letters POW.

"I know," he whispered back and mocked her astonished look, then smiled. "Your jaw's 'bout on the floor."

She took a few steps back, turned and leaned over slightly to catch a glimpse of the prisoner. His head was turned to the left so she couldn't see his face. His right shoulder and arm were bandaged. He had cuts and burns on his arm. She leaned back and pushed Oklahoma quickly out into the hallway and on toward the garden.

"It's a POW!" She said, her voice full of wonder.

"Got injured pretty bad in the laundry. Heard his arm almost got ripped from his shoulder when it got caught in a vat of spinning hot laundry and he's got burns all over him from the flames. Nurse Judy said he's lucky to be alive."

"Jeez."

"He's been out since they brought him in yesterday afternoon. They had to sedate him after the surgery. He wouldn't stop screamin' from the pain and they're concerned for when he wakes up. So far all he does is snore. I ain't even got a good look at his face, but I know the doctors are worried about how much blood he lost 'cause I heard 'em talking."

"You worried? Being so close to him like that. What if he tries something, like I don't know, attack you or steal your wallet and run away?"

"He wants to escape, he'll have to do it after his arm gets better and as far as attackin' me, I'm not much of a threat so he'd have no reason. If he wanted to leave, I couldn't stop him in my condition."

They stopped at a shaded spot under an awning. "I wouldn't like it. Dad says they're dangerous." Frances stood behind his chair, holding onto the handles as if bracing herself from falling and using them to grip tightly to release her tension.

Nearly a month had passed since she watched them brought into town and there'd been no sight of the Italian POWs since. Frances would've forgotten they were there if not for her father continuing to complain at dinner. She thought of when she looked through the binoculars when they'd gone into the barracks and she said to Mary that they were gone like ghosts. Until this moment, it seemed as if she'd never be in actual contact with one and she didn't know how she'd take it. It was all terribly exciting.

"I'm not worried," said Oklahoma. "Keepin' my food down's got my mind wrapped up. Gotta git some meat on my bones to get out of this damn place."

"You will," she assured him.

"This whole war business, I'm done with it anyway. If he's not a Nazi or a fascist, them the only two types I'd have a problem about, we'll get on."

"I don't know what to think anymore, it's just so awful."

"What?"

"The war."

"What part?'

"All of it. Damn stupid war."

She wanted to tell Oklahoma how she wished he'd never got injured because of the stupid war and that she was worried about him, Nicholas—everyone. The stress was getting to her the longer the war dragged on. The first year she was just in high school and didn't pay much attention to it because America was neutral, but it was still something she thought about often as she went about her life, trying out for cheerleading, kissing a guy for the first time, all the high school firsts. She never imagined all these years later that it'd still be going on or that her life after high school would be helping guys write letters back home or reading to them. Too long—that was how long the war had gone on.

"Got a letter from my momma I want you to read," he said, "but let's get out under that sun. I wanna warm up my bones and have you sit so I can see your face when we talk. You're always behind me with this wheelchair pushing you do for me." He removed the letter from his shirt pocket and when she went to take it, he pulled it away, "Uh-uh, not until you git me over there." He pointed to a spot in the garden, which really wasn't a garden anymore but that's what it was called when the place used to be the hotel. He liked a spot by the Joshua tree that gave him a view of the San Jacinto Mountains.

"All right." She pushed him towards the spot. They weren't alone. The garden, surrounding sidewalks and overhangs were all filled with other men getting their health back from whatever brought them there with other nurses or Red Cross volunteers helping. But it wasn't a social scene where they all chatted and talked. This was a place where sorrows of the war could be seen by the injuries or the sickness the men had. A reminder of the magnitude of the matter, not just at Torney, or all over America, but also the world. That war was hell even if it was necessary.

"Happy?" she said as she placed him in his spot and sat down beside.

He waved the letter he had in his pocket. She took it and pulled it out of the envelope. "Now I want you to read that last line out loud when you get to it," he said.

"Then I'll get to it first since I can see it's about me." She smiled and read: *"Tell Miss Frances she's a doll for taking care of you for me."* She put the paper down. "She sounds sweet."

"Ooooweee, she is if you follow her rules. You get a high falutin', she'll bust you a

good one. That's why no one messed with mama."

Frances laughed. "Well, she likes me, so I'm not so worried… yet."

"How's Nicholas these days?"

"Don't know. Haven't heard from him in a while." She answered, holding in the mouthful of comments she'd like to add to the answer but decided not to.

"You're bothered but hidin' it. You got a thorn you gotta get out. Tell me, what'a he do to upset you?"

"Five letters!" she blurted, like she'd been holding her breath and would just burst if she didn't say it. *"Five!"* She got up from her chair and paced in a circle. "I think over and over, is he dead? Does he not like me anymore? Did he meet some gorgeous girl over in those

Solomon Islands that he's fallen for? Is he injured? It doesn't stop inside my head, around and around. I feel like I'm going crazy sometimes."

"Wouldn't worry. Guy's got you. He'll come home. No way he's not comin' back even if he has to crawl or swim or flap his arms and fly like a bird to get back to this godforsaken desert."

"But why hasn't he written to me? I sent him five letters and not one back from him."

"He's a marine. Don't get much downtime to write letters," he assured her. "You just gotta keep the faith."

"You're right. I have to keep the faith." She smiled at him. He was keeping the faith and his situation was so much more dire. But it was so hard not to be at her age. Selfishness came to her as easily as wanting to go to sleep after twenty-four hours awake. "Let's write back to your mom," she said to him, now in a better mood. "I'll get it in the mail right after we're done so she'll have it in her hands in no time."

"Nah. Would rather just talk." Oklahoma seemed drained, as if their visit was too much already. "Could you go get me a pain pill on my nightstand? I didn't take it 'cause I'm tryin' to get by without it much as I can, but... "

"Do you wanna go back inside?"

"Nah, not yet."

Frances realized she'd need to go into his room with the POW.

"Frances, he ain't gonna hurt you."

"It's just weird that there's a guy from Italy in your room. What in the world is the world coming to, really? There. I said it. Now I'll go get your medicine in that room all by myself and hopefully I'll live to come back here."

"Sassy Miss Frances."

"Well, just pointing out the gravity of the mission you've given me. So, I'll go and do as you ask. If I don't die, I'll be right back."

"You gonna die now?"

"It's a dangerous mission." She headed towards the room, then called back: "Don't go anywhere."

"I only go where you put me."

Frances stood at the door of the room, listening to the swell of his lungs and excel of his breath. The still-beating life of a foreigner who survived the battlefield against us, then came to our home-field to be among us. His battle cry now the sound of his breathing as he tried to live out a wound gotten in America, land he never thought he'd step foot on when he went off to war. Now he was here. Near death. Near the enemy. Near her. In this small room. Breathing the same air.

She could see the paper cup with Oklahoma's medicine next to his writing pencil and paper on the table only fifteen feet inside, but she was scared to walk in and get it. Alessandro Reggio was hidden behind the curtain so she couldn't see him but felt his presence even though she didn't hear him snoring or even breathing. Her heart pounded and she felt stupid.

She glanced over at the nurse's station, which was just a desk set up on the side of the hallway with chairs and buckets of charts and coffee cups and paperwork. She felt someone watching her and saw Nurse Judy avert her eyes to hide that she'd been observing. Frances hurried over to her and whispered like she'd just told her a secret no one else knew.

"Judy? There's a POW in Henry's room."

"Uh-huh?" Nurse Judy had been around for a long time. A retired nurse, she put on the uniform and came out of retirement to help, but she'd long ago lost any natural sense of naivete or ability to be surprised.

"Is it safe to have one of them here without a guard?"

"So, they say."

"But they don't know?"

"I just work here, Miss Frances." She pointed to the nametag Frances wore that said Miss Frances. "He's a patient. Got his arm nearly pulled off and he needs our help. That's all I care about and unless you're told otherwise, that's all you should care about too."

"Certainly. I completely agree. It's just... do we know anything about him?" She felt embarrassed for being so catty and insensitive, yet Nurse Judy couldn't help but notice her efforts to cover-up her curiosity.

Judy half-smiled and placed a patient's chart in a bin and said to her, "Human beings are human beings, suffering is suffering, Frances. First rule of what we do, swear to protect our patients. He's a patient. If you have a problem with that, I suggest you rethink what you're doing here?" She walked away, leaving Frances embarrassed.

"Yes, ma'am." Frances called after her, always the first person to cave when confronted with conflict. She didn't like this side of herself.

What am I doing here? she thought. This had been the point she was making to Oklahoma earlier. She felt so lost lately and she didn't like it. She was losing her optimism and she'd get irritable for no reason. Now she felt ridiculous for being such a tattle.

She walked down the hall to the room and stepped inside as if she expected to see no one there, when in fact she knew he was there. It was an act to cover up that she was scared, which also made her feel ridiculous because no one was watching. The room was silent, just the sound of her sandals on the floor and nurse Judy humming "My Country Tis of Thee" down the hall. Frances took the small cup with the pill off the nightstand with shaking hands as she kept glancing over to the right, where the POW was behind the drape.

Turning to leave, her sandal caught on a blanket hanging off the side of the bed to the floor, causing her to stumble. Her hand raised up as she caught herself, flinging the cup up so that the pill went to the other side of the room and rolled under the POW's bed. Frances bent down to see under the curtain, searching for the pill, seeing it was now on the other side of the prisoner's bed. She scooted closer on her hands and knees, grabbing, but it was out of reach. She stood, contemplated, decided, then slowly walked around the dividing curtain, glanced at him, only able to see bandages, a brace on his arm and shoulder. His face was covered by the rise of the blankets and turned to the other side. He remained a mystery.

She moved a few steps forward, bent down on her knees and reached under this gurney to grab the pill. Her heels lightly tapped the floor as she stood and paused to see if she'd awakened him. He was quiet. The faint rise and fall of the bedding the only confirmation that he was alive. She stepped forward to see him. Her heart pounded as she leaned over his body, slowly, carefully, to get close until she could see his face and she stood there looking, trying to understand him.

He was young, tall, brown-black hair, strong square jaw, olive skin. She realized he was one she saw sitting in the back of the vehicle who looked so scared. She recognized the face, even though his eyes were closed. She leaned closer and looked down at him sleeping with unrest, the pain he felt evident on his face even when sedated and she looked at his left hand to see if he had a ring on his wedding finger. He did not. He stirred, moaned and turned his head to the other side and she backed away quickly, her steps loud on the tiled floor as she hid behind the curtain.

"*Acqua.*" She heard him whisper. "*Acqua, per favore.*" He said it louder.

His language—so melodious and new to her ears. She stood there frozen, behind the curtain, chest heaving, nervous.

"Water, please." He said in English, his Italian accent heavy still.

Frances looked out in the hall. No one was around. Nurse Judy couldn't be heard humming. She was the only one near to give him water, so she stepped out from behind the curtain.

"Water?" She said innocently as she poured it from a pitcher into a cup. He struggled to sit up, the pain evident on his face. "Wait," she told him, then she helped raise his back up and placed pillows behind his shoulders so he was sitting upright. She brought the cup of water to his lips. He drank it all. "More?" Frances asked and then realized he didn't speak English. She filled the cup up again and brought it to his lips. He drank the second cup as fast as the first, but some water spilt on his neck. Frances set the cup down and grabbed a towel on a side table and wiped the spilt water from his neck. There was one- or two-days' growth of coarse dark hair from his cheekbones down to the collar of his patient smock. Tangle of chest hair peeking out. He looked at her as she did. His large brown eyes following her as she moved about.

"There." She told him. "You don't understand me probably, but I'll get a nurse to help you."

He reached for her hand, which caused her to jump back, fearful. She looked at him, trying to understand his intention. She held her breath, as she looked into his face, his thick eyebrows, dark, with heavy strands of coffee-colored hair, cut jaw and broad nose, his stubble. Then she shifted back to his deep brown eyes.

Nicholas had blonde wispy hair that sort of floated on his head and moved around because of its weightlessness. His face was round and his features were soft without edges you could see, no cuts of definition and he was smaller. Alessandro was tall and while thin from the war as all POWs were, he was big-boned so that his frame had a presence even in this thin form. But it was his hair that she noticed the most as being different from Nicholas. Alessandro's hair had weight, strength and swirls—not curly, not straight, but a *force*, a mass on his head that was on its own attractive. He was strong in features and colors in all the ways Nicholas was soft and light.

"I speak English." He told her, his accent making his words to sound heavy. "A little," he added as he lifted his olive skin hand towards her. "Please."

She place her hand in his, feeling the warmth of his body, heated from fighting infection. Her tan skin, the mark of a desert girl, held pink undertones different than his European hue. A ping of shame hit her as their touch was intimate, as if he was kissing her.

His thumb rubbed her engagement ring, a plane gold band Nicholas gave her that last night when he proposed. "Married?"

"Engaged, not married yet," she answered as her fingers curled around the edge of his palm, holding him closer, as if kissing him back.

"Soldier?"

"Yes."

"Away?"

"Yes," she answered, feeling she'd just betrayed Nicholas. "A marine. Somewhere in the Pacific now," she added.

Nurse Judy could be heard humming down the hall. "Nurse Judy!" Frances called out. "The POW is awake."

She tried to pull her hand back, but he gripped it tightly. "*Grazie,*" he softly said, like their meeting was a secret. "I am Alessandro Reggio."

Nurse Judy's footsteps got louder as she came closer. Time was running out. He looked at her and nodded his head as if to gesture *And you are?*

"Frances Clark," she said, a bit unsure of herself.

"*Grazie,* Frances Clark."

Nurse Judy entered the room just as he let her hand go free. "He asked for water," she said, stepping out of the way. "I gave it to him."

Nurse Judy began checking his vitals and a doctor came in right after. They'd been concerned that he wouldn't wake up and now that he had, it was good news. Frances backed away as the medical staff chattered on about his condition, asking him questions about how he felt. Just before she was about to step out of the room, he called out:

"Bye, Frances Clark."

She felt embarrassed. She wasn't sure why. Her heart raced as she stepped out into the hall so that she had to stop a moment and catch her breath. What would her father say if he found out about this? She would not tell him. He'd stop her from volunteering there as he'd already threatened to do so when he heard the prisoners were being brought in. She looked at her hand that Alessandro had just held and smiled.

It had been the most thrilling, unexpected moment of her life so far in this small desert town.

. . .

She returned to Oklahoma. She'd only been gone for fifteen minutes, but he'd drifted asleep and his head had fallen forward so that his neck was at an uncomfortable angle. She raised his head back against the wheelchair back brace, the way a lover might hold onto her beloved's head as she leaned in.

He abruptly opened his eyes. "You're tryin' to kiss me, aren't you?"

She could feel herself blush. "No. I'm trying to keep you from getting a kink in your neck. You fell asleep." Then she handed him a cup of water. "And you know I can't kiss you. I'm engaged to be married."

"So, the monster didn't attack you?"

"No. But he did ask for water."

"He's awake?"

"He is."

"And did you give him water or did ya run screamin'?"

"Did you hear a scream? Of course I gave him water. What kind of monster do you think I am?"

"A monster that looks like a chicken." They laughed.

She held out the pill on her open palm that she'd taken out of her pocket. "Take this pill, you goofball." He took it from her. There was a table nearby set with water for those convalescing in the garden. They were set up all over the hospital as hydration was a major part of getting healthy especially in the desert heat. Some of the Gray Ladies oversaw filling them up as one of the non-medical tasks they handled at the hospital. Frances preferred library duty.

"Just like I'm doing for you, Oklahoma, I gave him water. Not just one cup, but two. And when it spilled on his neck, I took a towel and wiped it up."

"Don't believe it. And I'm so disappointed in you for lyin' just 'cause you don't want me to call you chicken again?"

"Well, I'm not lying. That is a true story."

"And you lived? He didn't attack?" He added, then opened his mouth, popped a pill on his tongue and took the cup of water she held out, taking it in one gulp.

"Two cups, as reported. I even helped wake him out of his beauty sleep, saving the day since you all thought he wasn't gonna wake up, like you said." She didn't feel comfortable telling him that she held Alessandro's hand and decided to keep it a secret.

"Miss Frances. I'm proud of you." He said in a goofy way, affecting a cartoon character's voice.

"You're a card."

"Just teasin'. I was a little worried you were too soft for this world, but not anymore."

"You think I'm a sheltered girl?

"Not for me to say."

"It is if I'm asking it? Do you think I'm a sheltered girl?"

"Hard to say."

"No. Not if you just say it."

He shifted in his chair as if he was sitting on spikes. She was making him remember a time and place he didn't want to ever think about again. The memory of blood splattered on the face of a kid only eighteen who just days before had talked to him about his first kiss with a girl in his neighborhood, a girl he planned to ask to marry him the first day he was back home. That was just one memory of many he didn't want stuck in his mind, but they were there, probably for the rest of his life, he knew, however long that was. These were the times he didn't talk to her about, preferring to read kiddy books about pigs and tease her with light banter over her being a chicken monster.

"The world, you think you understand it." He let what he was going to say go, because he didn't want to be the one who told her she was a sheltered girl, but that was good because knowing how horrible people could be, that wasn't something he wished he knew, but the war had taught him. He wasn't just a sheltered Oklahoma kid anymore but wished with everything that was in him that he could be that boy again.

"Don't lie to me," she teased.

"Let me ask you a question and dependin' on how you answer, I'll tell 'ya."

"Depending on the question, I may not answer."

"Did you donate blood the other day, or did you go yellow?"

"An entire pint of blood was pulled out of this arm. I didn't faint. I didn't cry. I went straight in there, despite my humiliating episode on my visit before to which I was laughed at by the nurses, but I took it on the chin and laughed with them."

"You're brave. You can't be sheltered if you're brave. Remember, above all else, Miss Frances, when you think of me." And his eyes welled up, as if he knew his time on earth wasn't long and that he'd never go home, that he'd been someone who meant so much to her that in the future, she'd think back to.

"Henry," she said, "Oklahoma." His nickname was the only way she knew how to respect him with these emotions and feeling guilty that she'd helped bring it on by her selfish question.

"No, no, Miss Frances. I'd like you to remember this. It's okay I might not be going home. I'm just one man of many who won't if that's my fate, but this brought me here to you, so I'm grateful for that."

She reached out and took both his hands in hers and squeezed them to reassure that she'd be there for him.

"But always be brave," he said. "Gotta remember that?"

"Why?"

"Because I said."

"Besides that. Why do I have to be brave? Seems like a hassle."

He laughed., "Can be."

"So, why then?"

"When I was young, there was this mean man that lived down the road who kept his dog on a leash in the yard his whole life. I tried to take him, but the man said no. I would sneak over there at night and give him food, play with 'em. Then that man died, and that dog became mine and I never put him on a leash. He'd run around the yard like a happy pup even though he was old by the time I got him."

He stopped talking and looked at her as if she should understand.

"That's the story?"

"Yeah."

"That's the story!" she yelled out again as if he was losing his mind. "I'm sorry, but what's the point?"

"Don't be a dog on a chain, doing what everyone expects you to do."

"Easier if you're not a woman. It's not a choice for us. It's just how it is most of the time."

"If you say." He answered, like he felt she was giving an excuse. "Go in now?"

She stood up, moved behind him, unlocked the wheels and pushed him from the dirt onto the walkway. She leaned down to his ear and whispered, "Fine. I can't promise, but I'll try not to be a dog on a chain."

Oklahoma smiled, not even from what she said, or her face so close to his, her warm breath in his ear, her sweet perfume scent fanning him briefly. It was that she listened to him. He could talk to her about anything and for every second of every day if he didn't get so tired, and that helped him, more than any book she'd ever read to him or any pain pill with a cup of water she handed to him. She saw him. He mattered to her, for some crazy reason. They'd clicked together like an ammo cartridge to his M1 rifle. He took it like he was getting a taste of what falling in love might feel like before he went away for good. Oklahoma felt he was dying – in his gut – as a truth he just knew, no matter what the doctors told him.

Chapter Four

Frances waited for Mary at the Palm Springs Tennis Club where her family had a membership. She did this every Saturday at 8:00 a.m. before the sun scorched the town so that playing tennis outside would not be possible. Palm Springs in the summer hit a high temp midday to anywhere over a hundred degrees, often even higher than 110 degrees. A villager her whole life, Frances was used to it and simply modified her schedule so that she wasn't outside midday, adjusting her way of life around hot weather. She waited on the court sideline, pressing the tip of her tennis racket into the tip of her toes as she leaned forward and commented to herself, "Always late, always late." She was saying this to herself because Mary was late again.

Frances opened a bag of new tennis balls, missing the crack of the aluminum can popping and the swish sound of the air pressure releasing from the cans new tennis balls used to come in. All through the war, new tennis balls came in bags of three because the metal was needed for the war effort. They went flat quickly in a bag. She missed the airtight cans, which had a key on the top like a tin of sardines.

Not one to waste hitting time, Frances took the bag of tennis balls and went to the serve line and began hitting serves like a horses tail swats away flies repeatedly. Smack! Her first hit sent the ball slicing through the air, low, just over the net and to the left, landing in the farthest corner of the court without going out of bounds.

She began hitting practice serves from the serve line, forcefully, her serves fast and dropping just before the line, slicing through the air and hitting against the chain link fence, some balls getting lodged in the diagonal squares, sticking against it like magic . She continued serving from the basket of balls set, sweat bubbled up on her forehead and upper lip already. She worried they wouldn't be able to play too long since getting a late start. When the ball basket was emptied, she headed across the court to gather balls as Mary at last came onto the court holding the newspaper.

"Portrait of the week! Frances, how could you not tell me?" She held out the newspaper page where Frances' photograph was added as the portrait of the week in the back page of the paper with a caption that read, Miss Frances Clark. It was her high school senior picture when she was seventeen and looked so sweet.

"My mom did it," Frances said as she gathered up tennis balls. "And my dad does what she says so there I am. It's so embarrassing. And you—" she pointed her racket at Mary " —are late again."

Mary placed the newspaper on the bench and took off her racket cover. "You're famous," she added as she grabbed a ball between her shoe and tennis racket, raised her foot up, which tossed the ball in the air when she pulled her racket back and she dribbled the ball up and down against the court before putting it in her pocket.

"You're late."

"I'm always late."

They went to their sides of the court and began volleying. "I don't need to warm up. I've been hitting balls for 20 minutes."

"So?" Mary asked her like she was waiting for details of a torrid matter. "You've got to tell me more. I could keel over from expectation."

They'd talked on the phone briefly the night before about the POW, but Frances couldn't say much as her father was listening.

"He's so... I don't know... just different."

"How?"

"Just different," she said and thought about her hand in his. She felt a tingling in her arms as she did, goosebumps from thinking about that moment. It surprised her that she still had this feeling the next day that she'd had all last night. The magic feeling from that moment was still strong and this made Frances a little nervous. She pointed her racket to the other side of the net, "Get over there! Let's go! Only got an hour probably because you're late, again!" Frances yelled jokingly.

"Are you in love with him?"

Frances chased Mary with her racket and a ball in her hand, trying to throw it at her as she did, but Mary giggled and ran side to side to escape. "Get over there!" Frances giggled and Mary finally did get to the other side of the net as she avoided her best friend's attack and returned it by picking up balls and throwing them at Frances, who dodged them and she pushed on with her mission to peg her with her ball, finally throwing it and getting Mary in the butt, which was too hysterical to each of them.

"Let's talk about it after. I wanna play."

And she thought of him again, as she had all last night, remembering his face, his deep round eyes, a chocolate brown hue so warm. Alessandro Reggio, she'd said his name too, in her mind, many times, prisoner of war, POW, a person to fear yet all she wanted since meeting him was to see him again.

Set up for the match, Frances bounced the ball repeatedly, trying to get her feel before starting, preparing to serve, taking too long, trying to focus.

"Come on, Frances." Mary said as she paced side to side, waiting to receive the ball, knees bent, game face on.

These Saturday matches were serious. Both girls played tennis in school and the Palm Springs Clubs and were serious on the court. Mary considered going on as a professional tennis player, but the war happened and her parents couldn't afford the training.

"Someone's angry. I don't think I'm going to win today." She said as she went back in place to receive the next serve which was equally as powerful and unattainable.

"I'm not angry. I just like to win."

"So do I," Mary said, slicing the ball to the corner of the court, out of Frances reach, yet Frances leapt to try and get the ball still, hitting her racket on the court and stumbling down onto the court. She yelled out in frustration.

"Gotcha!" Mary piled on, declaring war.

"Yeah, we'll see." Frances answered as she got up and readied for the next serve.

The battle progressed and Frances lost, but it was close. After the rousing and bragging from Mary settled down, they wiped their brows and necks in the lady's room, washed their hands and headed over to the coffee shop for lemonade and eggs, both scorched hot from playing intensely.

"Spill the beans."

"I told you everything."

"Nope. Nope. Nope. You missed stuff... a lotta stuff."

"I gave him water. He shook my hand to thank me. He said his name. I said my name. And I called in the nurse."

"Ridiculous. No details. You're hiding something. I know you."

Frances just smiled.

"Spill it."

The girls huddled closer. "You can't repeat this to anyone. Promise?"

"Cross my heart."

"Cause I'm engaged to be married and it wouldn't be right if it got out that I said this."

Mary closed her lips and mimed locking them.

Frances whispered, "He's really cute."

And both girls smiled, squealed, and grabbed each other's hands as if they were sharing the world's most exciting news.

"And when he held my hand, he held it... for a while."

"How long?"

"A minute. Two maybe?"

"Oh, my heart is pounding."

"So, it was long?"

"And I can't stop thinking about him—it, I mean."

Mary looked astonished at this news.

"I'm still in love with Nicholas, don't get me wrong and this is why you can't tell anyone that I'm telling you this."

"I promise."

"But it was the most exciting moment of my life. I was so scared. And my heart was pounding. And he was so different than Nicholas, you know. His hand was big and warm." Frances took a sip of her lemonade and fanned her face. "I just never thought in my lifetime something like that would happen to me. Right here in boring Palm Springs."

"It's unbelievable."

"So that's why I can't stop thinking about it... and he's really cute. I mean, really cute."

"Crazy."

Satisfied that she'd gotten the juicy details finally, Mary put the newspaper on the counter in front of them and they flipped through it, commenting on the advertisements to do your part for the war bonds and have you planted your victory garden? Frances borrowed a pen from their waitress, who was also one of her friends from high school and the three of them had a hoot drawing a mustache onto Frances's picture in the paper and then Mary added alien antennas.

"Look at this ad?" Mary flipped to an add that said: *Free a marine to go fight. Join the marines and be a conductor.* It had an image of a woman in uniform working on a train. "That would take me out of here. I'm signing up."

"I don't want you to go anywhere." Frances pretended to beg. "Please, please, please stay with me Mary."

"Stop it."

"Wanna ride over to town, see a matinee? I don't want to go home just yet. My mom is fit to be tied about dinner tonight and the longer I stay away, the easier it'll be for me."

"Who is it this time?"

"The mayor, president of the bank, a General from Torney. And of course their lovely wives."

"Boring."

"Yep."

Finished eating, they slung their tennis rackets over their backs, the front straps of the case across their chest like a cross-over bag and strode to the front of the club where they'd parked their bikes and took off.

They made their way down Palm Canyon Drive riding their Schwinn bikes. Frances' parents had given her the "The Hollywood" model last Christmas. It came with all the equipment the men's bicycles had, yet allowed the buyer to choose the color of the bike and offered a two-toned version. Mother picked two-toned blue and ivory. The bike had a horn and a light, a feature she'd often use when sneaking out at night to meet up with Mary to get into no good, as her mother called it. But these nights were the most magical of her life so far. These sneaky late-night outings where Frances and Mary would hike up trails on the edgy mountain terrain that bordered the west side of Palms Springs, taking sips of liquor they stole from their parents, breaking out into singing whatever song was on the radio that week or even dancing arm and arm the West Coast Swing. They didn't think it was being up to no good. It was the best time they had. They sang with loud abandon—no one for miles around.

Now, with spending time at Torney to liven the mood for the insured soldiers and to raise money for whatever the need was at that moment—funding a war loan or raising money to help pay for the cause of the week—having fun was scarce. Always rations for simple things like sugar and coffee. Never-ending pleas to support the war bond drives advertised in the paper. *Today 570 of our boys will pay for war the hard way. They still die—will you buy. The biggest job is still ahead. Buy bigger bonds, now!* The words with an image of soldiers carrying wounded. *On to Tokyo. Let's all get behind the greatest march in history. The march to Tokyo and Victory. Let's echo that cry with bonds! Buy at least an extra $100 war bond! Palm Springs quota is $354,000.* Images of soldiers with rifles and an army tank driving forward. And the worst, names of people in town who purchased bonds were listed so if your name didn't show you're your neighbors knew you didn't buy.

They came upon a group of high school kids playing handball against the wall in the alley next to the ice cream shop that knew Nicholas. A few boys back for the summer from university called them over when they saw them riding by, wanting to know how Nicky was doing overseas and what could she tell them about him. She filled in the usual information, keeping quiet about him not sending a letter in a while. Bad news was to be avoided unless it had to be told. It was the way people seemed to cope best.

The girls parked their bikes, lowered kickstands and sat on the steps to the still-closed ice cream shop to watch. They guys goofed on her about her picture in the paper by the kids to which she told them all to shove off, all in fun. They then turned their focus to gossiping about the families going in and out of the coffee shop across the street. Did you hear about her and did you know this about him? They didn't go to church last week. She has a new dress on. He lost his job. The kid is annoying. That one was spotted talking to so and so and that one wasn't on the list for having purchased the war loan.

"Listen to us," said Mary. "Even our gossip sounds small town. We should bust out of here. Head out to Los Angeles and live in the big city, maybe get discovered in Schwabs like Lana Turner."

"That would be dreamy. A movie star, can you imagine?"

"Sounds better than being one of those conductor marines so that's an option."

"I'd be afraid to leave here. It'd be exciting, but it'd be scary."

"Nah, you'd get over that easy. I think. I don't really know 'cause I've never been anywhere."

"And you never will because you can't leave me," said Frances and gave her a big hug as a sneaky way to grab hold of her and give her a noogie on her head.

"Frances!" Mary screamed and chased after her as Frances knew she'd be in for Mary's revenge to which the girls laughed as they ran about.

"You'll never catch me."

"Will too!" And the chase continued down the street until Mary caught her and gave her a return noogie.

'Uncle! *Uncle!*" Frances yelled.

"There. We're even." Mary let go of her and they found themselves on even footing that they could walk back to their bikes without worrying about revenge.

They walked back to their bikes just as the ball came their way. Frances grabbed it and threw it back to the guys. They yelled their goodbyes to each other, the guys asking Frances to tell Nicky his boys at home are rooting for him, which she agreed she'd do and they rode on to the Palm Springs Theater, parked their bikes and slipped into the movie without paying because Chip, who had a crush on Mary, was working the ticket booth. Unabashed flirting for a favor and Frances had to stop herself from rolling her eyes. She faked a smile as she watched Mary use her female charms on a seventeen-year-old boy to scam free tickets.

In the lobby they bought sodas and popcorn, the butter scent drawing them in like a snake charmer and headed into to theater that was already filling up fast because it was so hot outside. The girls giggled at the fact that they got in free and snacked on popcorn as the lights dimmed and red curtains opened so the screen was visible and the Movietone News played a report titled "Girls at War" on those in the Women's Army Auxiliary Corps. Halfway round the world in Italy, it showed WACs getting medals and praise from their general for what they'd accomplished and how their friends and families back home could be proud of them. The girls watched, slapping popcorn into their mouths as they viewed women just like them who decided to be brave and travel across the globe to serve.

Mary leaned close to Frances and whispered: "I could be a WAC."

"Stuck in some camp with all those women gossiping about each other?"

The movie moved on to show Army nurses in the Pacific doing exercises together in their army uniforms and then going swimming in the ocean in their bathing suits as the narrator talks about how swimming is slimming. With this, the girls started laughing.

"Swimming is slimming?" Frances said.

"Jeez."

The newsreel continued, talking about the allied troops invading Normandy by air, land and sea, in order to surprise the Germans.

"Some of it's gotta be a lie," Frances whispered to Mary.

"What?"

"What they say about the Nazis and all the horrible stuff they say's going on and done to the Jews? Doesn't seem possible."

"Yeah, sure doesn't."

The lights dimmed as the Movietone News ended and the film *Going My Way* began. Bing Crosby was a singing priest and WWII wasn't happening. They ate their popcorn and Mary snuck out and got them Lik-M-Aid Fun Dips that turned their tongues blue so after the film, as they walked in the village pushing their bikes, they kept sticking their blue tongues out at each other as a goof. An ambulance raced down the road, sirens blaring, with a police car behind it, no doubt rushing to the train station or the airfield to transport a newly incoming soldier who needed medical care.

"It's so loud here anymore with the planes and ambulances." Frances said.

"Used to be a quiet town." Mary said.

The sound of planes overhead was always there now, more common than the sound of birds chirping. Soldiers and supplies were constantly brought in and out of the air base. The wounded or sick that didn't come in by air were brought in by train. Sounds from the military invasion of the village had escalated so much in the few years since Torney had been set up that Palm Springs was at its highest population ever. Locals talked about General Patton being the ringleader for the population boom by driving the setup of ten desert training camps in '42 to train soldiers for the North African Campaign. The desert had harsh conditions with its heat and dry land that helped soldiers acclimate, so they were prepared to fight in Morocco and Algiers.

"I better get home. I'm sure my mom is staring at the clock wondering why I'm not there."

"See ya," Mary said and stuck her blue tongue out at her.

"See ya." Frances stuck out her blue tongue back.

It was a short ride to the house. With temps over 100, five minutes seemed like 30. Once home, Frances parked her bike in the garage and stepped in the side kitchen door and hollered:

"Mom... I'm home!" The house was set to host guests. The punch bowl was ready, the nuts and pretzels were in bowls and casseroles were in the oven.

Their house had a mid-century modern style, clean lines, minimalist furniture, pops of yellow and turquoise on the davenport, cushions on the exterior furniture surrounding their pool. Her mother had styled their home Palm Springs chic before the war broke out and Frances knew the history of the items in the house because at every dinner if there was a person new to their home, she went into lengthy discussions of the pieces, their history and how her designer helped her choose the piece so that it fit in with the room to accentuate this and that.

Frances went to her room and looked in her closet, pulled out a navy dress and held it up in front of the mirror. "Mom!" she hollered out again.

A woman kept in all ways, her mom Helen entered wearing heels and a dress, prepared for the dinner party she was hosting.

"This one?" Frances asked.

"Too casual. Can you wear your pink dress, the one we bought at Lykken's with the lace on the arms?"

"Mom, you like that dress. I don't." She answered, fully knowing that she'd be wearing that pink dress because Mom wanted her to, and Mom always got her way. She was charming about it, but she got her way in all family matters.

"Why are you home so late, Frances?"

Frances, frustrated, put the navy dress back, annoyed that her mother was so demanding with how things should be, always. "I saw a movie."

Her mother left, moving on to prepare for the dinner party of nine, three couples always, Frances and her parents. Frances wasn't in the mood to mingle and serve drinks and appetizers for the night. But as the daughter of the owner of the only newspaper in the town, it was part of what she did in her life since little. It'd become as common as brushing her teeth.

With Mom out of sight, Frances plopped down on the end of her bed on her belly, feet, head and arms flung over the sides and stared at the floor as if boredom had taken over.

"Guests arrive in 30 minutes," her mom said as she walked by in the hall and saw her daughter. "No time for dilly-dallying."

"Can't I skip it?"

"No!" Her mom hollered back. They'd had this discussion several times and had come to a compromise. She was to stay through refreshments and dinner, then she could retreat to her room and skip dessert. "Get going, Frances. Don't make me...!" she said and looked at her sternly. She didn't have to finish the sentence because Frances knew the ending. And if her mom finished the sentence, it meant she was at a level of anger Frances didn't want to be around.

Frances dragged herself off her bed and over to her dressing table where she took out the bobby pins from her hair and placed them back on the cardboard packaging for her Gayla Hold Bob Bobby Pins. She had seen in her father's paper a ridiculous ad in the lifestyle section for women to keep their bobby pins in a safer place other than their sink so that they didn't rust. She told her father it was trite, to which he replied that trite is exactly what people want right now. "Too much with the war," he added. This was a line he said often, to her and to everyone, as a way of talking about a lot without saying much. There was so much with the war, he would say to her when she'd tried to talk to him about things in her life that he dismissed as trite, often saying to her that there was "so much with the war." She couldn't break into him since the war began. He changed so drastically. She missed how he used to be before Hitler turned everyone's lives upside down. She hated Hitler.

Her hair fell onto her face as she pulled the pins out and balanced against her cheeks. A brunette, her skin tanned from desert sun, she had blue eyes that weren't light or dark, they were both – and every color between – ombre – and her naturally long lashes framed them so that they looked bigger than they were. Her face was wide, in a way she disliked, but others found beautiful because it gave her a striking presence. People found it hard to look away from such a prominent face with crystal blue eyes. She didn't look like her mom or dad. She looked like them both – a genetic meshing of each of them into one, so that people often looked at her and ask, which one does she resemble? And after trying to pin her looks to one or the other, they'd give up.

After she brushed her soft curls out of her long hair, she scratched her head with both her hands as if scratching a dog's ears to win over the dog's affection. She always did this when she got her bobby pins out, as she pinned her hair back every day. It felt good. Then she put on her shower cap and headed to the bathroom where she quickly rinsed off the sweat of a tennis match and biking in the hot day. She returned to her room in her bathrobe.

"Dilly-dallying Frances." Her mom commented as she walked by her room again.

"Mom, I'm getting ready." Frances hollered, then closed her door. "Dilly-dally. Dilly-dally. Really!" She said to herself as she stepped up her pace. She was dilly-dallying because she was not in the mood for a discussion at the dinner table about the war loans drive and Hitler and all the conversation that came with these dinners. She got dressed quickly, the lace on the pink dress irritating her because it was itchy and stepped into her evening heels. She parted her hair on the side and rolled her curls back from her face and pinned them into place before applying rouge and lipstick, finally ready to be her mother's hostess.

The dinner parties her mom organized started over a month before the evening. She would have special invitation cards printed up announcing the event that she mailed to her first select group of participants. Her dinner parties were always planned for a total of six guests. If there were declines, she had a second set of invites that were mailed to assure that there would not be any gossip at the women's club that Mrs. Helen Clark had planned a dinner party that no one attended.

The women could be quite the gossips, looking for the tidbit of the week they could spread to other women that would lead them to be more in favor for being in the know. Her mother had played the game for so long and so exceptionally well that she was able to see all the potential angles of gossip or disgrace. That is also why she was always on top of Frances with overbearing rules and expectations. Frances' part in the evenings was to help her mother provide beverages on a demand basis. Her father would say *What can I get you to drink?* as they lounged in the living room having cocktails and appetizers before moving into the dining room.

Since it was wartime, it wouldn't have been prudent to serve an ostentatious dinner. Coffee and alcohol were rationed and dinners were often casserole, which it was this night as well, along with a salad made from her mother's victory garden she'd planted in their yard. Her mother liked to make a big deal over it, letting her guests know that she was doing all she could to support the war effort and was willing to make sacrifices. This was often a bit hard to swallow for some guests, as it was clear that the Clark's had money so her mom's sacrifice was hard to swallow at times, but no one would ever say this to her.

Father came in from work and made a big ta-do about how beautiful his women looked, which her mom just ate up and Frances tolerated because she wanted to get out of the itchy dress, yet her mom refused to allow it despite Frances saying that it was uncomfortable. "Do what your mother says, Frances," Father said to her before changing for dinner. That was what he always said so she shouldn't have even asked, but then her father gave her a kiss on her cheek and said, "You look lovely in pink." She would now have to stay in that dress for the duration of dinner because that's how their home worked.

The evening started with the guests on time. It would be considered rude to be late. Drinks and appetizers at 5:30 followed by dinner at 6:15, then the women would retreat to the kitchen and outside by the pool and the men would stay in the living room to discuss politics. As always, the dinner went as planned and Frances and her parents played perfect hosts to their guests who never tired of talking about Hitler and the Germans, the raid on Normandy and its success a few months earlier in June. It was all in the right vein, no one straying from their area of expertise: her father the newspaper man, the mayor concerned about civic matters and the women discussing the Women's Club and the upcoming fall festival dance they were hoping would uplift the spirits of the men and women working so hard at Torney. It was standard conversation that could be forgotten easily as it was said so often it was as common as saying the sky was blue. Frances hadn't been bothered by any of it, only the lace on her arms that was causing her to scratch and pay attention to the time left until she could take it off.

But then the Lieutenant spoke:

"A POW hurt his arm in the laundry facility. Had to admit him so now he's taking a bed from one of our boys."

She paid attention, listening as if each word that followed had the value of a one carat diamond.

"Those traitors need to go," the Lieutenants wife added, leading the conversation into a long discussion about the discomfort villagers felt having them near and how women had been talking about being fearful that one might escape and come into their homes late at night, vulnerable because their husbands were off serving. The pay the POWs received of 80¢ a day was discussed at length. Was it right? Were they taking jobs away from villagers? The deepest discussion rose about if they truly were on America's side. *Those WOPs shouldn't be here. America has lost its edge with these Italian Service Units. I don't buy it. They'd slice our throats in a moment if they could.*

Frances heard his voice in her mind as she listened to the persecution of him.

Water.

He was being called a WOP, Dago, Guinea, rapist, killer, alien, traitor.

Water, he said again in her mind, pain evident in his tone, like it had drained his voice of confidence. She remembered her hand in his and how warm his palm felt.

"Frances?" Her father said, pulling her out of her daydream. "Did you hear me?"

"No, Dad."

"Have you seen him at Torney? This man?"

And she thought of his face, his wide eyes, his razor stubble on his cheeks, his thick black hair framing his face, ending before the line of this strong jaw and understood he was none of the things they'd said.

"No, Dad. I haven't seen him."

"Good. I don't want you anywhere near him."

"It's not safe, Frances," her mother added, echoing her father as she did in all matters.

And she didn't say more, as it would've been useless and dumb to open her mouth and tell them of her secret meeting. She knew the men and women at the dining room table were the ones the Italians should fear and Palm Springs was not safe for men like Alessandro Reggio.

Chapter Five

The lobby bathroom walls had a colorful wallpaper left from the days when the hospital was a hotel, coating the building materials under it with a thin paper lining of extravagance. This was where guests who arrived after the long drive in from Hollywood would freshen up—Mary Pickford, Douglas Fairbanks, Ginger Rogers—before spending their days poolside with other notables, the Hollywood leaders worshipped for their good looks more than merits.

Frances imagined women stepping into the lobby and into that powder room to touch up their faces, brimming with anticipation but acting blasé. El Mirador Hotel no longer existed, but its walls were still dressed in high-end wallpaper, the shell of its former glory, a hangover from fancy days. Frances liked the yellow and green design of palm leaves on that wallpaper, a large mirror above the sink that made the bathroom feel glamorous and was the best place to check your hair. Frances adjusted her hair and pinched the apple of her cheeks to create a natural rouge. She walked out to the hospital, doing her rounds to track down outstanding library books, stepping into rooms to gather them or get the reason they're late, a hunter of lost stories she was committed to returning. A month before she and Mary had hung out in the tower waiting to catch a glimpse of the enemy prisoners entering their world. Had it been so long already?

She made her way towards the one person she'd thought of obsessively since he held her hand, Alessandro Reggio, the forbidden man, the spark for a fire she was trying not to start. That was five days ago and every day since then she stayed away because she knew she may have a problem. Of what sort? She was interested in him and this was a problem. But she was unsure whether this feeling was excitement over the encounter or something more. She worried it was the latter. That's why she stayed away, despite Oklahoma needing her. She hoped the Italian would be released before she visited again and she wouldn't need to deal with these feelings because the guilt was killing her. She thought about Alessandro, wanted to be near him. It was wrong. She wasn't comfortable with wrong. These feelings had been in the mix of her thoughts, which in turn became five days of figuring out who she was. She didn't come to a resolution and this in and of itself, made her understand that she was dealing with something entirely new. And exciting.

The door to Oklahoma's room was nearly shut all the way, which was the message that the patients were getting treatments or consultations with the doctors, which was confirmed when she walked past and could see a physician and a few nurses with Oklahoma. *What is going on with him?* she thought and felt guilty for not visiting for so long, a failed caretaker.

She knew Alessandro was still in his room because word got out to the other women that he was there and for a few days suddenly a parade of Gray Ladies stopped in to check on Oklahoma, to which Edith put a stop. He'd become the reason for huddled girls in the halls, whispering and giggling, dreaming with excited breaths of lust Frances was assigned to him and a few others so she was allowed to visit the room, but now she couldn't go in because something was going on with Oklahoma. She could feel it wasn't good, but she felt it wasn't her place to ask.

Biding time like a hovering eagle waiting swoop down on its prey, she went to other rooms to investigate the whereabouts of this book and that book, catching one soldier quickly hiding a magazine under his blanket as she neared and she had no doubt this was a smut magazine smuggled in by her best friend. She acted as if she knew nothing and carried on to other rooms, getting a few fellas to laugh when she told them Phyllis the librarian was going to have her arrested for returning books late and explained they'd need to round up money for her bail. And when the guys asked if she was joking, she explained, not at all because stealing from the library was a federal offense, which got an even bigger laugh. This wasn't the first time she'd used these lines to lighten the mood with the guys and it wouldn't be the last because as she'd learned over time, next week, next month, these guys would be gone and new ones would arrive to take their place.

When she saw Oklahoma's room was at last cleared of medical staff, Frances gave it a moment before going inside, quickly pinching her cheeks again while glancing at her warped reflection on the side of a silver aluminum can of cleaning solution on a shelf. Tense, she almost laughed at herself, like she'd become a silly schoolgirl behaving so vainly because she was about to see a boy, but in this case, it wasn't her fiancé and this was the problem. The way she felt, the tingling in her stomach, the thrill of expectation to see him again, was the problem. She shouldn't feel any of these things, she knew, but she did. Five days away had only increased her desire to hold his hand again, not waning as she expected, so she headed back to him hoping that when she saw him she'd feel nothing. This was the test. The only way to get to some resolution for the question she couldn't face all week: Did she really love Nicholas? And if she didn't, what was she going to do about it?

When she stepped into the room, Oklahoma smiled, despite the pain she could clearly see he was in.

"Well, Miss Frances returns," he drawled with a week voice.

Alessandro was there, behind the room dividing curtain which was partially closed.

"Oklahoma? What's going on? Something wrong?"

"No. No. Doc's just checking my spark plugs under my hood again. Where you been?" He tried and failed to laugh.

"It's not funny. Not at all."

"Thought you forgot about me, Miss Frances." She kept looking over at the curtain, knowing he was behind it, to which Oklahoma noticed. "Oh, I see." He said with his midwestern drawl in a way that seemed slightly condescending.

"What?" she asked as she picked up a *Freddy the Detective* book and started flipping through the pages as a diversion from revealing herself. "What's our detective up to these days?" Alessandro's leg moved, catching her attention.

"Alessandro, you awake?" he called out. And Frances' eyes went large, as if she were excited and scared at the same time. "Got a visitor. Miss Frances, the one I been telling you I miss is here."

Alessandro pulled back the curtain and she saw him again, finally, after five long days. He held out his hand to her. "Frances Clark," he said and she reached out and he closed her small hand in his warm, large hand, as if hugging, not shaking it. "I remember," he said and then released her hand far sooner than he had before. She wasn't able to speak for a second as she took in this moment she'd hoped for, but it still felt so unexpected—even though she'd fixed her hair and pinched her cheeks to make them red. It wasn't needed as she was blushing fiercely. This was welcome in a crazy way, stopped her from feeling overconfident in the moment.

Oklahoma watched the interaction with an understanding that these two could be, maybe, experiencing some sort of love at first sight and the moment lifted his spirits. It lessened his fear of death in some way to see that life could be so sweet, so magnificent. Two strangers overtaken by affection for one another. So different from recent experience. This was a part of life he'd lost hope over. Was there love here on earth that validated all the horribleness of human existence? This moment told him yes.

"You speak English?" she asked Alessandro.

"Yes. Not good." It was that same deep baritone he'd had when in so much pain, he'd requested water days earlier.

"Better?" She pointed to his shoulder. It seemed to be swaddled in fewer bandages, burns still visible on his uncovered skin. His arms, neck and face were healing.

"Yes. *Grazie.*" He told her and when they spoke, for her, it was as if no one else was in the room. Oklahoma didn't exist. No one else in the world existed.

Oklahoma coughed. His lungs sounded full of fluid and this drew her attention immediately. "That doesn't sound good."

"I'm alright, Miss Frances." She grabbed a towel and handed it to him as he began a long coughing fit.

Blood on the towel, which he hid from her.

Alessandro sat up and flung his legs to the edge of the bed, ready to help.

"Like to get in the sun," said Oklahoma.

"Let's get you in the sun then." She pushed the wheelchair to the edge of his bed and let him lower himself into it. Alessandro watched, wondering if he should step in, his brown eyes followed Frances, voyeur to a friendship he was not a part of.

"Can I help?" he asked.

"No. No. I have this." But this time Oklahoma reached out to Frances for support as he transferred to the wheelchair, holding onto her forearm. This was not lost on her. This was not what she wanted him to have to do because it meant that he may not be going home to see his mom.

She decided it was time to do what she did best for him, which was to annoy him with sarcasm, get him to laugh on this day, which they both knew was one of the few days he had left.

"How does a pig become a detective?" she said as she pushed him out of the room under the watchful eyes of Alessandro, whom she wanted and needed to get away from. *Disturbing* was all she could say to describe her situation with him.

"Freddy is a genius pig. That's how?" Oklahoma answered as they turned out of the room and down the hall.

"Pigs are smart. Ever been around pigs?"

"Nope."

"Let me tell you about this one pig we had I named Sweetheart because she had all the pig fellas in love with her. Their eyes would follow her wherever she went and they'd follow her as she went around the pen. Sort'a reminds me of you," he said as they exited the building and were blinded by the warm sunlight of an August day to which he raised up his face and took in the heat on his skin as if it were a sacred gift.

She giggled and continued to push him towards his favorite spot in the garden, under the tree. "Did you just call me a pig?"

"Now, now. I did not," he said, but he knew it would get her going and she knew it too so she played along and started snorting like a pig which got him doing a belly laugh. This turned her day around and she forgot for a moment about Alessandro and her uncomfortable feelings for him. She felt back to who she was before he took her hand five days earlier and she liked that she was herself again. Safe for now.

"I love you, Miss Frances," he told her and she was surprised.

"Oklahoma?"

"I do. I love you," he repeated and started crying.

She took both his hands in hers again as he broke down. "I love you too, Oklahoma. I always will."

"Don't stay away again. Five days felt like five years."

"I won't," she said. "I'm sorry I upset you."

And he pushed off his crying so that he could get back to being what everyone thought was being: a man, not crying, bucking up, handling emotions like a rock.

Oklahoma said, "He's a star at home, you know, Alessandro. He plays the violin. People come from all over to watch him, I guess. A virtuoso."

"Alessandro?" Again, she was pulled back into those strange feelings.

"He knows English. Goes on tours all over before getting brought into the war."

"But his arm?"

"Yeah, it's sad." Oklahoma lifted his face to the sun again.

"Do you wanna read a bit? I don't have too much time as I have to go to a Gray Lady meeting with annoying Edith."

"How is she annoying?"

"She acts so superior."

"Is she?"

"No!" Frances sputtered.

The smile on Oklahoma's face made up for the pain she saw on his face earlier. "So why do you care if she thinks she is?"

"Hmm. Never thought it that way. Maybe I'll go back to bein' a dumb pig." She snorted like a pig, then added a few oinks.

"See? You make me feel better. This is why you can't stay away."

"I won't. I told you. I won't again."

"Fair enough. I forgive ya."

"Why thank you, sir. Now do you wanna get back to Freddy's case?"

"I believe I do."

"All right."

She opened the book to the leaf bookmark and they read for twenty minutes or so before she returned him to his room. Alessandro was again behind the curtain and she could only see that he was there but didn't want to be seen. After she helped Oklahoma into bed, she placed the book beside him, picked up the basket of books she'd rounded up earlier along with the chart showing which had been signed out and were overdue. She set it on the wheelchair and wheeled it out of the room.

"Bye Henry."

"Oklahoma," he corrected.

"Bye Oklahoma."

"Bye Frances."

Then without thought or hesitance, she said, "Bye Alessandro."

He pulled the curtain back and her heart skipped when she saw his face again, his chiseled features, his square solid jaw, his smiling, handsome face.

"Addio, Frances."

"You two stay outta trouble," she told them before leaving.

She parked the wheelchair in the spot in the hallway where they were to be returned when not in use. Then she grabbed her basket of books and headed back to the Gray Lady library where she put them in a book bag. Mary showed up.

"Let's go, Fran." Mary shouted at the doorway. "Edith doesn't like it when we're late."

"Coming." She said as she put the heavy book bag on her shoulder.

"Leave those here. Get 'em after so you don't have to carry them."

"I guess." Frances set the book bag down and followed her.

"Let's go."

They headed out of the main building and walked two hundred yards to the left to an Army tent that was the Red Cross training room. A mandatory meeting had been called for this week and many suspected it had to do with the handsome Italian POW in the hospital that they'd all been trying to get a look at by stopping by room 54 to be helpful when it wasn't their place. Edith was always the wise one on what was going on with the girls. She had frequent check-ins with the nurses to get a handle on any bad behavior that was brewing.

"Saw one of your smut mags today," Frances reported as they walked through the hospital.

"No!" Mary laughed.

"Yes!"

"I told the guys to be super safe or it's curtains for me."

"Hope it's not what this meeting's about."

"Ready for Edith?"

"Never ready for Edith."

"She's longwinded."

"Edith the Bore."

"Frances, I do believe you're becoming corrupted."

Frances smirked and rolled her eyes. "She's not nice."

"No, she's not, but what's going on with you? You never talk like that."

"I do, a lot. In my head." She pointed to her skull. "Crazy things goin' on inside here."

A flow of Gray Ladies converged upon and entered the Red Cross tent set up for instruction, their gray uniforms merging to form a drab flowing sea that pooled inside. Forty or so women filled the room and sat in chairs that were lined up in rows. Most of the Gray Ladies were young, but there were a few actual gray-haired volunteers in town who'd joined out of a sense of duty. Mary and Frances had often suspected that they were recruited by Edith to spy on the girls' behavior so most stayed away from them. There'd been many times a girl had been told on for something Edith had no way of knowing about, unless it was from one of the spies. Knowing this, the girls had squeezed them out of their inner circle of trust and assigned a code name that would change when they thought they were being found out. Right now, it was *Jane*. They would say to each other, *Jane here today? Jane nearby? Jane alert.* They thought it was funny to say *Jane Jane approaching!* which meant two of Edith's spies were nearby. Whenever Edith and her women would question the who Jane is, they'd change the name and pass the information along: *Jane out* and would assign a new name they'd pass it along in notes they'd hand to each other in the halls.

"Quiet down, Gray Ladies," Edith said as she stood in front of the chalkboard.

This was the same room the Italian POWs were brought to for their English classes. It was considered part of treating the men with dignity under the Geneva Convention, which was also why they received 80¢ a day for their work. They weren't considered prisoners since they'd switched sides and joined the Allied Forces, but many considered this a band aid on a bad situation. Many Americans still considered members of the ISUs to be with Germany and had simply switched sides for better treatment in America. *It's possible*, Frances thought at times. But she couldn't imagine Alessandro being for Hitler. He didn't have that kind of heart, it seemed to her, even though she barely knew him.

"Quiet! Quiet, girls," said one of the three Janes. She was the one most of the younger women really didn't like. Her real name was Marla Square, which Frances thought was so funny because she *was* a square. She was a childless widow who lived in the older part of town and ran a stationery store in the village for decades, screaming at kids to stop touching everything in her store and to stop hanging out there if they weren't going to buy anything. She then clapped her hands loudly, twice and fast and the room quickly settled.

Edith started writing on the chalkboard and said the words as she did, "*Inter Arma Caritas*. Who here can tell me what this means?"

The women answered in unison. "In War, Charity."

She shook her head up and down, as if she were hearing an evangelist preach the Gospel. This was how they started every meeting. Every woman there knew what the words meant.

"It is a difficult day, ladies." To which the women looked alarmed. "While I know many of you think I called you here for this impromptu meeting to discuss the behavior around Room 54 and our injured prisoner of war, or that there has been someone who's been bringing in reading materials that... "

She looked to the other Janes for support on this.

"Disgraceful," said one of the three Janes.

"Inappropriate," sniffed another.

These adjectives gave Edith a reason not to be the heavy and lower herself into actually saying the words "disgraceful" or "inappropriate."

Frances kicked Mary's ankle. "Ouch!" Mary yelped, to which the women in the room turned and looked at her for a reason for her outburst. She reached down to her calf and quickly covered herself: "Charlie horse." She rubbed the spot, then turned to Frances and gave her a look that said, *knock it off, will ya.*

Edith continued: "If the news wasn't as important as it is that I have to deliver, I would go into these matters more fully, but I'm sure there won't be a problem with either going forward." Edith looked directly at Frances and Mary. Frances wanted to die. She was so mad at Mary because she told her she didn't want any part if this fiasco in the making and now she had Edith and three of her Janes giving them the stare down which was the same as accusing them.

Mary came back with, "I'm fine now. The pain's gone. No need for you all to worry." And Frances had to hold back a chuckle, turning her head away and covering her mouth with her hand to hide her smile and then she coughed intentionally to hide her response more.

"The rule, women, when we have an unusual injured, is that same assignments hold. If you are not supposed to help room 54, then you should not be in room 54, or standing outside room 54 and trying to see the man inside room 54. Do I make myself clear?" The room was quiet except for the three Janes who agreed with her that she was clear. Edith looked at the women in their gray seersucker uniforms. "I'm sorry." She said with her fit to be tied voice that often Frances heard her mom use when she was about to get angry.

The room responded with agreeing in a series *Yes, Got it,* or head shaking up and down. This seemed to satisfy Edith and the Janes.

"Now that that's settled." Edith said, which made Frances and Mary annoyed because she always did this. She started out by saying she wasn't going to talk about something that she talked about in a roundabout way. The girls often joked that it was getting slapped in the face, but you only realized it after it happened.

"She got us again." Mary whispered to Frances who whispered back:

"You better not bring anymore magazines, Mary, or you're gonna get kicked out."

"She doesn't know it was me."

"Well then she thinks it's me because she looked right at us."

"Girls, problem?" Edith yelled out, as their whispering was audible, despite the words being inaudible.

"Nope. Nope. Just talking about my iron. Frances says low iron can give you muscle cramps so that might be why I get charley horses."

"Oh, geez," Frances said under her breath. Mary was going to get her kicked out of the Gray Ladies and she for sure was going to have to answer to her father as to why she allowed Mary to bring in her father's girly magazine. Frances' family and Mary's family were from different sides of the tracks, as her mother and father put it, which was a nice way of saying that Mary's family wasn't as upstanding as them. Frances always knew what they meant and Mary always felt that her parents thought that Mary didn't come from the kind of family they felt their daughter should be associated with. Frances didn't care about this. She'd go to the ends of the earth for Mary and that included going against her own snobby parents. She loved them, but they were snobs. Frances couldn't deny this.

The women started talking, different groups forming in the room as more and more began whispering to one another, bored with the meeting all ready.

"Girls. Girls. Down a notch," Edith instructed as she raised her hands up high and pressed them toward the ground, as if conducting a choir and asking them to sing softer.

The Janes clapped their hands and directed the women to pay attention.

"We are about to be involved in an important mission."

The room got quiet.

"We get to help even more of our injured boys." She continued, getting emotional. "There's an evacuation being planned from all fronts, coming here to Torney, flying into the air base. We'll be asking more of you as we help." The room erupted with concern and comments: *Of course! Yes! Whatever's needed...*

"I knew you all could be counted on. Such a team. Such an amazing team."

The meeting ended shortly after. Edith was waiting for more information and her strategy for today was to make them aware that things were about to get more difficult. The war was headed their way. The war that happened after the fighting in the field, like Oklahoma and his sickness that wouldn't get better and the men who didn't have a limb or couldn't get over their rheumatic fever. It was the second phase of the war, the lasting one that stuck with the men for the rest of their lives and also for the women who spent time with them. History in the making. For all her shortcomings, Edith was a good leader, preparing them emotionally for battle.

As they walked back to the main building, the two paired in conversation amongst a flock of ladies moving here and there, Frances finally said it:

"Oklahoma told me he loved me today."

"Uh, ah... That's not right. You're spoken for."

"He didn't mean it like that."

"How else did he mean it?" Mary came back in her horsing around way, not understanding that this was a serious moment. "Frances plus Oklahoma sitting in a tree. First comes love, then comes marriage, then comes a baby in a baby carriage," she sang.

"STOP IT." Frances yelled.

Mary realized she crossed a line.

"It's not funny."

"I'm just teasing."

Frances turned around and walked in the opposite direction.

"Come on. It was a goof." Mary went after her. "This isn't the way."

"I know." Frances yelled at her, but kept walking fast, fury propelling her forward.

"Then turn around."

"No."

Mary rushed up to her, grabbed her arm and stopped her. "What's wrong with you?"

"He's dying." Frances said and tears welled up in her eyes.

"Ah, Fran," Mary said and pulled her into a hug as Frances broke down.

"I love him too." Frances mumbled; her face braced against her best friend's shoulder. "He's my friend and he's dying."

"I know you do." Mary told her as they embraced. A river of military personnel rushed about around the midstream island of grief. A frequent occurrence at Torney.

Chapter Six

True to her word, she returned the next day, but Oklahoma was not in the room. "Where's Henry?" She said out loud to no one, panicked with fear that he was dead evident in her inflection.

Alessandro was behind the curtain and he moved it to speak to her, but she bolted out of the room when she saw a nurse walk by in the hallway that she knew.

"Judy! Where's Henry?"

"He's in recovery from surgery."

"For what?" she asked.

"Stump infection cleaning."

"Oh."

"He'll be back, Frances. He did well. Try not to get too attached."

"I won't. I'm not." She answered. "Just surprised me. I didn't know about the surgery and when he wasn't here..."

The nurse moved on and Frances looked back at the room to Oklahoma's bed, then noticed Alessandro looking at her. Should I go in? She asked herself, unsure if it was something she should do. Was it appropriate for her to be with him alone?

"*Ciao*, Frances." He said, pulling back the drape to see her better.

"Hi Alessandro." She stepped inside the room. "*Ciao*? Hello?" she asked. "Is that the translation of hello?"

"*Si*," he replied. "*Ciao* is hello."

"And *si* is yes?"

"Yes. *Si* is yes." He smiled. She smiled back.

She walked to Oklahoma's bedside where she found a note on his nightstand. *Franny, I'm getting a tune-up today. Be back soon. Oklahoma.* He was a charmer. She placed the note in her uniform pocket, made his bed, fluffed his pillows, filled up his water pitcher and took out the trash, knowing Alessandro was watching her through a narrow space where the curtain did not close shut. When she looked back and caught his eye, he looked away.

She wrote a note for Oklahoma on his pad. *Oklahoma, so glad you are getting an oil change. I'll be here when you are back. Frances.* And she drew a sketch of Freddy the Pig, which was a good resemblance, then added to the note. *And Freddy.*

When she was done with refreshing Oklahoma's side of the room, she went to leave, then thought twice about it. She glanced over at Alessandro's side of the room. He'd closed his curtain more so that she couldn't see him and he couldn't see her.

"Alessandro? Do you need anything?" She asked and stepped on the side of his curtain so that he could see her completely. She ignored the feeling in her gut when she saw his incredibly handsome face.

He shook his head side to side. "No."

"No in Italian is the same as English?"

"*Si.* No '*et no.*"

"Yes. No is no." She translated back. "How come you close your curtain all the time?" She could see he didn't completely understand what she had said, so she grabbed the curtain, open and closed it to illustrate her question and when she closed it, added "Why closed?" and he understood her now.

"The women," he answered and held his hands up to his eyes and made circles with his fingers so it looked like binoculars.

"Ah, the women," Frances answered and they laughed. "They like you."

"*Si.*"

"We're not used to having men from other countries in here."

"*Si.*" He told her. 'I am '*e* circus."

"A circus?"

"A show?" He changed his word to fit his meaning and she understood.

"Si." She admitted because he was a show for the young women at Torney not only because he was an Italian POW, well Italian Service Unit member if she addressed it correctly, but his looks were what crushed the girls looking for some interesting way to go about their days. Gossip about him had been happening since his first day being injured, even to the point of how to handle this situation in the future if there were more men injured and should there be a section of the facility for the POWs. His situation had opened the issue that he may not be the only POW who needs hospital care and what would the process be for Torney to deal with this. It had come up especially with Edith Marshal in the Gray Lady meetings as when there began to be a parade of them trying to assist Oklahoma, but it was just a ruse to be near the foreigner. Alessandro didn't know all this, he just knew that women kept staring at him as they walked by his room, so he closed his curtain.

Alessandro's water pitcher was low. "You need water." She walked over to his bedside table where his meal was there for him to eat. "And you need to eat. You're not hungry?" She asked him.

"No."

She grabbed his water pitcher and went out of the room and filled it and brought it back in. She poured water in his cup. "You'll get dehydrated."

"Dehydrated?" he repeated.

She pretended to drink from the cup to show him. "Thirsty."

"Ah, thirsty. *Assetata.*" He took the cup of water from her that she handed him.

"You should eat." She pushed the table over his bed, closer to him so he could eat his meal which was peas, some typed of casserole. It didn't look too good to Frances. He took a bite and made a face.

"No good?" she asked.

"No." He shook his head.

"Tuna noodle casserole. Not my favorite."

"You like peas?" he said.

"Yes."

"Eat your peas?" He scooped up the peas onto the spoon and lifted it to his mouth, but many rolled off his spoon as he was using his left hand to feed himself and he was right-handed.

"I'll get them." She told him and picked up the peas that had rolled all over his bed and onto the floor.

"Sorry." He pointed to his right arm that was still bandaged and unusable.

"You're right-handed." Frances answered, more to herself than to him, as she understood why getting the spoonful of peas in his mouth was hard. "Here." She took the spoon from him and fed him the rest of the peas, four spoonsful.

"Thank you," he said.

"You are better?"

"Yes."

"Good. I'll see you tomorrow, Alessandro."

"Bye Frances."

She took the food tray away, and left the room, knowing she'd been in there far longer than she should have been, alone, with him. Not because of who he was, but because of how he made her feel.

The next day, she returned to find Oklahoma in his bed which eased her heart. She relaxed and acted as if nothing had happened. "Oklahoma, how are we today?"

"Look at my favorite Gray Lady."

"Seems you've returned."

"Yes."

"Hi Alessandro," she called out, now more comfortable acknowledging his presence.

"Hi Frances," came the gentle baritone from behind the curtain.

She sat beside Oklahoma's bedside in a chair and opened the book where the leaf was written on. She said, "I got your message."

"Yep. Figured you would."

"And you too have returned."

"Live to see another day."

"Good tune up?"

"So, they tell me. All the gunk's gone and I'm lookin' pretty."

"Why yes, you are." She smiled. "I have to go do library shift, but I just wanted to check on you first."

"Make sure I was alive?"

"Nah, I knew you were alive. I've got friends in high places. I can find out all about you without you telling me a word. Plus, you're Superman, so I knew you'd pull through."

"What are my powers then? Can Superman grow his legs back?"

"Nah, It's charisma."

"I knew it. You're in love with me."

"See. Charisma is your superpower. I'll come back in a few hours and we can figure out what this pig is up to next. Freddy is a very busy pig."

Frances patted his hand like he was a puppy. He grabbed her fingers and squeezed her hand, sweetly. "You're gonna be okay," he said to her before she pulled her hand away and it was a statement that said more than what it said. He meant when he died that she'd be okay, but she didn't want to hear it.

"Such a charmer. I'll be back in a few hours."

"I'll be here. Waiting with my superpower. Thinking how I'll charm you next."

"Bye Alessandro," she called out.

"Bye Frances."

Frances returned the next day and the next. Oklahoma didn't have too many days left. His time was close. Even Oklahoma knew it as the finality of life had a way of making itself known before it arrived, as if it had messaged them and said, *I'm on my way. Be there soon, just not sure on exactly which day, hour, minute, but I will be there soon.* A clock ticking down to the end of life, without sharing how many seconds were left. So she went every day and stayed for hours, to make him laugh and not feel alone.

Alessandro shared these hours with them, playing pantomimes which Oklahoma always guessed. A chicken? A tree? An Elephant? All three understood exactly what they were really doing without speaking of it, because if any of them tried to bring it up, Oklahoma would cut them off.

"Some things you don't wanna talk about," he'd say and after a consult with a nurse or doctor for his vitals or pain medication, then he'd add, "So 'ya don't talk about 'em."

He would remind Frances. Then if she got mushy eyed at all, he'd get after her and tell her, "And 'ya don't *cry* about 'em." He'd remind her between laughing and smiling and coughing, the infection heavy in his lungs, causing him within days not to have the strength to get out of bed. If he had legs below his knees, he wouldn't be able to stand upright and walk. That was how weak he'd become.

Still, every time he'd give her an order, she'd say, "You can't tell me what to do."

And he'd say, "I just did."

"But I just told you that you can't!" And she'd giggle as she dabbed a tear.

This exchange was good for a laugh no matter how many times they bantered this way and it happened often in Oklahoma's last days.

Getting better, Alessandro would laugh with them and try to

guess Frances' charades, answering in Italian when he forgot to speak English, which would make them all laugh. It was hilarious to play charades with answers no one understood. He could be right or he could be wrong, no one knew. Frances asked him about his upbringing in Italy, curious about him, yet trying to hide that she wanted to know all about him. Oklahoma could see Alessandro was a spark for her and she was for him, each lighting up at the sight of each other, as if sunshine to each other. He watched them from his corner of the room navigate their undeniable attraction, a little jealous, a little sad, a little in awe. The mixture was full of every emotion expected in a young man soon to pass, without having fallen in love. It was unfair.

Alessandro answered her questions. He had a magical childhood. The son of a baker who woke at three a.m. each morning to start the day at the bakery named after his mom Bella. It was on a famous street in Milan and the sun shined on it between two tall buildings so it looked like it was lit by the Gods. Here he spent his childhood after school, working with his parents and his little sister, Natali, when he wasn't studying violin. He spoke of Milan, a city he loved like nowhere else he'd seen in his travels across Europe performing and how much the war and everything Germany stood for was horrible. And the shame of it all he'd bring up, and would get sullen, like it was something he'd never get over, and he say, but I had no choice, as if reasoning with himself.

His arm was so much better that soon he'd be released according to the doctor. The only concern was mobility and how useful would his arm be once out of the brace. He'd have to do exercises to rehab the injury, but his prognosis had changed from fear that he may lose his arm to concern that it may not work as it did before the injury. "A fair trade," she heard the doctor say to him one day from behind the curtain which was more painful for him to hear than losing his arm, she knew, because he'd told them, "I am a violinist," as he pointed to his bandaged arm and repeated, with terror in his eyes

"I am *violinist*." He'd say with the crackle of fear in his voice that he wasn't now. Frances heard it, the desperation to be a violinist again, as if he was begging for his life.

It was on day seven that Oklahoma's pneumonia became so bad that he couldn't sit up and rarely talked. Frances tried her best to keep his spirits up but he knew, as she did, that his life would end soon at Torney at the young age of 22. His fever rose. His jokes became comments. Sentences became words.

"How's Oklahoma doing today?" she'd ask every time she returned and he always replied, "Better—now that you're here."

On the seventh day he didn't answer her right away, then spoke lightly, "Better." And smiled. "You're here."

All the words were whispered after that.

On the seventh day breathing was almost impossible.

And it was also on that day that Alessandro was released back to his barracks. His arm in a brace, prognosis good. His burns had healed with minor scars. But the violin—would he be able to play as before? He asked the doctors and nurses repeatedly. They answered that they weren't sure and he should be grateful he still had his arm and that its movement was returning.

This is not what Alessandro wanted to hear.

"I am a violinist."

He said this constantly to doctors and nurses, Frances and Oklahoma, as if playing again were as essential to him as air. But to this affirmation, they couldn't give him a better answer. Nor, it seems, did they care too. Alessandro was a prisoner of war and not their main concern. As promised, more American soldiers were already coming in. Torney would soon be overwhelmed and doctors had to prioritize.

Before Alessandro was to be escorted back to the barracks, he stood beside Oklahoma's bed. "Bye, my friend." He cautiously patted Oklahoma's hand.

Oklahoma whispered, almost inaudible: "Come close."

Alessandro leaned down and Oklahoma whispered in his ear. Alessandro stood back and answered. "*Si.*" He grabbed Oklahoma's hand and squeezed it. "*Addio*, Oklahoma."

"Addio, Alessandro."

It was all Frances could do not to break down in sobs—for both of them.

Military police waited at the door to escort him back to his barracks and politely asked him to move along. Even they felt the heaviness of the moment.

"Bye Frances." He said with tears in his eyes. "I will miss you," he said quietly, so the military police didn't hear. "Don't forget me."

"I won't." she answered, wanting to hug him goodbye, but that wouldn't be right and it would set off the gossips. And she wiped tears from her face as she smiled. "I'll never forget you." she whispered quietly, but he knew what she felt for him with the tears, and that was enough for him to leave knowing he mattered to her.

She watched him leave the room and wanted to run after him.

The faintest of voices— "Frances. Come here." Oklahoma asked.

She leaned down. His breath already had the staleness of death.

"I need a favor."

"Anything."

"Leave."

"No."

"Don't come back till I'm gone."

"No." Now the tears couldn't be stopped.

"Please."

"You don't mean it."

"I do," he said, smiling through tears.

She picked up the book. "We haven't finished." She opened the pages, moving the leaf that they used for the bookmark.

"Finish it. Then you have to go." He was begging now. "Promise?"

"Yes."

Frances read only one page. Oklahoma closed his eyes and fell asleep. They had about twenty pages to go still, which gave her the excuse to come back the next day and the next and the next because she planned to read the book so slowly that they wouldn't get to the end. This way she wouldn't have to honor that promise, just yet.

She closed the book, stared at Alessandro's empty bunk, curtain pulled back now, the sheets and blankets messed from how he'd left them, and waited an hour for Oklahoma to wake. He didn't. She placed the book on a side table and stood over Oklahoma, watched his chest barely rise and fall, struggling for each breath.

She kissed his forehead and left.

The nurses told Frances he never woke up.

She showed up the next day. He was already on his way back to Oklahoma to his family.

Hey Oklahoma, how you doin' today?

Better now that you're here.

She had grieved each day she stood by him during his decline so that now when she was told he'd reached the end? She was prepared and took the information in as if she were being told something as simple as the sky is blue. It's what he would've wanted.

She went into the room where she'd spent days talking about far off places the two men had been—Italy, Africa, the middle of the Pacific. Their lives had been so sad and grand already, beyond what her life would be and the excitement of hearing their stories had been some of the best days of her life. Now, Oklahoma was gone and Alessandro was unreachable. She'd lost them both on the same day.

Frances remembered about the book. Someone had taken it out of the room. No one seemed to know where *Freddy the Detective* had gone. She searched under the bed and in the drawers. Nothing. She walked out of Room 54 for the last time, glancing at the chalk board which was now clear. No names remained. Oklahoma and Alessandro erased just like that, with a swipe of a towel and it hit her just how fast it had all happened.

Life was a blur. So short.

Frances wandered the halls to the sitting room off the front lobby where the library was and saw the lime green cover with the silly pig holding up a magnifying glass to his eye and wearing a plaid detective's hat, walking upright on his back hoofs. She took it out of the basket and hugged it like it was Oklahoma and closed her eyes as she took a wave of grief so hard that it made her scrunch her face up as she fought off tears and the hurt. She drowned in grief as it suffocated her. She bent forward as if needing to vomit, then slid down to the floor where she sat against the desk for a long time listening to the sounds of the hospital around her, hidden from site, holding the book and staring forward at the shelves, reading titles and names of authors. A welcome diversion as she waited to get the strength to stand and move on with life.

This was the hard part a person not in a battlefield had the luxury to choose: when to move on after death has arrived. You move or you die. Time to grieve can't happen in the moment. She thought about this, then returned her attention to the spines of the books in front of her. Oklahoma was the first person she'd known who'd died and the finality when a life ended seemed so strange. Mortality had been an abstraction. Oklahoma's death made it a reality.

Standing finally, she placed the *Freddy the Detective* novel in her bag and walked to the main building. Passing through the courtyard where they used to sit, Frances was stopped by several girls who gave their condolences—then Mary spotted her.

"There you are!" She grabbed Frances's arm and pulled her through the group of gawkers quickly. "Stick with me. I'll get you out of here."

"Where are we going?"

"The tower. We need privacy."

The girls climbed the stairs to the landing spot under the bell.

"Okay, let it out. No one can see you cry up here but me."

"I've already cried," Frances said—then she started crying again.

"Uh-huh." Mary hugged her. "You're not done."

"I knew he was gonna die, but did he have to die?" Frances said as she walked around under the bell, the majestic mountains behind her.

"It wasn't his choice, Fran."

And Frances started laughing. "I know that."

"None of us get a choice."

"Yeah."

She got herself together and they both sat down and leaned back against the wall. An army transport flew overhead towards the airfield. Frances watched it pass. "Steel bird in the sky."

"Going by," Mary added.

And together they said the end: "Let's watch it fly, bye, bye."

"That's what I did with Oklahoma this week. I watched him fly away."

"He's... "

"Out of pain." Frances stood up and looked out at the mountains. "Now I'm the one in pain."

"It won't always feel like how you feel today. Tomorrow it'll get better and the next day... "

"I know," she said automatically, then shook her head. "Why did I say that? I don't know. I've never known anyone like this who's died. I didn't know it would feel like this. How long will this terrible feeling stay here?" Placing palms to chest as if having a heart attack. "It's here, in my chest and God, it's bad, it's bad," she said as she crumbled forward to the floor and lay on her side, infantile, desperate.

"Frances, Jesus," Mary said as she reached over and pulled her broken friend onto her lap. "You don't have to feel this alone. You have me." She brushed Frances hair away from her face and leaned down and kissed her on her forehead. "I love you, Frances."

Frances calmed. "You ever think about dying?"

"Try not to."

"People disappear. In minutes. They disappear. All their memories, gone. All their stories just gone. It's the end, just like every book says at the end of the story. THE END. It's so simple but I can't understand it."

"You don't have to, Frances. It's death. No one can understand it." Frances rolled towards Mary, placing her head in Mary's gut, reaching arms around her waist and held on tight. Mary rubbed her head, smoothing back her curls, placing them into a soft mass of spiral paths that led to the open world.

"It's just the end."

"Maybe. Maybe not. I don't know. It's complicated."

She and Frances let out a laugh as she rolled her head back to look away at a plane flying by. "I just said it was simple."

"I know, but it's complicated too."

Frances wiped her eyes. "It is." Then turned back so that her face was buried in Mary's lap. "I just want to stay here."

"We can."

"With you." Frances reached her arms around Mary's waist again and hugged tight.

"Okay." Mary leaned forward, body shielding Frances, arms wrapped around her like a mother and child. "It's simple too though. That's what makes it all so confusing, and I don't think we'll ever understand it."

"It can't all be explained, I don't think now that I'm feeling this. This is... there's no words, no explanation."

"Well. Maybe. But you'll be okay, Franny. I do know that. In a while, you will." She said as she leaned her head forward so that she covered Frances completely.

Weeks passed with the *Freddy the Detective* book sitting on her bedside table in her room. The illustration of the pig on the cover made her smile as the pig was drawn to be almost standing like a human, wearing cape and hat, holding a magnifying glass. This book was close to her every night on her bedside table while across the room on her desk was Nicholas' photo. She kept it at a distance not because she didn't care about him, but because it was so painful to worry about him.

Oklahoma was gone and his death made it so real to her what the dangers were for Nicholas that she couldn't stand it hardly. *Why is this happening?* she'd ask and think back to life before the war. It wasn't supposed to be this way and yet it was. How she wanted life to be and how it really was, this occupied so much of her thoughts. The dream and reality fighting inside her, reality always winning.

Oklahoma's mom's heartache must be indescribable. Frances thought of her often and wished she could speak with her and tell her all the moments of Oklahoma's last days and how much he laughed, but it wasn't her place. One thing she could do, she decided, was send the last book her son read. So one morning she sat down at her desk with the book and, next to the picture of Nicholas, she opened the front cover and wrote on the inside.

Dear Mrs. Smith,

Holding you in my heart. Henry had become a dear friend and I want you to know how much he talked about you and home. He requested I read this book to him because you read it to him as a boy and it brought him comfort so I want you to have it. He will be missed.

Deepest sympathy,

Miss Frances Clark

Gray Lady, American Red Cross, Torney General Hospital.

She wrapped the book in vanilla paper, tied it with a string and addressed the package to Oklahoma's mother, which was an address she'd engraved in her brain from sending so many of Oklahoma's letters for him and took it to the post office. She'd done all of this in a moment of emotion where she'd been in a sort of frenzy for an hour as she thought of the idea to send her the book and then went through with it. Now as she stepped out of the post office and walked back to her bike, coming down from the last hour which was so full of emotion, she remembered the only advice Oklahoma gave her.

Always be brave, Miss Frances.

It was as if he were there with her, speaking those words again. She stopped and absorbed his imagined presence.

Alright Oklahoma, I'll give it a shot.

Chapter Seven

Frances stood in the hospital yard like a cactus trying to get a break from the busy work inside.

Torney had been a madhouse since the Army put in place the massive air evacuation of casualties from all fronts being sent to Torney. They'd been landing men at the air base at a pace she'd not seen before and it'd been going on for weeks keeping everyone busy. This was good for Frances, though, as it stopped her from dwelling on Oklahoma's passing. Her Torney library responsibilities had escalated. So many men wanted books to read that Frances went to the library daily to return books and check out more. Each time she had to hear from Phyllis that the *Freddy the Detective* book was overdue and raking up late fees. Frances almost spilled to beans and told her that she'd sent it to Oklahoma's mom, but she was a little scared of Phyllis. Finally, she lied, telling her the book was missing and paid the five cents lost book fee as *Freddy the Detective* would never be returned.

"Fucking war," Frances said to herself as she walked down a path. "I'm so done with this fucking war!" She tried to remember what life was like before the war started as she kicked a rock down the path.

Swimming as a little girl in their pool came to mind, giggling, smiling, no worries as she'd dive to the bottom of the deep end to touch the drain first before her friends.

A desert breeze rolled through, blowing hair in her face. She smelled the dust in the air, gritty, parsed by the wind into microbes carried in the air. Infrequent gusts had been pulsing around the valley on and off all day. A summer storm brewed, the heated kind that made one confused on if it was summer or fall. Heat mixed in the wind and gurgling cloud clusters threatening rain shimmied above. Frances loved these summer storms that came after the brutally hot summer and this weather state fit her melancholy mood. It was also thrilling to think of flash floods coursing down the mountains and canyons.

She'd walked far, realizing she'd unconsciously meandered over towards the training barracks where she knew Alessandro lived. This was not the first time she'd been walking hoping to see him, even though she didn't admit it to herself. She turned a corner not too far from the training barracks, the part of the facility grounds that she'd never set foot on where the ISU was housed. Five prisoners in blue jumpsuits were working the grounds, pulling weeds, sweeping pathways, turning soil around the plants, aerating dirt. American army personnel supervised, but the ISU's were under light protection, having been allowed to have more freedoms since they arrived and the community became more comfortable with them working at Torney. Frances approached, hoping one might be Alessandro, but as she got closer and could see the men's faces more clearly, none of them were him.

"Ma'am." A soldier said to her as she walked by and the prisoners looked at her, "Would you please move out of this area while we're working here? Be done in 'bout twenty."

"Yes sir," she said. Not one to like attention, she'd never have come this close if not for her longing to see him.

Frances turned around and headed in a north-east direction, thinking about Alessandro. She'd never been to the laundry and was unsure of which way to walk. She wanted to see him just one more time, see how he was doing. As she walked around the grounds looking for the laundry building, asking people for directions, she found her way towards the last building on the north side of the grounds. She stood outside, pacing, nervous, not knowing if she should walk in. Her palms were moist. She felt afraid and brave at the same time and it made her think of how this must be a sliver of how Nicholas feels everyday as a marine in a foreign land, not knowing which day he'd see combat. Guilt hit her hard then, that she was trying to see another man she cared about but rationalized that this was just to see if Alessandro was doing well. He'd been a patient. She was being thorough, going above and beyond. Also, she wanted to talk to him one last time as he understood her feelings for Oklahoma like no one else, not even her best friend Mary, because they spent the last hours of his life together in that hospital room and no one other than those three understood this profound experience.

Frances opened the door and stepped inside, hidden behind shelves filled with buckets that had labels on them: bleach, ammonia, detergent. When the door closed behind her, the room went dark grey as sunlight was shut out. The building smelled of chemicals, musty from hot moisture in the air. She could hear men talking in Italian. Between the buckets on the shelves, she could see large bins of laundry that blocked her view of the main area where the men worked. She moved out from behind the shelf and sneaked closer. Standing behind the laundry bins, she peered around the side slightly to watch the men. She scanned the room, looking for Alessandro. There were fifteen or so men working, sorting laundry, placing it in cleaning vats, moving out to dry and be folded, POWs providing human labor for the hospital.

Frances searched first for his large frame, tall, masculine bone structure, his thick head of hair. *Not him, not him, not him,* she thought as she knocked off contenders quickly. Her nerves had her in a fit that she'd be spotted, heart pumping with adrenaline. How would she explain why she was there, spying on men from behind dirty laundry bins? This wouldn't look good if she were found.

A POW, head down, folded laundry at the other edge of the room with effort, his arm handicapped with small range of motion. *There you are*, identifying the thick black hair, the square jaw profile. Looking down at the massive pile of white towels, Alessandro picked one up, folded it and placed it in the laundry bin to his right and did this over and over. *Look up*, she shouted in her mind, a silent command. She'd been inside for a while and wanted to leave, but wouldn't until she saw his face one more time. He paused and rubbed his arm, wincing as if it were causing him pain. *Turn around, Alessandro.*

Two guys brought over a new bin of clean towels for him to fold and pushed his large bin of folded towels off after replacing it with an empty bin. The men blocked her view of him during this so she couldn't see him at all.

The summer storm that had threatened to rain all day started its downpour. The rain beat against the aluminum roof and sounded like an orchestra of tiny drums. Her heart was the second beat she was monitoring. She felt it inside her chest, not knowing how she'd get beyond this moment to the next without fainting. This behavior wasn't something she normally engaged in, but she'd been doing things like this with increasing frequency lately to the point where she was beginning to lose control. The beats of her heart, the rain, the clock ticking silently in her mind pushed her to want to get out of there.

Each minute that passed increased the chance of getting spotted. She leaned out from behind the laundry, partially revealed and whispered his name, "Alessandro!" He turned in her direction, as if he could sense her, looking towards the area she stood. When she saw him, she had so many butterflies in her stomach she felt she could fly. It was still there, that feeling that he belonged to her and she belonged to him. If she could, without risking everything in her life, she'd walk up and kiss him and never be away from him again. She stepped out from behind the bin, revealing herself, but he'd turned away and didn't see her. The door opened. She jumped and let out a small scream when she saw behind her a POW who'd walked in, now perplexed by her presence. She moved past, pushed open the door and ran out.

Raindrops the size of quarters hit her as she rushed away, between the buildings, amongst others who hurriedly moved inside, bodies rushing quickly in different directions. She breathed hard as she ran, as if a killer were on her trail and only gathered herself together after finding coverage under an awning around a corner. She braced her backside against the wall, hands pressed back on each side, like she was being suctioned to it, tense muscles turning her body into a straight board. She waited. Footsteps could be heard, moving fast, approaching, yet she was cornered as to her right was a fence. Scared, she moved closer to the fence, but there was no way to escape. The footsteps came closer. She waited. Closed her eyes. Breathed deep and then she saw Alessandro round the corner.

"Frances?"

He wiped the water out of his eyes after taking shelter from the rain next to her under the awning. "Frances." He said again, not questioning this time, but stating her name as if he were finally being spared the pain of not being able to see her.

"Oklahoma died," she blurted out, eyes welling with tears. The emotions she'd been holding back rose at the sight of him, remembering the three of them sharing the last week of Oklahoma's life. That vigil. Seeing Alessandro brought up the raw pain she'd been suppressing.

"*Si*," he said. "Yes." He gazed at her as if unsure of who they were to each other.

It was a relationship that was forbidden and inappropriate. Frances wasn't clear on how he felt about her. She knew she had feelings for him. Did Alessandro feel the same way?

"I wanted to see you one more time," she finally said, but could tell he was confused. She placed a hand on his shoulder. "I miss you."

"I miss you," he answered.

Silence followed. They assessed one another, trying to understand what was really happening.

"What did Oklahoma say to you?"

"*Cosa?* Eh, what?" he said after, trying to remember his English.

In the distance, a man called "Alessandro!" Someone was searching for him.

"Oklahoma, what did he say to you that day when he whispered in your ear?"

The man called out for him again. It was an American accent. Alessandro looked nervous. "Must go." He pointed in the direction he came. "Bye Frances."

"No." She reached for his hand and held him there. "No." She wanted him to stay. They might never see each other again. This was war—it happened all the time.

Alessandro reached with his free hand and brushed his thumb along her cheek. Then rested his hand on the back of her neck, pulled her to him, leaned over and kissed her. The man continued to call for him, his voice mixing with the sounds of the heavy rain. Alessandro let go of Frances, pulled his hand from hers, took a step back.

"Bye Frances." He placed his hand over his heart, turned and disappeared around the corner.

"No." Frances whispered. "No." She went after him, coming round the side of the building in time to see him meet up with the American soldier who'd been searching for him. After exchanging a few words, Alessandro shrugged and they went back inside the laundry.

But before he entered, he looked over his shoulder for a moment, as if searching for her face.

Frances stood there, soaked, feeling the pain of Alessandro's absence. He was there. He kissed her. Now he was gone from her life again.

She didn't know what to do other than just stand there wishing he would come back. She waited. Frozen.

Rain pooled around her feet as she stood in the path of a graded sidewalk designed to direct the precious water there before guiding it into the surrounding landscape. She looked up at the swirling storm blending about in the sky with awe. She thought of Nicholas for a second and he seemed to be a stranger, someone from long ago she knew and now didn't. The kiss, Alessandro, felt real and right.

"He loves me." She said out loud and smiled.

The day had become different and she was captured by its unpredictability and what it meant for the rest of her life.

Realizing she was late. Frances rushed back to the main building, scheming of how she might see him again, stepping in puddles, splashing her calves with muddy water as if she were a child again without a care in the world.

She made it back with only minutes before she was supposed to meet her mom out front. She gathered her bag from the corner on the bookshelf where she stored her things when she volunteered and headed off to the grand bathroom in the lobby where she changed out of her wet gray uniform and into a nice dress. She brushed her wet hair out of her face and cleaned the mud off her legs, then stopped for a second and thought about Alessandro's lips on hers, him close to her, his face, hands, his masculine tall frame around her, finger sliding across her face, the warm hand behind her neck. She smiled, felt scared, laughed, became serious, a tumble of emotions as her mind recalled the encounter.

Reality slowly asserted itself. She continued getting herself together. "I'm gonna get a the 'what in the world' for sure," she told her reflection in the mirror. Then she paused for a moment and said, almost absurdly: "You. Are. A. Woman," she said this without mugging or goofing. No giggles.

It was like greeting a new person.

She cleaned up as well as she could, headed out the front of the hospital toward her mother's car which was already in the round-about in front of El Mirador Tower, the spot where she always waited for Frances. The rain had ceased. A warm wind had dried much of the ground already so that if you didn't see it, you wouldn't believe that within the last hour rain doused the valley.

"What in the world?" Her mom gasped as Frances approached the car and opened the passenger door. "Why is your hair wet?" she asked as Frances got in the car, then reached out and touched strands of her hair to confirm that it indeed was wet, though drying quickly.

"It rained."

"Well, Frances? I don't know what to do?"

"Let's go."

"No. I can't have you coming to our Women's Luncheon with wet hair and not even a lick of lipstick." Her mom went into her bag and pulled out lipstick and handed it to her.

Frances got out of the car. "Then go without me."

"Frances, get in the car. You're being ridiculous."

Frances got back in the car and her mom started driving. "Why do you care so much about appearances?"

"It's how the world works. You should know by now that your reputation is everything. It always precedes you and once it's tarnished, there's nothing you can do about it."

"Now you're being ridiculous."

"Frances, ah, what's gotten into you?"

"Still the same girl, just with wet hair, God forbid."

They pulled into the parking lot of the Women's Club. After parking and turning off the engine, her mother turned to her, "Frances, maybe you should drive home and fix your hair and makeup and come back."

"Are you really that embarrassed to be seen with me?"

"Of course not. I'm just sure you don't want to go in front of this group of women like this. They seem sweet, but it's a room full of sharks."

"Like this?" Frances pulled out her pocketbook mirror and looked at herself. "I think I look pretty good. Let me just fix my hair." She took her palm and rubbed her hair so that it went all over and became messier. "There. That's better." Frances went to open the car door.

"Stop! And stop now!"

Frances pulled her hand away from the door handle. "I'm teasing." Frances brushed her hair and put on lipstick as she looked in her pocket mirror under the watchful eye of her mom, who'd gone silent —a strategy she employed when pushed to her limit. It was time to get in line or she'd hear it from her father later that night. With her appearance fixed as best as possible, Frances and her mom stepped out of the car, waved and smiled at the other women as they headed into the hall.

Inside, women milled about saying their hellos and finding their seats. As Frances walked between groups of them, they eyed her up and down. They smiled and said hello, but the look on their faces told her they were shocked that her hair was wet.

Mother was right, sharks for sure.

Frances moved quickly to the back of the room where the punch bowl table was set up and got a glass simply to have something in her hands. She stood against the back wall to tried to blend in with the wallpaper.

Mrs. Draper, Nicholas' mom, came into the room and, as if equipped with a homing device, made a beeline for her future daughter-in-law. Frances wanted to die as Mrs. Draper cut between the swarms of women moving here and there, chatting up the news of the town that week. Frances felt stuck to the floor, numb, unable to move as the enormity of what she'd done that afternoon passed through her like a virus making her feel instantly sick. If any of them found out what had happened with Alessandro, Frances would become the biggest scandal in town. Her parents would be publicly shamed and probably disown her. Her fiancé would leave her and all these sharks in this room would call her an Able Grable behind her back and possibly to her face.

"Frances. Hi Frances. The future Mrs. Draper. My future daughter-in-law. I didn't know you were coming to this boring luncheon today," Nicholas' mom said loudly as she gave her a hug. "Frances, dear, you have to sit by me, dear. It's so good to see you, but dear your hair is wet. You'll catch a cold for sure. What happened? Did you take a run in the rainstorm we had an hour ago and get yourself a mess?" Mrs. Draper was longwinded and known for jabs expertly inserted into verbose greetings. "Dear? Are you alright? You're about catatonic. I just can't get you to talk for the life of me."

"Yes... I, I... yes, I got caught in the rain."

"My Nicholas, our Nicholas, I should say, I got a letter from him just two days ago. He misses you. Oh, I can't wait until he's home and you two can start your lives together and I can be a grandmother. This blasted war. I'm so tired of this blasted war, taking my baby boy away from me and how I worry."

Frances had also received a letter from Nicholas a few days before and she was so happy. She read it to Mary and went on and on talking about how glad she was that he was still hers. There'd been months prior with few letters and the ones she got he seemed detached from her which is why she wondered if he even loved her anymore. He'd come out of whatever he was going through and was back to acting how he used to when he called her his sweet, which made her want to call him her lover boy again. She'd seemed so sure of her future with him when she got that letter. Today changed that. All she wanted now was Alessandro.

"Please get your plates! We'll begin shortly."

The ladies began breaking off their conversations and heading over to a table that had a line of casseroles and Jell-O masterpieces to choose from. Frances and Mary jokingly called the colorful blobs masterpieces because you never knew what leftover food was tossed inside so each one was so unique that it could never be duplicated. Meals were always casserole as it made it easier to stretch ingredients to their maximum. Rations of sugar, butter, eggs and meat made it essential to making sure every scrap of food was used and throwing scraps into a casserole assured food wasn't wasted. The Women's Club has been a big promotor of women planting victory gardens to help. Most every home grew their own vegetables and fruit, which was challenging in the desert. A recipe book for casseroles was created by the women and printed by Frances' father and he featured a recipe each week in the paper and held a casserole competition during the rodeo days. Her mom won for her tuna noodle casserole which she served every Monday for dinner.

After the women made their way back to their tables, they stood and said the Pledge of Allegiance and her mother who was the President, went to the front of the room and led a prayer to protect our boys before going into club matters.

"Billy Rostin had his bike stolen so any of the baked good items sold at the meeting would go towards buying him a replacement or if anyone knows of someone who has a bike they could donate, that is preferred. The Women's Club has been asked to lead the decorations for the New Year's dance at Torney. If you want to volunteer, there's a list on the back table to sign up. The Red Cross blood drive needs more donations. Please be sure to encourage any family member who is due to visit the Red Cross donation center at Torney."

Frances, sitting next to Mrs. Draper, appeared to be listening to her mom, but was thinking of Alessandro. She replayed it again, how he reached out for her and kissed her without asking because he knew she cared for him just from the way she looked at him. Flashes of his eyes looking into hers, his arms around her, their lips touching. How he said *Bye Frances* in such a way that she knew he didn't ever want to leave her and the pain she felt when he pulled his hand away from hers.

He loves me, she thought, believing this to be true beyond any doubt.

Chapter Eight

They were alone in the room and Edith was hard to read. Frances, hands in her lap, fingers linked, tapped her foot as she processed what was just said to her. "It happened once. That one time." She teared up. "Please, don't tell my parents."

Edith had called her in to have a talk and now they discussed the kiss she had with Alessandro that was witnessed by someone unnamed.

"Who saw us?"

"I can't tell you, but the person has agreed not to tell anyone else and to let me handle the matter."

"Everything's such a mess now," Frances said to herself, more than to Edith, as she felt the danger she'd brought into her life with her actions. She was no longer a sheltered girl.

"Tell me about your relationship with Alessandro. I need to know everything so I can figure out what is best for this matter."

"Am I in trouble?"

"It's not like that, Frances. I need to assess how this happened, so you need to tell me everything. He shared the room with Henry so I know this is how you two met, but can you tell me what happened in the hospital room, so I understand why you went to the laundry to find him?"

"When Oklahoma got pneumonia, I knew his time…" She paused as she didn't want to say that she knew he'd be dying soon, but Edith understood. "He knew his time was ending and it made him happy when I showed up. I didn't know what to do for him except be there and make him laugh if I could. It was odd."

"How so?" Edith asked.

"It felt like I was the wife he'd never get the chance to have, and…" she dabbed her eyes with a tissue. "He was dying and he needed me so I went every day and read a book to him that we hadn't finished and the three of us would talk. Alessandro speaks some English and kept talking about how worried he was that he might not play the violin again. He's a famous violinist in Europe, like a child prodigy, I guess. He was devastated."

"What else?"

"Nothing else. We just talked a lot. Helping Henry so he wasn't alone. Alessandro got better and Oklahoma got worse." She stopped, unable to go on.

"What? Frances? You can tell me?"

"On the same day, Alessandro got released and Oklahoma died. I lost them both forever within hours."

"It's hard." Edith agreed, giving Frances a moment to catch her breath. "Tell me about you and Alessandro? Did anything happen in the hospital room that I should know about that you haven't told me?"

Frances became even more alarmed as she understood the meaning of the question she asked. "No. God no. I swear. Nothing. I swear."

"Frances?" Edith said, "I need to know these things so I can understand what to do."

"You don't have to do anything. There's nothing *to* do. It was that one time and I only went there to see him… to see how he was doing and he followed me outside and we kissed." Frances stopped talking for a moment, the loss of all this hitting her again but compounded with guilt from her betrayal of Nicholas.

"Why did you go to the laundry?"

"I just wanted to see Alessandro one more time, to see how he was. Tell him about Oklahoma. I missed him and it was stupid, I know and I'm sorry. I didn't mean for it to happen. It was the first and only time, I promise."

"Do you have feelings for him?" Edith asked.

"I think I may be in love with him, but my father would disown me, so please don't tell my parents and I'm engaged to Nicholas. If we'd met under different circumstances, but we didn't. I'm engaged. I'm going to marry Nicholas Draper when he returns. If this gets out..."

Edith lifted the trashcan up for Frances to put her tissues in and then lifted the tissue box for her to take more. She was silent and this disturbed Frances more than if she'd said something. Edith stood up and walked back and forth for a minute, thinking on what to do, then sat back down across from Frances.

She stayed silent for a long time before speaking.

"It was back in 1924 when I fell in love with a... colored man who worked at my parents' store, bringing in supplies, stocking shelves and lifting heavy items that my dad couldn't. We spent a lot of afternoons alone when I'd work at the store, talking about everything. Seemed we were never at a loss of words between us and the time would fly by when I was with him. I would've married him if I could and thought about running off. One night we almost eloped, but I got scared and didn't meet him. He left and I never saw him again.

"What was his name?"

"Clarence."

"How old were you?"

"Eighteen. He was nineteen. Lived on the other side of town so we never would've run into each other if he didn't work at our store."

"I'd never meet Alessandro if POWs weren't brought to Torney. I didn't plan for this to happen. It just happened." Edith was silent again. Frances tried reading her. Was she in trouble? Would she be cut out of the Gray Ladies? What would she tell her parents? She'd never felt so uncomfortable.

"We've been looking to start a program here, but I've been too busy with so many girls to oversee. Some chapters of the Gray Ladies help soldiers with recovery by using music to improve their spirits. It's been in my mind for some time to add musical instruments to the book library that the boys can play in the garden as a way of physical therapy for their injuries as they heal, as well as helping to pass the time they spend here. I believe we have a piano. But we need other instruments. Have them playing guitar for example, harmonica or… violin."

Frances looked up, hopeful. "What are you saying?"

"I'm saying it could be good mental and physical therapy for the patients and I'm sure Alessandro's doctor would prescribe that he be given access to play the violin as part of his rehabilitation for the injury to his arm, if a violin could be found. And I'm sure that I could arrange one final meeting with Alessandro where you could deliver the violin, on doctor's orders—if that would be fine with you?"

"Yes!" Frances had to restrain her joy. "Of course."

"Good," Edith said and stood up again. She walked around as she talked, as if she too were excited by the idea. This meeting had suddenly turned into something thrilling. "You oversee our library and you've done an exceptional job so you would be the best person to lead the drive to find instruments for our musical instrument library, especially with your father's paper. We can post notices in there to get the word out."

Frances looked up at the woman she'd dismissed as dry and cold for so long with relief. "I agree. I *would* be the best person and I'm sure my father will help." She told her and then reached out and grabbed her hand in hers, put her head down as she processed her emotions. "Thank you."

Edith pulled her hand away after a second, as if this intimacy were a bit uncomfortable for her. "No, no, Frances. Thank *you* for helping. It's in my best interest to have you handle this for the Gray Ladies, being such a dedicated Red Cross volunteer."

Frances smiled. This woman was a gem. She didn't know what to say.

"Well," Edith said, hoping she'd get the hint that their conversation was over, but Frances didn't pick up the cue. "You may go now." Edith told her, her face still stoic.

Frances stood up, a bit bewildered still about this turn of events and slowly walked to the door as she processed what'd just happened. It dawned on Frances that Edith had taken a big chance in sharing her story of Clarence. It suggested a level of trust that shocked Frances. She would never have imagined Edith living through such a matter or that she was so compassionate. The town was full of gossips. *Sharks.* Frances was determined to not let Edith down. Then Edith threw her a parting curveball:

"And Frances."

"Yes, Edith."

"This meeting, if a violin is donated for you to deliver, will be the last time you see Alessandro."

What? Thought Frances. *Oh no...*

"Yes."

"And this is the last time we'll speak about the matter of the kiss between us or to anyone else."

"Yes."

Frances stood, waiting for the next order from Edith.

"Time to get back to your work."

"Yes." Frances said as she walked out of the room, astounded and somewhat crestfallen. When Edith had suggested musical therapy, it sounded like Frances would be an active part of it. She'd fleetingly imagined watching if not assisting Alessandro in his musical rehabilitation.

No matter. This was how it was. She'd take it.

· · ·

A few days later the announcement in the paper was placed:

Do you have an instrument not being used? The Gray Ladies need you to loan your unused musical instruments to Torney so wounded soldiers can play while they recover from injuries received while fighting for your freedom. Bring your donations to the Gray Lady lending library at the hospital main entrance and help bring joy to the boys in the service recovering from their injuries overseas!

Within a week, instruments began to be donated or given on loan: a banjo, two harmonicas, three flutes, a trombone, three ukuleles, wind chimes—but no violin. Frances heard all the stories that went with each instrument as they came in and made a notecard for each with the details of where they came from and notes on what the person who donated had told her. She had not expected to hear so many stories about the instruments, but it seemed people were often emotionally attached to them. Frances tagged each instrument with a number on a card so she might easily match the instrument to the person who'd loaned it to Torney and details of the look and condition of the instrument:

#1 Banjo, on loan from Sarah Kelly. Pearl neck inlays, light wood, scratch on back of body, missing one string, belonged to her grandfather, on loan for 6 months.

#2 Flute, loaned by Patty Trixby, belongs to her son, soldier Carl Trixby servicing in the Pacific. Return when her son returns home.

And so on...

Frances had gone to high school with Carl Trixby. He was one of those guys who didn't look at her much or talk to her much as they aged. They'd been chummy in kindergarten. He liked nap time and would suck his thumb as he fell right to sleep. She'd struggle to stay quiet, tossing on the mat like she was being held down by some horrible monster trying to kill her. She'd toss. Carl would sleep. Then after, they'd go back to playing house where he was her husband and she was his wife. Now this war, him in danger—nothing she'd ever imagined for him back then when they were so sweet together. Frances wanted to make sure to note important details as her father placed updates to the advertisement in the paper with a list of those who donated. The newspaper advertisement was updated to include:

The Gray Ladies would like to thank Patty Trixby for donating the flute of her son, Army soldier Carl Trixby, to the recovering soldiers at Torney while Carl bravely fights for our freedom in the Pacific!

This strategy then led to more people donating so they could see their name in the paper for their good deed. It was the strategy her father's paper employed for publicly shaming those who did not contribute to the War Loans. He listed the names of all villagers who donated to the War Loans, shaming those who didn't by not having their names on the list. Having an instrument to donate was different than having money to donate to a War Loan, Frances knew, but was still disappointed when no one donated a violin. She'd hoped to be able to at least help Alessandro play the violin again because she cared about him.

It was in the fourth week after the first announcement went in the paper and two weeks since there'd been any notice in the paper at all, when a beat-up fiddle was donated by old Mr. Keller who used to play at the local rodeo, but his arthritis had become so bad he wasn't able to lift the bow into position and his back hurt too much to keep his neck in position against the fiddle to play. He'd named his fiddle

Maisey Baby and told Frances long stories of his days playing it on the rodeo circuit for decades. Mrs. Keller stood quietly next to him yet rolled her eyes sweetly as he reminisced about his days playing for the crowds. She finally piped up when he said he could still play the fiddle like the devil and she reminded him that he couldn't. Old Mr. Keller told Frances that he and Mrs. Keller never got so lucky to have kids, but if they had a fiddle-playing boy at Torney and playing the fiddle makes him better, then he can have his Maisey Baby on loan. She accepted it, with guilt, as she didn't tell him she'd be delivering his fiddle to an Italian prisoner of war. She'd heard so much discrimination about the POWs even at her own kitchen table, that she didn't want to know if that made a difference to Mr. Keller.

It was only days after the Keller fiddle was donated that Edith got Frances a meeting. As she walked down a hall holding the instrument case towards the door, she hoped when it opened that she would behave correctly. Why did she worry that she would not? She had difficulty focusing when uneasy. She knocked on the door. It opened.

"Francis Clark" she said to the tall man who opened the door just barely.

"You're late," he said and she realized she knew this Sergeant. He was a bit of a lady's man and had many dates with the other girls at Torney, despite that some say he had a wife back in Nebraska. He was one of those men an upstanding woman would avoid if she intended to remain without a tarnished reputation and this was, contrary to the example her mother gave her about her hair, a surefire way to ruin your reputation that you couldn't fix with a hairbrush.

"Yes sir. I had a last-minute matter come up. My apologies." This was a lie. She became queasy as the time came closer for her to head over and suddenly found herself in the lady's room vomiting because she was so on edge over seeing Alessandro again.

"Understood—however, punctuality can't be ignored. It's a sign of disrespect. I'm only entertaining this meeting because Alessandro's doctor requested it."

"Yes sir."

Satisfied with her humbling, he opened the door wider and inside she saw the back of a beige uniform with a green and white stripe arm band with ITALY on it. He was sitting in a chair facing the wall. This was a small office inside the ISU barracks where it seemed the Army men responsible for the ISU overwatch worked. It had a few desks and patriotic postings on the wall from the newspaper. Ads for the war loans her father made sure were consistently placed in the paper and articles about the local villager kids who had lost their lives in the war under a banner that read *Our Heroes*. In the chair in the corner, as far away from the door she just entered as possible, sat Alessandro, the man with the ITALY armband, looking meek under the watchful eyes of Sergeant Hamlin, who was clearly not a fan of the ISU or of having to be bothered with Frances.

"Please, sit over there, Miss Clark. For your protection." He pointed to a chair on the opposite side of the room, as far away from Alessandro as possible, as if he were too dangerous to be near. It annoyed her.

Alessandro wouldn't look up, as if he'd been taught to do so when a lady was around or because the sergeant told him too. She wasn't sure, but she was unhappy to see him behaving this way and it reminded her that he was a prisoner of war. She hadn't look at him that way since the first day she saw him ride into the village on the back of the truck months before on that scorching hot day in August. He'd used pomade in his hair that day to smooth down his hair, but tips of his hair were now beginning to come free and flip up. She noticed this and found it endearing. Her hands became sweaty. She clasped them in front of her body after she sat.

The Sergeant took a seat and pointed to the man. "You have a matter for Alessandro Reggio according to Mrs. Marshall?" Alessandro didn't look up, even though his name had been spoken. She found this disturbing. "He don't know what we're saying," the Sergeant said to her when she looked at Alessandro, waiting for him to look at her. She feared he didn't like that she was there. She couldn't read him and worried she meant nothing to him now.

"He does," she said, then looked to Alessandro who still didn't raise his head. She wanted to scream she was so frustrated. "*Sì, Alessandro?*" she said directly to him, despite him not looking directly at her. What was the matter with him? She stood up and walked to him, "Alessandro?"

"Stay on the other side of the room Miss Clark," the Sergeant barked.

She stopped and looked at him. He went on, "I'd prefer it. We don't know this man. Could be a vicious killer and I don't feel comfortable having the daughter of Mr. Clark injured and then read about it in his paper the next day. That wouldn't be good for my military career."

He said this last part with a stupid laugh.

Frances could see she was dealing with a terrible guy who delighted in treating the prisoners badly and that was why Alessandro didn't want to step out of line. "My father can also write about the mistreatment of prisoners, if that becomes known." He was an arrogant ass, she felt, who needed to be brought down a few notches.

"I'm sure you are not accusing me of anything."

"Of course not," she answered, feeling unsure of how she just stepped out of line, but she sensed that Alessandro was being abused in some way and when it came to him, she seemed to be a different person, someone she'd never been in her life before; a person who was brave, said what was on her mind and took chances for someone she cared about.

Always be brave, Miss Frances.

"Because these men here, Alessandro here, are protected under the Geneva Convention. We do not mistreat these men and I take great offences to any insinuations otherwise."

The room was silent as the Sergeant and Frances waited to see who should speak first. She considered agreeing with him by saying "of course" or "understood" just to get him back into a reasonable attitude—but she couldn't kowtow, especially because she was right.

She held her tongue.

Alessandro remained silent, eyes pointing down.

The Sergeant eventually cracked.

"Let's get to the matter. Alessandro has to get back to work."

Frances pulled out a piece of paper from the pocket of her uniform, unfolded it and handed it to him. "From Dr. Tennant, who did surgery on Alessandro's arm."

"What is this?" He read the paper and started laughing. "These times don't give a break on any day." He handed the paper back to her.

She wasn't laughing. Alessandro looked up, wanting to understand what was happening.

"Sure." He laughed more. "Why not?"

Frances said, "Fine." She knew he'd agree, it was essentially an order essentially he had to obey. Frances stood up and grabbed Mr. Keller's fiddle, sitting beside her chair. Alessandro, sitting at attention, hadn't seen the case. When she placed the case on the desk in front of Alessandro, he tried not to look shocked. She opened it up and took out the fiddle and the bow and handed it to Alessandro. "This has been donated for your physical rehabilitation." He looked up into her eyes, so taken away with emotions and not wanting the sergeant to see.

"A fiddle," she said.

"Violin," he corrected.

"A fiddle is a violin?"

"*Si*, fiddle is a violin."

He rubbed the wood with his fingers, feeling the instrument as if it were a work of art, but it was so beat up and old that most would consider it barely useable.

"For your arm. To get it better," she said. "Your doctor insists that you play every day."

He didn't put the instrument on his shoulder, under his chin, nor place the bow in position to rub it against the instrument body. He seemed terrified and she knew it was because he feared he couldn't play anymore—and the knowledge of what had passed between them that day in the rain.

"We have work get to here, Miss Clark."

"Right." Frances stood up. "I'll be going."

Alessandro tried to hand the instrument back to her. She pushed against the fiddle so it

went back towards him. "For you. It's yours to keep for now." She said, then looked to the Sergeant.

"If he don't want the damn thing then take it." The Sergeant leaned way back in his chair. "Violin, fiddle, whatever the damned thing is, he don't want to play it which is good because I don't wanna hear it."

Alessandro looked up at her briefly, fear in his eyes that his talent might be gone.

"He can play."

"How do you know."

"He said so."

"He said so?" The sergeant lit a cigarette, tapping his foot so that his pant fabric hit underneath the desk softly, a drum-roll it seemed. "Just 'cause he said. Ha! He said. Let's see, so someone can just say anything without proof and you believe him. just 'cause he said?" The sergeant pushed the instrument case with his boot. Show me, then I'll let you keep it."

Alessandro looked down at the case.

"Ain't got all day. I give you fifteen seconds to get that fiddle singing, boy. Countdown's started already. You lying? You a spy?" he said as he leaned forward and placed his hands behind his ears as if ready to listen. "My ears are open. Play if you don't want to be brought up on charges of espionage."

Frances looked to Alessandro, panicked.

"ten, nine, eight..."

Alessandro flipped open the case, grabbed the fiddle and positioned it under his chin, yet struggled to lift the bow with his injured arm, pain searing into his shoulder so that he wanted to cry.

"... seven, six, five..."

"Alessandro, play!"

"... four, three..."

Dying of pain, he raised his arm and placed the bow against the strings where he played Beethoven's 5th, softly at first, then harder, louder, the pain in his arm causing sweat to bead on his face, the song building, ba-ba-ba-baaa, ba-ba-ba-baaa, until he collapsed in excruciation.

The sergeant clapped his hands and laughed, lit cigarette dangling between his lips as he chortled from his chest.

Alessandro, sweating, head down from humiliation, looked sideways from the corner of his eye to Frances, who smiled and he nodded—though she was enraged.

"There's your proof, Sergeant." She left without giving him a sense of acceptance. She didn't like the guy and if her father wasn't so against the Italian prisoners being there, she'd go to him and tell him his reporters should investigate if any of them were being mistreated by their overseers, but her father wouldn't care she knew. She stood up, knowing this would be the last timed she'd ever see him."

"Goodbye, Frances Clark," he responded which made the sergeant surprised that he knew her name and that he spoke English.

"Goodbye, Alessandro Reggio."

Frances left the room with knots in her stomach again, ran down the hall, then outside to the landscaped area the POWs were clearing the day she went to the laundry and they kissed. She leaned over the cactuses that had been planted, feeling her nausea coming back and breathed in deep to catch her breath, then got herself together before someone noticed her.

The compromise she agreed to with Edith would be the compromise she'd live with despite knowing now, after seeing him one more time, that she was in love with Alessandro. She was resigned to living the rest of her life with the pain of having to let him go.

After this day, she'd have to stay away from him. She settled her expectations of what was possible for her life. Frances resolved to stay the path she'd been on before ever setting eyes on Alessandro Reggio.

Chapter Nine

Frances looked forward to the New Year to trigger the sweet feeling of hope needed after a year with little of it.

1944 had been hard for everyone: Normandy, the Philippines. Even now on New Year's Eve, word was coming in about the Battle of the Bulge that happened over Christmas. The bad news seemed to never stop. Yet everyone kept saying 1945 was the year the war would end. Every time Frances heard someone say this, she'd remember that they said this time last year and the year before that. People acted as if there was a magic spell that happened when the clock clicked even one minute into the next year.

Frances saw this magical thinking over and over at Torney. Young men would hope their lives to go on, despite facing death, or that their lives would go on to be even better than before they got injured, even against impossible odds. Sometimes hope was all you had. That was the spell that captured everyone on New Year's Eve and Frances was guilty of being taken by it too. '44 was brutal. She couldn't wait to be on the other side of midnight and step into 1945.

Frances liked the holiday season in the desert. Downtown Palm Springs was a festival of lights all over, crossing over Palm Desert

Drive from one side to the other. Everyone put lights on their homes and businesses. Santa Claus appeared everywhere: on a window treatment in the store; in a sleigh on top of a house as a cartoon in the paper with his jolly smile and plump body making the world feel softer. Holiday music in every store. Villagers said Happy Holidays! And Merry Christmas!

There were homes with a gold star in the window, meaning someone had died in service. These homes received gifts of food and caroling to help them through the difficult holiday. The world just seemed better in every way—even if it was just a façade. There was an urgency to the celebration, the nagging truth that life was short and this Christmas could be your last.

Frances took it in like a hot chocolate, savoring every drop. But 1944 had been hard for her too. She thought about Alessandro every day.

She tried to keep herself busy, attending gatherings for Thanksgiving and Christmas at her house, hospital, Racquet Club, the Women's Club. She served food at the church to those less fortunate and gave candy canes to the kids at the library. Turns out the librarian, Phyllis, did like her, despite losing the *Freddy the Detective* book. She asked Frances to read stories during holiday story time events. Turns out Frances had a talent for this and enjoyed it very much. She enlisted the nearby elementary school kids at Torney to deliver letters to the soldiers.

Frances did these good deeds to prove to herself that she was still a good person. She still had tremendous guilt about betraying Nicholas and the fact that someone saw them kissing left her on edge. Who could it have been? Any day her secret could be revealed and she had no control over it. Would her tryst with Alessandro remain a secret forever or would it be exposed when she'd least expect it? That someone had the power to interrupt her life worried her daily.

Frances talked to Mary about this fear often, the one person she trusted to never betray her, that she was worried about the story getting out.

"It's done," Mary told her. "It's done and there's nothing you can do now except don't make another mistake like that again. One day soon you'll be walking down the aisle with Nicholas and all will be as it should be."

This message changed a month later when she got tired of Frances talking about Alessandro and how she felt about him. "I don't wanna hear it anymore, Frances!" She yelled at her. "Alessandro's bad for you. He's a bad influence and I don't understand why you just won't let it go. Do you wanna ruin your life? You've skated by, making one of the worse mistakes of your life with little consequence. Just let it go and consider yourself lucky."

After that day, Frances never brought up Alessandro again. Maybe Mary is right, she considered, when trying to discern if Alessandro was bad for her. Frances acquiesced and never spoke of him to Mary again. She decided to keep Alessandro locked in her memory of 1944, just as Edith kept Clarence locked in 1924.

"How many dances do you think we'll have?" Frances asked as the girls got ready for the New Year's Evening dance at Torney. They'd been practicing the Lindy Hop with their hair still in rollers, passing hand to hand, turns and steps, giggling as they did before they plopped down onto Frances' bed.

"Many fellas at Torney are well enough to dance," Mary added.

"So, we'll have many dances, I'm sure."

"Maybe with Frank Sinatra or Cary Grant."

"Those are rumors," said Frances.

"Someone saw Frank and Dean playing golf at O'Donnell's, so they're in town."

"Rumors, but if they're here, they just might visit the guys. They've stopped in before."

Mary grabbed her purse on the end table and pulled out their lists from past New Year's where they wrote things to remember and forget about the year. The girls started this tradition in junior high.

"Oh jeez," Frances said as she picked up their list from 1940.

"Things to remember. Chad's blue eyes. Things to forget, Eddie farting in class." The girls started giggling uncontrollably.

"It was a big fart," Mary added.

"It was horrible."

"1941 things to remember: Chad's blue eyes listed again," said Mary.

"Too bad he moved away sophomore year. One of us could've married him. Probably best because we were both so in love with him it would have ruined our friendship."

"Nope, never happen. We'll always be best friends and don't you forget it," Mary told her as Mary went over to Frances' desk and took out a notepad from the drawer where she found Nicholas' picture in his dress blues. "Franny, why'd you put his picture away?"

"Seeing it makes me upset. I'm afraid he'll be killed and I think of that less if I don't see him every day."

"Oh Franny. Don't worry so much. He'll be fine," Mary said as she placed the picture on the desk without asking if she could. Frances noticed and it bothered her, but she didn't say anything. Sometimes it was easier that way. Mary wrote on the notepad:

New Year's Eve, 1944. Things to remember. Things to forget.

"I am not doing that this year."

"Come on, Franny, it's a tradition."

"Made to be broken. Nope. Uh-uh."

Mary smiled and went back to the notepad. "Things to remember: Nothing." The girls giggled. "Things to forget," said Mary.

"Everything," Frances sneered.

Mary wrote everything on the notepad, "Everything." She held up the list and looked at it. "This list isn't good."

Frances rushed over and snatched the list out of her hands. Mary chased after her as Frances ripped the note up into pieces and threw them at her before the cat and mouse play was done.

Mary looked at the pieces on the floor. "So, let's skip this year."

"It's about to be done."

"Finished!"

"'44 gone forever!"

"I do have one thing to remember, maybe," Mary volunteered.

"What?"

"You know that cute doctor who transferred here last month."

"Dr. Reilly?"

"Yes. I'm pretty sure he likes me."

"What! Tell me everything."

"He's always staring at me and trying to talk to me. The other day he followed me down a hall. I think he was getting up the nerve to ask me out."

"Did he?"

"No, but Franny you know when you can feel that you're super special to a guy in that way that no one else looks at you. He looks at me that way. You know, how Nicholas looks at you."

She doesn't know me, Frances' thought, as she heard her best friend dismiss what she'd been trying to get her to understand. Nicholas never looked at her that way. Only two men had looked at her that way in her life so far: Alessandro and Oklahoma.

"What if I marry him! A doctor!" Mary screamed, "And when Nicholas comes back, we can be wives together and have our babies and be moms. I can't wait."

"Boogie Woogie Bugle Boy" came on the radio. Frances turned it up, happy to change the subject. "And a one and a two and a three." Frances timed and then reached her hand out to Mary and they practiced swing-dancing again.

"After this song, we have to start our hair."

"After this song," Frances agreed.

It was a cold New Year's Eve in the desert. While the summers were scorchers, the winter nights could be frigid and this evening chilled Frances to the bone as she walked towards Torney from the parking lot with Mary, wrapped in their dress coats that didn't provide enough warmth for such a chilly winter night. It was in the low 40s with clear skies and wind gusts that were so strong it took effort to keep their skirts from flying up. Both wore their high school graduation dresses, reusing what they had in their closets as that's what the lean times called for. Mary's dress had a white bow on the back of the bodice and was light pink. It complemented her auburn hair. Frances had an ivory dress that had lace-covered buttons going down the back of the bodice and had a tulle skirt that made her feel like a princess. Their hair was pinned and sprayed into place, parted on the side and curled back into bobs.

No clouds blanketed the sky, so the stars sparkled bright as Francis looked up to catch her final site of the 1944 sky before going into the hospital. The Big Dipper and Little Dipper hovered above, cups made up by an outline of stars, forever ready to pour something down onto earth but never do. The same Big Dipper and Little Dipper as when she was a little girl and laid in her yard and examined the stars. Nothing had changed in the sky in all those years, but she'd changed so much. But the cups in the sky being the same as when she was little made her feel good, like this was something she could rely on in this unstable world.

The mood in Torney was lively as they passed through the main building to the Red Cross tent, where they met with all the other Gray Ladies. Chatter rumbled around the room, every other word was high pitched as women were bursting with the excitement over how beautiful everyone looked and the night of dancing that awaited. First, however, they had instructions from Edith as to which halls they were responsible for walking or wheeling over soldiers to the party. The Gray Ladies were on point to make sure any soldier who wanted to dance had a girl to dance with and to try and convince those who had no interest in going to celebrate to change their mind. Frances and Mary hurried off to the rooms they were to check in on and helped bring over patients. The guys were impressed with their fancy outfits, which Mary loved, but made Frances blush since she wasn't ostentatious. This was another reason why she worried about her secret getting out. She didn't know how she'd be able to handle living a life where everyone noticed and spoke about her.

The girls rounded up the soldiers and brought them to the party that was in a large room which used to be a dining hall when the hotel was open. The Women's Club had put up the decorations and the place had colorful surroundings matching the spirit of the night. Hospital decorations from past years were used. Banners that said *Happy New Year* and ribbons repurposed from holiday gifts had been taped to the ceiling and dangled down over the dance floor which made the room look festive. There was a band set up on a raised platform playing swing music to get the night going. Jumping, sliding, shaking, the room was abuzz with happiness and movement all over, not just on the dance floor as people tapped their feet at the punch bowl. They snapped their fingers standing the side of the dance floor as the swing band played upbeat tunes to bring in 1945. The biggest hit of there was "In the Mood" and every time the band played it the crowd went nuts.

Frances went from guy to guy, making sure they had a partner if they wanted to shake their injured bodies despite the pain. Mary however, soon disappeared when the doctor showed up and finally got the courage to talk to her. The two of them sneaked off for over an hour. Franny wondered if she'd come back for the countdown to midnight. If she didn't, Frances was sure to give Mary the interrogation of a lifetime over where she went and what she did. She did worry about her reputation, as a few of the girls were talking that they'd seen her leave with him and not return. There was never a loss of gossip happening and none of the girls seemed to miss an opportunity to give their two cents about a matter. It made Frances wonder if it was a Gray Lady who saw her kiss Alessandro.

The shorthand on the clock moved closer to twelve and the long hand was 28 minutes away from midnight. Hours had passed and Frances was getting a bit spent. Mary still hadn't returned and they had a tradition of bringing in the New Year together and she wasn't going to miss it this year. She asked around and a girl said she'd seen Mary in the garden with a group of people. Frances headed out the back of the building and stepped outside, in the cold and looked around in the dark for Mary. There were groups of people in different spots talking, smoking cigarettes and mixing about. She stepped onto the dirt area, which was the garden in times past and spotted the place Oklahoma had liked to sit that was always in the sun so she had to constantly remind him he was turning red as a cherry. She hadn't thought much about him for months, time taking away the intensity and pain of that experience and now as she thought of the year behind her, she realized it would not only be Alessandro locked away in 1944, but Oklahoma too. "Happy New Year, Oklahoma," she whispered to the tree and remembered him sitting there with her and how much they made each other laugh. She heard a familiar voice across the courtyard.

"Mary!" she hollered.

"Frances, over here!" Mary called back.

"There you are!" she said. "I've been looking for you." She rushed over, forgetting about Oklahoma again and moving on with her life. It happened like that now, where she'd think of him quickly and then he'd leave her mind. She liked it so much better than what she experienced the first weeks after his death where there was hardly a minute that she didn't get choked up.

"Over here!" Mary called from the dark corner of the garden where shadow figures of about ten people could be seen from her spot. Frances ran over and joined the group of young people from the hospital, some doctors, some nurses, Gray Ladies, Army soldiers who were chatting and smoking cigarettes.

"This is Frank," Mary said as she introduced the young doctor to Frances. "This is my forever best friend, Frances."

"Nice to meet you," Frank said and held out his hand to shake.

"Nice to meet *you*," Frances replied, then shivered. "It's cold out here. Mary, I came to get you inside. It's almost midnight, you all."

The group went back into the dance hall and soon the countdown to the New Year began until the entire room yelled out in unison, *10, 9, 8, 7, 6,5,4,3,2,1, Happy New Year!* Hugs and kisses began and Frances turned to Mary to hug her, but saw she was kissing Frank as confetti floated down. *Maybe Mary would marry a doctor after all*, Frances thought as screams of Happy New Year were yelled out a hundred times. Frances hugged soldiers and spun those in wheelchairs in a circle in celebration. Mary soon skipped out of the room again with Frank into the garden with a group that had pirated a bottle of whiskey.

Frances suddenly felt very alone.

It was here finally, the new year with new hope, but only ten minutes into 1945, Frances found her exhilarated mood crash. She grabbed her coat off the chair and headed out the front of the building. She looked to the right at the El Mirador Tower silhouetted against the blue sky. She headed over and climbed up the stairs quickly, in the dark and looked out at the view of a starry night and a large moon against a deep blue background. She closed her eyes and whispered, "Dear Lord, please keep Nicholas safe." She opened her eyes and could see the fog her breath created in the cold. She closed her eyes again and added: "And without too much damage to his heart. Amen." She'd seen men at Torney where their injuries would heal, but they'd been left with a sourness and sadness that seemed permanent, even if they were laughing. She worried Nicholas would return to her like this and didn't know how they'd ever build a life if he came back like that.

Frances looked out at the view and listened to the partygoers in Torney settling down to singing "Auld Lang Syne," when she heard a high-pitched sound in the distance, then it stopped. She listened for the sound again and she wondered if she imagined it. Happy New Year was being said repeatedly around Torney from the party inside and others who were gathered in the garden. In the distance, fireworks went off and pans were being banged in the streets and then she heard it again, unmistakable high-pitched notes.

A violin was being played in the distance, beautifully, from the far side of the hospital grounds where the ISU was housed. "Alessandro," she said and smiled, filled with amazement as she listened. He played on, his beautiful notes passing overhead like swift winged creatures, untouchable, out of reach.

Part Two

War

Chapter Ten

Frances sat in the garden in the spot where she used to sit with Oklahoma, but now she was with John, a fella from San Diego who'd been wounded in the leg and foot, but even after his wounds had healed, he didn't want to talk much and cried often. He'd never be a fighting soldier again since his injury to his foot got gangrene before they were able to get him medical help and were forced to amputate three of his toes to save his life.

His military career was over, but he couldn't be returned to his parents as a shell of a man, so the doctors sent him to Torney for R&R, hoping that time to decompress would fix him up. He had what they called shock from the war, battle fatigue. It was so bad he could hardly function. The sunshine and warmth of Palm Springs, they hoped, would help him recover. He'd been getting better since he arrived the week before, but it was still obvious that he struggled with anxiety. His sadness was so palpable that anyone who interacted with him could feel it's weight.

John was a Hemingway fan and unfortunately for Frances his favorite Hemingway book was *For Whom the Bell Tolls* which the US Postal Service had banned in '41 as unmailable so of course Phyllis took it out of circulation. "If the US Postal Service refuses to mail it because its pro-communist, then I'm certainly going to refuse to allow it in this library," she told Frances when she asked if they could order a copy. Frances had filled every soldier's request until this one, but this was a book that would not be welcome at Torney. Instead, she brought John *The Little Prince* in the hopes the light story could help pull his spirits up and asked him if he played any musical instruments. He played the harmonica, so she brought one when she visited him and tried to get him to play.

John was hard to be around. He made a clicking sound with his mouth that annoyed her, but she never told him to stop. It wasn't her place. Working at the hospital for a year had changed her, especially the experience with Oklahoma. What she felt when he died, she never wanted to feel again. In hindsight, she worried that she flirted too much with Oklahoma and gave him the wrong message about her feelings for him. She wasn't sure, but what she did know now was her influence over the men. She was that pretty, young woman they dreamt about coming home to while walking over endless miles of dirt in a foreign land, knowing the end could be at hand. She represented the cliché they wanted to live for, the girl, family, white picket fence. The mythical American Dream. *Don't get close*, she reminded herself daily and didn't speak about her personal life and asked nothing about theirs. The less she knew about them, the better for her and the less they knew about her, the better for them. The only way to not be heartbroken as the men passed away or moved on to live their lives elsewhere was to stay a stranger as best as she could while still compassionate. To do this, she behaved towards the men like Edith, caring yet reserved and this had allowed her to escape debilitating and continuous heartache.

Political conversations were off the table too, especially as the world was trying to grasp the concept of nuclear weapons after Hiroshima and Nagasaki. Any talk of Fat Man and Little Boy put her in a sour mood. It had been weeks since the atomic bombs were dropped and even after this devastating hit, Japan wasn't giving in.

The Potsdam Conference in July, just a month before, with Churchill, Truman and Stalin, determined only unconditional surrender by Japan would be accepted. Even after the bombs that followed in August, the world was still waiting for Japan to admit defeat.

Frances had horrible thoughts about people burned alive. So devastating were the bombs that no one even knew the death toll. Reports said within minutes anywhere of 100,000 to 200,000 people were killed. It seemed senseless to Frances and she couldn't understand how this could be the only way America could get out of the war. Japan couldn't win, everyone knew it, but they wouldn't stop fighting – wouldn't accept defeat and surrender to save themselves.

At home, her father talked obsessively about the bombs, praising American innovation and how dropping them would save American lives. He'd go off before they were used daily about how Japan needed to surrender, how that son-of-a-bitch Hirohito needed to "kill himself like that son of a bitch scum coward Hitler and finally end this goddamned fighting." Spittle would form in the corners of his mouth as he'd rant and nothing her mom said got him to stop. After the atomic bombs were dropped, he'd rant about when would that son-of-a-bitch Hirohito surrender. Frances would retreat to her room and would lament to Mary about how human beings are terrible to each other. These conversations had been ongoing between the girls for months as newsreels played about the horrors of Nazi concentration camps. They'd talk about the cruelty of the Germans, about nuclear bombs and how they had no control over anything that went on in the world. Everyone was still reeling from Roosevelt's sudden death. It was overwhelming.

Frances watched John as he sat silently in the garden. His face hinted at stories from the battlefield, brow furrowed in anger, then his eyes would go wide like he was scared, then tears as his mouth hung open and he'd take in a huge breath to calm himself. His face told the story but she never knew what he was reliving as didn't ask. She didn't want him to have to talk about atrocities. Her job was to make him smile, so she pulled out the harmonica from her uniform pocket and handed it to him. He took it and looked at the instrument like it was beautiful. "You wanna play a bit?"

"Nah. Not today. That's the same type of harmonica my dad played." He handed it back to her and she put it in her pocket.

Last year she would've asked about his dad and when he played the harmonica. In the morning? Evening? What songs did he play? But not now. "You sure you don't wanna play?"

"Got it hard today, Miss Frances." He said and he took his right hand and made a fist and tapped it against his heart. "Heartache."

"Yeah, I know," she said. "It'll get better."

"Hope it does."

"It does. I've seen it get better for guys again and again."

"How long you been here?"

"Ah, long enough to know that if you play the harmonica, it'll help make you feel better."

She took the harmonica out of her pocket and handed it back to him. "Play a little." He didn't take the harmonica from her, so she put it back in her pocket. "Tomorrow maybe."

It didn't matter which instrument a soldier played—guitar, harmonica, flute, banjo—the music often was a pathway to healing. Even an old fiddle so battered one might put it in the trash had healed Alessandro.

She promised Edith that she'd stay away from him, not knowing then that she couldn't. Like craving water in the heat, she craved Alessandro.

It started with climbing to the El Mirador Tower in the evening to hear him practice. He played every evening at the back side of the barracks building that faced an open field. When his celebrity grew, people went to the barracks to listen to him play Bach, Mozart, Prokofiev, Bizet. She'd be in the crowd often, watching, and he wouldn't see her when playing, his art his focus, but when he finished and bowed to their claps, he'd see her there, watching him. It seemed no one else was around as they'd look at each other and smile.

And later at night, if it was quiet enough, no planes flying overhead or ambulance sirens wailing, she could hear him playing faintly from the road on the other side of the field. She would lay back on her hood, her back up against the windshield, and look up to the stars and think back to when he kissed her. She wanted Alessandro. All of Alessandro for all time, and she'd have to fight the urge to run across the field and into his arms. He'd be in trouble and she'd be shunned by everyone.

And after considering that fallout, she'd think of Nicholas. He'd been writing her more frequently, declaring his love for her again and talking about their life together when he returned. Every time she went to write him a Dear John letter, she just couldn't. It seemed cruel to leave him that way, while he was out there fighting, and decided to wait until he returned.

She looked up at a cargo plane moving by and thought, what if Nicholas is on that plane. It was nearly a daily thought, when would he return and how would she get through letting him go?

John was quiet and after minutes like this he closed his eyes and rested. She stayed quiet too, under the warm sun, next to him and read *The Little Prince.* Twenty minutes later he woke and realized he'd fallen asleep.

"Sorry, Frances."

"You getting enough sleep?"

"Nah, don't sleep through the night."

"Figured. You seem tired. Try counting sheep. You have any sheep in your head you can count? I've got like three herds in here walking around that I round up every night and count them jumping over a fence." She pointed to her head and he smiled. "Ah, gotcha to smile."

He chuckled. "You did."

She could still get a guy to laugh which was what she always tried to do when working with the men in uniform. This gave her purpose. Her special mission.

"No sheep in *my* head. Wish it was just sheep in my head."

"This book I got you has sheep in it. Try reading it before you go to sleep."

"You always trying to fix me."

She held back telling him that she couldn't fix him, only he could make himself better, but checked herself. You could push too hard. "You wanna head back to your room and rest? You seem tired." Frances noticed there was something going on as she glanced around the garden. A few staff had rushed into the building.

"Nah. I'm good here for a bit." He put his head back, closed his eyes and looked up to the sky. "I like the sun on my face."

She thought of Oklahoma when he said that, how she used to get after him for sunning into a cherry.

"We can stay then. If you want."

"I'd like to, for a while." He closed his eyes and leaned his head back.

Frances noticed people began moving from the garden into the hospital and there were words being said that she couldn't decipher but she could sense something important was going on.

"John, something's happened." She said as she tapped his arm. "Let's go inside to the radio."

"You go without me."

"John, come on." She put her hand out to him. "I'll help you."

"Nah. I'll stay"

"I'm not going without you, so if Japan surrendered finally, neither of us will know."

He looked up at her, realizing that this could be the moment the war ended. Others waved at them to come in and people were yelling different words they could pick-up: *surrender*, *Japan* and *radio* as everyone hurried into the building.

"Let's go together." She put her hand on his arm and the other hand she wrapped around his hand. "On three. One, two, three." She pulled him up as he put in the effort to stand.

John kept hold of her arm to help him walk. His wounded leg and foot still caused him pain even though it was fully healed. The doctors diagnosed it as a phantom pain, which was another way of saying that it was all in his head. Frances didn't question if his pain was real or not when he complained. She'd softened about the issues the guys had, even though on the outside she seemed to have become less caring. She knew that if John couldn't stand on his leg without being in distress, then it was real for him, so she didn't question if it was in his head. She'd developed compassion and maturity over the last year, becoming seasoned in a way only experience could teach.

"Think they surrendered?"

"Don't know. John, can you walk faster?" Frances walked him towards the building but kept having to stop for him to catch up. She wanted to have him use a wheelchair, but the nurses refused, saying he was fine according to the doctors and if she pushed him around in a wheelchair, she'd be placating to him not getting over his phantom pain.

"I'll try," he said and picked up his pace a little.

Sirens went off in the town. Frances and John looked up at the sky.

"I think it's real, John."

"My God." He whispered as he gave his full effort to move faster.

A hospital loudspeaker beeped repeatedly followed by a woman saying: "Stand by for an announcement!" followed by a beep. This repeated as Frances and John got inside the building where the radio was being broadcast through the com speakers in the hospital. Inside the hall, patients, nurses, doctors, everyone stood still, waiting for the message to be delivered. This exact scene had happened back in May when the German's surrendered, V-E Day. They waited in the halls for the news, V-J Day would mean the end of the war.

The reporter spoke:

Japan has agreed to unconditional surrender to the allies on this, the 2nd day of September, 1945. World War II, the bloodiest war this nation has ever seen has ended. I repeat, the war has ended. Victory over Japan had been achieved with the Japanese admitting defeat, the bombing of Hiroshima and Nagasaki crumbling their resolve to fight *on. I repeat: Victory over Japan has happened. Franklin Delano Roosevelt, God rest his soul, would be proud of America of this day. I repeat, Victory over Japan has happened. The Japanese surrendering to the allies today. World War II, the longest and bloodiest war, finally comes to an end. The Imperial Government of Japan has surrendered, renouncing their vow to fight to the bitter end in the Pacific.*

Hearing the announcement, Frances was so shocked that she was unable to express any emotion, still holding her breath without realizing until the room lit up with smiles, hugs and cheers as it became a reality. She turned to John, "John, Japan surrendered." She kissed him on his forehead, like he was a little kid and hugged him. "The war is over." He lost his balance and fell back against the wall. She caught him and helped to get to a chair in the hallway.

"I'll be damned," he said. "Those bastards surrendered."

Frances hugged the others in the hall as the news became real and then when she turned back to John, he was standing at attention, shoulders back, arms to his side, head up.

"John?" She said and he looked straight ahead, stoic. "John?" She asked him again. "Are you alright?"

"Ten-HUT," John yelled out and those around looked at him. "For those we lost."

He then saluted. "For Chuck," another soldier said and saluted and other soldiers all down the hall followed, naming men lost that they fought with and saluting them. John collapsed back into the chair.

"John?" Frances yelled, catching him so he didn't fall to the ground as emotion hit him and tears came to his eyes.

"I'm alright."

"I know you are. We're all going to be alright now." She said to him as if she were finally admitting it to herself. "Come on. Let's get you out of this hall." Frances held out her hand to help him up and he waved her hand away.

"I can do this," John said and stood with more strength than she'd seen him have before and he walked without help towards his room.

Frances walked beside him, ready to assist, but he didn't want her help. When they got to his room, they were greeted by his jubilant roommate who was jumping up and down on his hospital bed like a gleeful kid which made Frances and John laugh.

With John taken care of, Frances rushed off to find Mary as the news didn't feel real until they shared it together. She looked around, seeing staff and patients in the halls in shock, some happy, some crying, but still a reserve with their emotions she didn't expect to see on the day the war ended. As she searched, she hugged people she knew, the thrill of it all becoming bigger and more monumental as the truth settled in.

Finally, she found Mary in the lobby. "Mary!" She yelled out and ran over to her and they hugged as if they were never going to see each other again and Frances found herself in tears. "It's over."

"It's over," Mary affirmed.

"1945's the year after all."

The air raid siren at the fire station went off, howling across the village. Frances and Mary went out front to hear the siren which had only been rung twice before, in '43 and one other time before that for a blackout, but this time was for celebration. People came outside to listen and it seemed most were in shock, as if they couldn't believe it. Some began crying. Some were stoic. There was overall happiness, but a feeling of underlying sadness too, like having the best day of your life—but you had to get through the worst days of your life to get there and you wouldn't ever forget it.

"Frances, give me your hand," said Mary, her face beaming with exhilaration.

Frances grabbed her hand and counted out, "And a one and a two..." and they began doing the Lindy Hop in front of the hospital in celebration.

"I can't believe it!" Frances shouted as they spun around.

"It's over!"

Others around them watched with glee as the girls danced in celebration. People ran up to the El Mirador Tower and waved out to the world with happiness, some yelled out to the village below, *Japan surrenders! V-J Day!* Men grabbed hands and danced with girls. Girls danced with each other. It was a moment that filled them with such joy, the hit of the reality took their breath away, then gave it back like a flat tire getting filled with air.

Frances almost didn't have the words to say all that it meant to her. "It's over," was all she could utter with a grin that crossed from her left to her right ear it seemed. It *was* over and it was glorious.

They stopped dancing and Mary suddenly broke down in tears. Frances hugged her tightly, patted her back. "I love you, gal."

"I love you too."

"I have to get home and see if my dad's come to his senses now that Japan surrendered. I'll meet up with you later."

After grabbing her crossover bag from its spot in the book library, Frances rushed home on her bike to see her parents, hoping to have her father back to normal now that the war was over. She missed him being the dad she knew. None of them had been themselves as the war dragged on and chronic stress changed all of them. She'd become a shell of the young woman she'd been fresh out of high school. Her father had become obsessed with politics and her mother plugged along trying to keep up with running all the local war drives. The war had taken a toll on them as it had affected everyone in some way. No one was spared.

When Frances came through the door, she was greeted by her father who embraced her. "Frances, your life can be the way it should be now." His voice cracked as he said this and his eyes filled with tears and she knew then that he loved her through all of this and that was what she needed from him right then. "I love you, sweet pea," he said and kissed her on the forehead like she'd done to John an hour earlier.

Life without war seemed nice, but she had no idea what that looked like anymore since it'd been so long. "I love you too, Dad," she said and hugged him like he was her teddy bear.

· · ·

There was a two-day holiday declared in the village, so the town shops closed and the flights overhead to the airfield stopped. It was the quietest it'd been in the village since the war began. Villagers celebrated mildly compared to the images that were published in the papers of people celebrating across the country, packed in the streets, men kissing women, people dancing and conga lines forming in the crowded streets.

Most celebrated in silence, especially at Torney where the men in uniform accepted this news as if it had stunned them more than elated them. It'd been a long and difficult journey and the scorched imprint left by the war could never be fixed. Reports about Hitler's treatment of the Jews were so shocking that she couldn't process what she learned as it seemed a far worse nightmare than anyone could dream, but this was real. There were fresh revelations that people within our own government, elected representatives who'd taken an oath to protect the Constitution had actually been in cahoots with the Nazis, paid to spread Hitler's propaganda. And the atomic bombs, the devastation of cities in seconds, the death and misery this created so great that she often couldn't eat. Gold Star families in the village who'd have to go on without their boys while the world celebrated the war's end.

The ugliness stayed and for Frances she was numb and unsure about how to move forward. Everything from the wretched war hurt too much and some days she wished she could go back to being that sheltered girl she was so very long ago. That girl was sweet and happy because she knew nothing of the real world. Now she did know and it was far worse than she could have ever imagined.

Chapter Eleven

Frances walked down the aisle holding a bouquet of pink carnations that matched her pink dress with cap sleeves, a lace detailed bodice with a large bow flowering out above her tule skirt. At the altar stood the priest, the best man Ned who was Mary's older brother and the handsome Dr. Frank Reilly.

The church was filled with Mary's family and friends, which included their core Gray Lady crew and Edith whom all the girls now held in high regard. Frank's family wasn't there as they lived north of San Francisco, so the honeymoon was to be a road trip driving up the California coast, stopping in Hollywood, Santa Barbara, Carmel and then the City by the Bay to introduce Mary to Frank's family.

Ned raised a fist at Frances which made her giggle. As children, he'd chase her down and give her noggin a bonk with his fist. He and his crew of stinky friends also enjoyed shooting spit wads out of straws at Mary and Frances, often camouflaged in a bush so they could attack when the girls least expected it. To be fair, she and Mary picked on Ned too. Their best prank was ketchup on Ned's sheets so that he'd wake up thinking he was bleeding. In the morning, he screamed for his mommy, sure that he was dying. The girls both got put on restriction from seeing each other for a week, but it was worth it as it gave them years of teasing him about crying out for his mommy. Frances could never have imagined back then that they'd be behaving so maturely, standing up for Mary at her wedding ceremony and it made her nostalgic for when they were young. Time seemed to pass with increased velocity year after year and this wedding was another reminder that childhood was getting farther away.

Frances reached her place on the altar as bridesmaid and smiled at Frank. She felt good about their match. He was a nice guy, a doctor, but a bit of a bore she admitted to herself as she looked at him waiting with anticipation to see his bride enter the church. But he loved Mary, made a good income and she felt solid about standing up for their union.

An organ player began "The Wedding March." All the guests in the church stood for the bride as she walked down the aisle with her father. Mary looked gorgeous and her smile was so big under the veil that it radiated out like sunshine. Frank was the man Mary wanted without a bit of doubt, she told Frances the day before when they met to play their last Saturday match as two single girls.

"I hated the war more than anything, Franny, but without it, I'd never have met Frank."

Frances wanted to tell her friend then that without the war she'd never have met Alessandro, but Mary was bigoted against the POWs. It was an intolerance that she revealed after Frances told her what happened that night in the rain, that he kissed her and she thought she was in love with him. Mary said he was probably a fascist and, anyway, was a foreigner. She would scold her often. How could you do this to Nicholas? How could you do this to your family? How could you do this to your country? And Frances couldn't believe that she was talking this way, especially after all her talk of marrying one that hot day in August when the POWs rolled in from Camp Haan under military guard.

"I was joking, Frances. I wasn't serious. How could you think I was serious? I'm an American girl," she stated like that meant certain things Frances should understand, but she didn't. An American girl? What did that mean for Frances if she loved Alessandro? That she was un-American? That she was a traitor to her country?

"Stay away from that man. He's trouble, Franny. He'll ruin your life. I just know it."

That was the last time they spoke of him. As Mary told her and as Edith told her, she'd tried to stay away from him and listened to his violin play across the night sky. Smoke signals telling her that he was there, playing the fiddle for her every night, his love letters to her until she couldn't stand it – then she started showing up near his barracks just to see him.

Mary reached the altar. The music stopped. She handed Frances her bouquet of flowers. "Wish me luck," she whispered.

"Good luck." Frances whispered back, her voice cracking with emotion.

"Don't cry, Franny. I'm happy," Mary whispered.

Mary turned toward Frank and lifted her veil and Frances helped smooth it back behind her. The people in the church sat, adding the sound of wood pews creaking and knocking as the guests got comfortable. The priest welcomed all to witness the union of Frank and Mary and proceeded to read from the Book of Genesis 2:18-24 of how God made animals and created woman from the man's ribs so that man would not be alone and that is why a man leaves his father and mother and clings to his wife and the two of them become one body. He talked about having dedication to each other in sickness and in health, a partnership for life, in the dark days and the light days, sharing in God's love until death do them part.

This is serious, Frances thought to herself, to make this vow for life. How could she make such a vow to Nicholas? They dated for seven months in their senior year. He'd been gone for more than two years now. They bound themselves to each other on a whim, young kids scared of what was to come and doing something that seemed what they should do before he went away maybe to his death. I'll know when I see him again, she'd been telling herself as her anxiety of him coming back increased. As an unmarried man without children, he didn't have enough points to be considered to return yet on the Service Rating Score which determined the order for soldiers to be discharged. Soldiers got 12 points for up to three kids so unmarried fatherless guys like Nicholas had to wait to get their ticket home. She hoped she'd love him as much as Mary loved Frank, so she could let Alessandro go. The waiting to see him, to know if she did love him, had been keeping her up at night and now hearing the priest ask them to promise to love and cherish each other, in good times and bad, until death do they part, made Frances want to run out of the church and she was only a bridesmaid.

Frank and Mary both said I do to the question without any hesitancy and placed the rings on each other's finger. Frank was given permission to kiss his bride. The guests sounded off with claps and cheers for the groom and bride as they kissed for the first time as Mr. and Mrs. Frank Reilly. The wedding processional song began and the bride and groom walked down the aisle to cheers and well wishes.

Frances and Ned followed them. "You next, Franny? With Nicholas?" Ned said.

"Nah, how 'bout you go next?" She told him as they walked behind the bride and groom. "Someone's got to love you someday even though you stink." She punched him in his bicep lovingly.

The wedding party met in front of the sanctuary for hugs and congratulations before heading over to the church hall for lunch. Food rations of sugar, meat and butter were still in place as it'd only been four months since the war ended. As the bridesmaid, Frances was charged with putting the meal together and relied on the help of her mom with the Women's Club for food donations and Edith stepped up to bake a lovely cake. A single woman, she'd rationed her rations so that she had the ingredients in her cupboard to bake a three-layered cake which she decorated with a white frosting and pink flowers. Wedding guests were asked to get their food and find a seat so there could be well-wishing toasts to the bride and groom. At the Gray Lady table, there was some talk about between two of the girls who'd gone on a date with Frank before Mary, but on this day they all agreed that when Frank saw Mary, he never looked at another woman again. That was true love. After speeches and the meal, the group went outside to the parking lot to send off the bride and groom for their honeymoon, throwing rice at them as they headed to the car.

Mary hugged Frances and whispered in her ear again, "Wish me luck, Franny." She said with a smile and Frances knew this comment was about one thing: sex. They'd had several conversations leading up to the wedding of how excited and nervous Mary was about her wedding night. They'd be staying at the Roosevelt Hotel in Hollywood for their first night as husband and wife and Mary had been on the edge of her seat about it all week long. "Not sure it's going to feel good," she confided to Frances. They both suspected the rumors that sex was fun was a lie because there's no way having one of those things in there could feel good.

The car pulled away, JUST MARRIED on the window, ribbons and bows mounted on the trunk and flowing behind. They honked repeatedly as they drove off.

The group dispersed from the church steps, many leaving for home, while Frances, her mom, Mary's mom and some Gray Ladies and Edith returned to the church hall. They cleared glasses and plates, gathered trash and wrapped up remaining food and those who brought any items took what was left home. Frances swept the floor, women wiped down the tables, while others took out the trash.

"Frances," she heard a man's voice call out to her. She turned around to see Nicholas standing at the doorway in his Marine service uniform, so nervous he was standing almost at attention. He took his cap off and stepped stiffly into the church hall.

"Nicholas," she said, so shocked she didn't know how to act.

"Hello Frances."

"Nicholas," she repeated, emotional and suddenly rushed to him, stopping short so there was still a foot between. "How?" Her bewilderment of him being there was so great that she almost couldn't process that he was standing right in front of her.

He stepped forward. "I'm so happy to see you," he said with desperation. "I've been waiting for this moment for... " His eyes had tears in them and so did hers.

"Why didn't you tell me you were coming?" Frances asked.

"I wanted to surprise you."

Both stepped forward and reached for each other, embracing awkwardly. She placed her head against his wide, muscular chest and suddenly felt like she fit there perfectly. The few women still left in the room watched this reunion with the enormity of the moment hitting them all. After their embrace, they came over and welcomed him home, their moms so moved with joy they started crying.

"Frances, you two go on." Frances' mom said.

"Thank you, ma'am," he answered. "Should we go for a walk?" Nicholas said and held out his hand.

She placed her hand in his and felt her heart skip. He was more appealing now, tan and muscular, with a confidence he didn't have when he left. A Marine, a man now, she was unable to speak hardly from the shock of him standing there, holding her hand.

"Shall we walk?" he asked again.

"Yes," Frances said as she looked at her feminine hand in his large, calloused hand thick and worn from his life as a soldier.

"I think maybe I've startled you," he said.

"Yes, I think you did."

They both smiled as he closed his palm around hers and they walked towards the door. His large hand was warm and sturdy so that she felt protected. "The wedding was the only big event I'd planned for today. Seeing you like this, surprised... well.... it's more than I thought would happen when I woke up this morning."

When they exited the building, he stopped and turned to her. "Frances, look at you. Look at you. You're so pretty. You're even prettier now... " He took his hand and placed it on her head and moved it down her hair like she was a sculpture worth admiring. "I've been waiting so long to see you. You have no idea." He leaned down and kissed her passionately for many minutes before they broke apart.

Frances giggled like she was nervous and a bit put off.

"Me too. I am so happy to see you. I just wasn't expecting this today. I just thought it was only going to be my best friend's wedding day, but you're here. I can't believe it. You're here. You've really come back to me after all this time. Is this real?" she said as her eyes again filled with tears.

"It's all I've been trying to do since I left," he told her. "And it wasn't easy getting back, Franny. It took everything I am to get back here to you." He told her as he stood strong like a soldier, fighting back his emotions, so handsome in his uniform.

Frances remained quiet as she looked into his eyes, searching for the boy who left and who they were together on the night he got down on one knee and proposed. She didn't see that Nicholas. Who she saw was a different man. That other Nicholas who left years ago was gone.

"I can't imagine what you've been through."

She spoke this with compassion, as she knew what he'd been through had been horrific. There was no other way it could've been different as all parts of war were horrific. Nicholas didn't answer, instead he looked off to the right as if a flash of what he'd been through passed before his eyes. The men at Torney did this. They'd look away as they reflected on what had gone on over there.

"I'm the luckiest girl in the world, Nicholas." She said and took her hand to his chin so that they could look in each other's eyes. "So lucky to have you back. Safe."

She hugged him his tight and they stood there in each other's arms, in a rush of emotion, letting tears flow. Happiness so sweet it made them cry.

"When we getting married?" he blurted out after he pulled her up from the hug into his arms like a groom carrying his bride across a honeymoon threshold, her tule gown fluffy like a wedding dress so that it looked like a Marine in uniform just got hitched and she was the bride. She laughed with delight. "Come on. I see the church."

"Nicholas, you're crazy!" she yelled out and giggled.

He carried her to the chapel which was still dressed in pink roses from the wedding at the end of every aisle. He set her down just inside the door. "Stay here," he said and ran down to the altar.

"You're crazy!" she laughed.

"Yeah, I'm crazy in love!" he yelled back as he stood at the end of the aisle at the altar. "Come on." He started singing, *"Here comes the bride. Here comes the bride...!"*

She walked down the aisle, smiling and waving to imaginary people in the pews as he repeated his rendition of "Here comes the bride."

"Here comes the bride, all dressed in pink, da da da da da da da da da da..."

He sang and she hummed along as well so they were both going da da da da together. When she reached the end of the aisle, she turned to him and he turned to her and he took both her hands in his.

"You ready for this?" he said.

"I'm ready," she said, giggling at the same time she said the words.

"One problem."

"Yes."

"No priest."

"Well, two problems. No priest and no witnesses."

"Right. Let me see what I can do. Stay here." He went to the back of the chapel and took a small statue of Mother Mary off a pedestal and placed the stature on the first pew. "The Virgin Mary is our witness."

Frances smiled. "Who is the priest?" she said to him as he came back up on the altar and took both her hands and faced her again.

Nicholas looked up to the stained-glass window that went high up in a pointed arch of Jesus on the cross. "Our Lord Jesus and it's perfect because he got me through it all, Franny, along with you, so here today in front of the eyes of God, Frances, do you take me to be your wedded husband until death do us part?"

She hesitated as in this moment, she thought of Alessandro. "Nicholas, this is too much for me today." And she pulled her hands from his. "I need to breathe."

"Frances, please. It's just you and me. Please." He took both her hands again.

She looked at him, a bit uncomfortable for the first time as he seemed a little mad, as if this over-the-top behavior was something more about him than just this moment of them reuniting. She knew all of what he'd been through without even knowing because she'd worked with so many men in uniform at Torney and in this moment she knew that while Nicholas had been returned to her physically unhurt, there was still so much going on with him emotionally.

"What'd ya say?" He looked down at her, he was so tall and hand-some, true, but he wasn't Alessandro. She didn't feel for Nicholas what she felt for Alessandro. "Please. Frances. Please say yes." When she was about to speak—

"Wait. Let's start over. You ask me first."

"To be married?"

"Yes. Go on. You first."

"Nicholas, do you take me to be your wife?"

"Through sickness and in health, till death do you part, so help you God." He prompted her to add.

"Through sickness and in health, till death do you part, so help you God." She repeated.

"I do."

He said this like these were words he'd been wanting to say so many times as he hunkered down in a field somewhere, hiding behind a bush, sitting in the rain, looking at her photo, dreaming that he would live to be here on this day. "Now me. Frances, do you take me, your Nicholas to be your husband, through sickness and in health, till death do us part, so help you God?"

"I do," she answered as there was no other way to answer now without hurting him.

"Then with the powers invested in the Lord our God, I pronounce us husband and wife. May I kiss the bride?"

"Yes. Nicholas, you may kiss the bride."

He leaned down and kissed her, the sweetest and most wonderful kiss, a long kiss and they faced the empty church pews.

"May I present to you, Mr. and Mrs. Nicholas Draper."

They giggled as they walked down hand and hand from the altar and pretended to be greeting all the people imaginary people there smiling and saying, "Thank you, thank you, thank you..." until they made it to the front steps to the church.

"I love you, Mrs. Frances Draper," he said and hugged her again.

And in his eyes, she could see that he did, maybe, or maybe he loved that he was able to be there for this moment with her, she wasn't sure. It was all too high strung with happiness that the truth of them together was masked by things such as a soldier coming back from war and years of a long-distance relationship and that they parted when they'd just graduated from high school having each just turned 18.

Now they were nearly 21 and different.

"This is real for me Frances. We're married under God's eyes. I don't need a legal piece of paper to prove that we are. You're my girl now, forever," he said to her. "You and me. Right?"

"You and me."

They kissed again.

"Thank you."

"For what?"

"For being so beautiful," he said.

Her heart melted as she looked up into his eyes and she felt, maybe, just maybe, that he was the one for her after all. Maybe Alessandro wasn't her true love, as she'd felt since the first day that she saw him in his hospital bed and every day since. Maybe she could love Nicholas the same way if she gave them a chance. She'd give Nicholas her heart, as best she could, to make it work.

The only thing that scared her now was: Who saw her kissing Alessandro and would they tell Nicholas?

Chapter Twelve

Frances looked at Nicholas' photo on the desk in her room and thought back to all the days she'd look at it just hoping he'd return. Eight local boys had been killed in the war so when she felt awkward around Nicholas, she'd remind herself she was lucky to have him back.

In their two years apart, each had matured into different people and they didn't fit together like they did in high school. It didn't help that her mother placed a wedding announcement in the newspaper that read, *Palm Springs High Homecoming King and Queen Soon to Wed.* She included a picture of the couple in high school and a picture of them supposedly on the day Nicholas returned, staging a picture at the church with Nicholas in his dress blues and Frances looking lovely in her bridesmaid dress.

Next to their front-page wedding announcement was an article on Nicholas with a headline that read *Village Marine Returns from Iwo Jima.* The reporter interviewed Nicholas about his time fighting in the Solomon Islands, yet the details Nicholas gave were light. He talked more about the pleasures of being back home with his beautiful fiancée than what he experienced abroad. He'd only talk about his fellow marines. "It's a brotherhood for life." He was quoted saying. "We did the job we had to do, together." Details of the offensive came from the reporter doing research outside of his interview with Nicholas, filling in information about one of the bloodiest battles in the war with sources he found elsewhere. Nicholas wouldn't talk about what went on, not to the reporter, his fiancée, or anyone who asked. Almost as if baffled by the lack of details he got out of his subject, the reporter ended the article giving his impression of Nicholas, saying "this young man is a national treasure and our local hero, too humble to boast about his sacrifices for the nation."

These two front page newspaper articles made them local stars. All the single girls envied Frances as the one who gets to marry the handsome marine. Everywhere they went, Nicholas would be thanked for his service and they'd be congratulated on their upcoming wedding. It had been thrilling initially. Frances loved the attention yet was worried about making it work out. With the spotlight on them, breaking it off and crushing what so many viewed as a fairy tale romance would be even harder.

Frances styled her curls so that they fell softly around her face, a nice change from being pinned back under her Gray Lady uniform cap. She applied a deep red lipstick that she last wore on New Year's Eve, the night she hoped 1945 would be the year the war ended. Her wish came true and life was returning to normal. The village felt alive and full of possibilities. Torney, on the other hand, was the opposite. Each day that passed, the hospital was closer to shutting down. Frances found herself saying goodbye to someone she cared for too frequently as an army nurse would be reassigned or a doctor discharged. When a patient was released, their bed remained empty. Soon the Gray Ladies were being decommissioned and the army was looking for a buyer for the El Mirador hotel. Without war, the Army didn't need a big hospital in their small desert town.

Frances heard a knock on the door and then her mother and father greeting Nicholas. She put her sandals on, grabbed her clutch and glanced quickly in the mirror at her new dress. Her mother bought it for her days before after insisting she clean up her appearance as Nicholas deserved to see her looking pretty after what he'd been through. This set off an argument. Her mom said that nothing was more important now than Frances taking care of him. This is your life now, her mother told her and all Frances could say back to what she now thought sounded so ridiculous was, "It can't be."

"Hey Frances, you look lovely, Frances," Nicholas said when she entered the living room. The timidness in his voice made it clear that what he saw in front of him was so beautiful that he couldn't believe it. "Your hair..."

"You like it?" She touched her hair. "It's a new style."

"Sure do." He held out his hand to her. "Shall we go? Dinner is at eighteen hundred hours and that's just minutes away."

When she took his hand, she felt a lift inside that made her smile at him and he smiled back. She didn't have doubts when she felt this way, but this feeling never lasted. Muscular and tall, Nicholas got her revved up inside, but when they talked this feeling went away and was replaced by frustration. They had little to say to each other. Nicholas being so closed off had her worried that they'd never click back together like they did in high school, but moments like this gave her hope that time together was all they needed to fall in love again.

"Marines don't like to be late," said her father.

"No sir," Nicholas answered as they walked to the door.

"You two have fun," her mother said with heightened giddiness.

"We will, Mom," Frances assured her as she walked out and rolled her eyes at the comment. Her mom's controlling hand in their relationship was beginning to grate on her as she and Mrs. Draper had dived in to wedding planning as her new obsession.

Nicholas opened the car door for her like a gentleman. "I could get used to this real fast."

"Well then, get used to it. It'll only be the best treatment for my wife." He moved the bottom of her dress that had landed where the car door shuts into the car.

"Thank you." She helped pull her dress further in.

As they drove, Nicholas was quiet again. When they were alone, he was often quiet.

"What did you do today?" Frances asked.

"Not much," he replied. "You sure look pretty."

I know I'm pretty, she wanted to say, as that was the one line he'd said to her most often since he came home and while she liked it at first... weeks in it was becoming annoying. "Thank you," she answered, hoping not to get into one of her prickly moods again. "The book I was reading, you remember?"

"Uh-huh."

"I finished it."

"Good."

They drove the next five minutes in silence. He'd look over at her and smile and she smiled back at him. Too much silence felt unnatural for a young couple soon to wed, Frances knew, but didn't know how to fix it.

"It was such a great book. The ending I didn't expect," she added, waiting for him to ask a question about the book, but he didn't.

"Nice to hear."

"Yes. It is," she responded. "Turn right, here. It's the second house down on the left." He followed her directions. "This is it." She pointed to a small ranch house a few hundred feet away.

He pulled over. "Stay here." He turned off the car and went around it to open her door.

"I can open the door myself."

"You don't have too though. You're my girl."

Frances stepped out of the car. He closed the door and put his arm around her shoulder as they walked up the path to the front door. Claustrophobic, she squirmed away slightly and he pulled her in tighter as Frank and Mary open the door.

"Come in, come in," Dr. Frank said as he shook Nicholas' hand.

"Finally got you two celebrities over for dinner," Mary said.

"Oh, jeez," Frances said to her as she placed her clutch on the entryway table. "Being famous isn't all you think it is."

"Please, make yourselves comfortable." Mary showed them to the living room where a pitcher of lemonade and four glasses on a tray were placed on the coffee table.

Frances and Nicholas sat down on the davenport and Frank and Mary sat on kitchen chairs she'd placed on the other side for their visit. Mary poured lemonade into each glass. "Here we are," Mary said as she handed each of them a glass.

Frances drank most of her glass immediately. "I'm thirsty," she said as the rest of them looked at her.

"We see," Mary said and the girls started laughing.

"Sorry. I should be more ladylike," she said to Nicholas.

"You're so pretty it doesn't matter." He responded and put his arm around her again, but she wished he didn't. She felt like this often, so hot then cold. She couldn't figure her feelings out. It was mind-boggling.

"Oh, that's so sweet," Mary gushed.

"Ah, hold up, I think this is the perfect time to tell you, my lovely wife, just how gorgeous you are," Frank told Mary.

The group laughed and their dinner conversation was off to a nice flow.

"Look at us Frances, here with our guys, having a proper gathering in my home. Let me refill your glass." Mary reached for her glass.

"I can get it." Frances pulled her glass back.

"No, no. You're my guest. I will get it."

"I'm not used to you treating me this good."

"I know. But it's my new role as mistress of the house."

"Mistress? I like the sound of that," Frank quipped.

"So, how's the wedding coming along?" Mary asked.

Nicholas and Frances both laughed.

"Our mothers are driving us mad with all their wedding planning," said Frances. "You can't breathe when those two are in a room together because they're so busy talking they suck all the air out."

"It's true," Nicholas added. "We already had our wedding, so I don't worry much about it, right?" he said to Frances.

"You're married already?" Mary said, shocked.

"No, not officially," Frances answered.

"We did our own ceremony in the church the day I came back. Far as I'm concerned, our vows that day were in front of the eyes of God himself as our witness, so it was real."

"Well, then you can skip out on the real wedding," Frank added, to which both guys laughed.

"Don't I wish," Nicholas said. "Been around so much hubbub, I just want things to settle down, be simple."

"I hear you," Frank answered quietly.

"I swear my mom is acting like this is her wedding."

"She's just having fun, reliving her life through you," Mary said with a giggle.

"Have you two thought about where you'll be honeymooning?"

"No," They both said in unison as they literally hadn't discussed this once, which Mary found odd.

"Well. Let me go check on dinner." Mary got up.

"I'll go with you," Frances followed her into a small kitchen inside their 1000 sq. ft house where a tiny round table was set in the corner for four. "This all looks so nice," Frances remarked as Mary got the casserole out of the oven. "Do you like being married?"

"I do. It's fun," Mary said as she placed the stew on a hot pad on the table. She called out for the men to join them. "Guys, time to eat."

The men came into the room and the group sat down at the table, little room for raised elbows.

"So, let's take a moment to say thanks to God." Mary held out her hands and they all joined hands and bowed heads. "Frank, grace," Mary commanded and Frances thought she sounded a tad bossy.

"Dear Heavenly Father, thank you for this food we are about to eat. Thank you for retuning Nicholas safely and for this time together. In Jesus' name. Amen." Amen followed from the rest of them at the table.

Mary scooped food onto Frank's plate which made Frances want to cringe.

"Does she always serve you?" Frances asked with a smile.

"She does. Don't need her to—"

"But I like too," Mary cut him off and kissed him on the cheek.

"I think it's nice," Nicholas added.

"Should I serve you?" Frances asked.

"Not gonna say no," Nicholas replied, to which Frances picked up the serving spoon and placed a few heaps of the casserole onto his plate. "Is that enough?"

"For now," Nicholas responded and she thought he should have also added "thank you." Frances was not amused.

"Well all, please dig in. I hope you like it. I just threw together some of what we had in the fridge."

"Delicious," Nicholas said after his first bite and the rest followed praising Mary for the meal she'd made which was followed by a long discussion of how she prepared the meal and all the ingredients she used which Frances didn't care about. She wanted to tell her to stop acting like this other person. She wanted her friend back who acted like herself, not playing a role of wife, hostess and casserole-serving mother to her husband. This was the beginning of them each becoming their mothers. A terrible turn in their lives, Frances now decided. Mary had morphed into a stranger right in front of her.

"I have to say, you sure like being married."

"We do," Mary said and then looked at Frank in a way that caught Frances' eye.

"What's going on, Mary?"

Mary looked a bit nervous. Frances turned to Frank.

"Frank, what's going on?"

"Why do you think something's going on?" Nicholas asked, unaware.

"Because she knows me too well," said Mary.

"We invited you over here for dinner because we have a few

things to tell you." She looked at Frank and he nodded to her. "I'm pregnant."

"Pregnant! Oh my, Mary." Frances stood and gave Mary a hug. "You're going to be a mom!"

Nicholas shook Frank's hand, "Congratulations."

"Oh, I'm so happy for you," Frances said to Mary, then went back to her seat.

Mary and Frank looked to each other again.

"That's not all," Mary added.

"Mary, what's wrong? Why do you seem like something's wrong? You're having a baby!"

Mary's eyes filled with tears. "I know. I'm so happy."

"Then why are you about to cry?"

"We're moving up north, Franny."

"Moving? When?"

"Next month. Week after your wedding."

"But you're having a *baby*," Frances said as if *how could you leave me when you're having a baby?!*

"Torney's closing. So for work, I talked to a few places and—"

"He's accepted a position at a hospital in San Francisco," Mary cut in. "We're moving to San Francisco, Franny."

"You're... leaving?" Frances said with disbelief, like she'd taken a bullet to the chest.

"Frank's going first, to look for a place. I'm staying back a little longer since my mother-in-law's a bit much. She never stops talking. And I mean *never*. If she doesn't have a word in mind to say, she just starts humming, right honey?"

"Can't lie," Said Frank.

"Excuse me. I need to get some air." Frances went out the front door and walked down the street. The evening had turned to night and the street was dark.

"Frances!" Mary came running after. "I don't wanna leave you, but I gotta go."

"We said we'd raise our kids here together," said Frances while trying to hold back her tears. "Everything's changing and I feel like I can't catch my breath."

"It's called life, Franny. You can't stop it."

"I don't wanna stop it. I just, I don't know. Everything feels wrong." Frances kept walking fast and Mary tried to keep up.

"Slow down. Let's talk. It's not too far. We'll still see each other."

"It is far and with the baby, I won't be there to see your baby grow up."

"It can't be helped, Franny. Believe me, I've tried to talk him out of this, to find some place closer, but it's a good job and hospital and for his career, he needs to go there and I gotta go with him."

"It wasn't how we planned it."

"I know."

Frances wiped the tears from her face.

"You're crying. Please don't cry or I'll cry."

"Mary, you ever think it'd be worse after the war?"

"What do you mean worse? Everything's so much better."

"It is, but I *feel* so much worse."

"You're adjusting."

"I don't think me and Nicholas work anymore."

"Sure, you do. You do. You're just adjusting."

"Maybe, but I'm sorry, this is your night. I'm being a fool. You're having a baby, Mary. A baby!" She said and reached out and hugged her. "I'm so happy for you. Really. So happy. I'll just have to visit all the time because I'm not going to miss seeing your children grow up."

"And I'll visit home all the time and we'll see each other all the time. I promise."

They let go of each other and Frances wiped away her tears. "I like your hair, by the way," said Mary.

"You do?"

"I do."

"What does it feel like to be pregnant?"

"Same as when I wasn't pregnant. If I didn't skip, I'd never know."

"You're still gonna be my maid of honor. I won't have that little one in your belly take that away from me too," Frances said.

"I've already had a talk with junior and explained that he can't go giving me morning sickness when I have a wedding to plan."

"Poor kid has no idea what he's in for."

They hugged again.

"All day long from his Auntie Franny, on the few days I'll get to see him."

"Ah, Franny, don't be like that. We gotta make this work. We're forever. That's all I know. It doesn't matter if I'm not here."

Frances reached out to her and just broke down into tears that didn't stop for a good while. "It's okay, Franny. It's okay."

Frances wiped her eyes. "Where did that come from?"

"Frances?" Nicholas called out as he hustled down the street towards them, with Frank following.

"I'm fine. Just crying over nothing."

"Not true. She's crying because she's gonna miss me."

"I am gonna miss you. I just got Nicholas back and now you're leaving me."

Nicholas gently brushed a curl out of her eye, standing so tall and muscular beside her as he sweetly said, "I'm not leaving you ever again." Which made Frances smile and lean into him as they walked back to the house to finish dinner and have coffee before calling it a night.

On the way home, Nicholas parked the car in a cluster of palm trees that provided coverage from anyone driving by and they made out and she even let him put his hand up her shirt and touch her bare breasts but stopped him when his hand went up between her legs before he reached her undergarment.

"Wanna do it now, Frances? We're already married, really, let's do it now." He'd push and push on her and she'd say no again and again. Nicholas was aggressive in this matter, almost a different person. Also more real. A peek behind the façade. It intrigued and scared Frances.

"You do it Nicholas? When you were away?" she finally asked. She'd long suspected. He was a marine, after all, who'd been to war.

"Don't ask me that," he said as he continued his aggressive groping.

"I have to get home."

"No. Stay with me." He rubbed the inside of her thigh.

"I can't. I have to go home." She pushed him off her, he came back in for a kiss. She pushed him back. "Nicholas!" she called out.

"Frances," he said as he moved his hand higher up her leg.

She pushed his hand away. "Home. Now." She told him and started laughing. He laughed with her and pulled her into an innocent hug.

"I'm so happy to be back here with you," he whispered in her ear and held onto her like a child. He took a large, contented breath and became limp in her arms, as if the breath took all the stress from his body.

She hugged him back and whispered in his ear, "Me too, Nicholas, me too."

He sat up behind the wheel of the car, abandoning the vulnerable state as if waking from hypnosis.

She said, "Nicholas, you can talk to me.'

"About what?"

"All of it. Any of it. I have a good idea what you've been through." He looked at her like she'd cussed him out.

"How do you know what I've been through?"

"I talk to the guys at Torney. They've told me many things. Still tell me things. What it
was like. The real hard days."

"Well, you shouldn't go back there anymore. I don't want you around a bunch of men
who'd like to take you from me."

"Don't say that."

"I can say that. You're my girl. You're about to be my wife. I got a right to make

decisions for you, like this and I don't see why you need to keep going there."

"It's my job."

"It's not a job."

"Maybe not a real job, but it matters. The guys I've helped, that matters still." She almost started crying as she thought back to the suffering she'd seen, especially with Oklahoma.

Nicholas relaxed a bit. "You're right."

Frances didn't want to speak or be with him now. "Take me home."

"Come on. Don't be this way."

"What way?"

"Where you ruin our good time."

"It's ruined already."

"It doesn't have to be." He leaned over and tried to kiss her. "Come on."

She turned her head away. "I want home, Nicholas, only to go home now."

He sat back, looked out the driver's side window, unable to understand how the mood had changed so that it was sour for the night.

"I don't wanna take you home."

"Take me home, please," she asked him nicely.

He started up the car, letting the engine idle, yet still not driving, like he was stuck there, unable to process what was happening. "I'm sorry. I don't know why I get like that." He reached over and rubbed her leg sweetly.

"It's normal after all that?"

"All what?"

"War."

"War," he repeated as if he were thinking about what that was, slammed on the gas and peeled out in the dirt, then onto the road.

"War," he said it again, like he was thinking of it with disdain now, remembering something he'd been through that he never wanted to think about again.

He pushed heavy on the gas. Frances glanced at him, wondering, what was his war like, the one he'd never talk about to anyone, the one he tried to wish away by pretending it and whatever horrors he'd experienced never existed.

"Stop driving," said Frances.

He looked at her like she was going crazy. "What now?"

"Nicholas, pull over." She grabbed the wheel and veered the car to the right.

"Are you crazy?" He said as he slammed on the brakes.

Frances slid over and grabbed him into a desperate embrace, holding him tightly, with meaning that was more than just about them. It was about Nicholas' war, the one going on inside him, the one he never talked about.

"I'm sorry too. I am. I'm so happy you made it back to me. So happy."

Shocked, he waited to embrace her back, finally doing so with a tight grip as she buried her face into his neck, in an embrace neither moved to end quickly, the type of coming home embrace Nicholas fought for and felt he deserved. Because maybe he did.

Chapter Thirteen

After pushing George in his wheelchair back to his room, she left him and headed to the library to place the harmonica back in the music instrument box.

She'd just played with him in Oklahoma's spot, the name she'd given to the area under the Desert Willow tree where she spent so many days goofing back and forth, getting time to pass as slowly as possible. She'd wanted to make a plaque that said, *Dedicated to Henry Oklahoma Smith*. Or carve his name in the tree to mark his special place, but she never did. It stayed as a thought only, one she'd think about over and over in the year since his passing, but never acted upon. The dedication lived only in her, which some days she thought maybe that's how it should be as every dedication plaque she'd read in her life always seemed to be for someone else as she had no knowledge of the person. That's how it would be for anyone who read *Dedicated to Henry 'Oklahoma' Smith* on a Desert Willow tree. They wouldn't know his sense of humor, how they got along like brother and sister, goofing on each other every chance they could get. They'd just know someone thought enough of him to make a dedication and nail it to the tree and that didn't seem enough of a reason to go through with it. She considered that it may be more special to keep thinking of doing it, because that meant she was thinking of Oklahoma again and again. She did still miss him. He was comfortable to be with as they had a chemistry she'd not easily found with another person and he was the first person she'd ever known who died. This was part of the reason for the deep imprint he'd left upon her.

George sort of reminded her of Oklahoma. He had a sense of humor that was similar when she could get him to goof. George liked to play the harmonica but wouldn't attend the weekly music program in the recreation room where local musicians would come to play with them to help the recovery of patients, so she assigned one to him to keep two weeks earlier the day he arrived and he would continue to have it on hand until he came out of his slump. Another one of those soldiers still in shock that he may lose a limb if his healing didn't go well, he was teetering every day with intense emotions that some days it made it hard for him to talk much, so he'd play the harmonica. That was one battle she'd won, coaxing and encouraging him. Since he didn't talk much, every time she visited him, Frances brought the other harmonica they had in the library and played songs with him as best she could. Frances did not have any musical talent in her, especially with the harmonica, so her horrible attempt at a duet would get him to chuckle here and there as he'd cover his ears to make fun of her. A giggle out of him each visit was her goal and she would stay until she got that one smile before moving on to check on the few remaining Torney patients.

Frances marked her harmonica, number 4, back in on the log. This harmonica was donated by the younger brother of Charlie Baxter who was still serving overseas. Frances had taken notes on the cards as well of the names of the soldiers who played the instruments and a little bit about them to share with those that donated them.

But the fiddle, what would she say to Mr. Keller? That it was played every day by a soldier, but not an American soldier? That it was used by an Italian Prisoner of War here earning 80¢ a day for a job an American boy couldn't do because they were risking their lives fighting for democracy overseas. It was more than a fifty-fifty chance that Mr. and Mrs. Keller were opposed to the prisoners being there if she took her odds from the people in the town, maybe 75% if she was being honest. She missed Alessandro. He still played in the evenings, but she stayed away since Nicholas came home. Some days she felt like she was coming out of her skin, she missed him so badly. Crippled with guilt and confusion over her feelings and with no one to talk to about it, she just set her mind to getting over him, and hope that over time, when settled with Nicholas so everything was as it should be, she'd forget about him. That was her hope.

Frances made her way around the corner, went through the lobby and outside to the El Mirador Tower where Gray Ladies and friends and family were gathered for an award ceremony. Chairs had been placed in rows and a podium had been brought outside, set up under the shade provided by the tower during that part of the day. It was fall when the temperatures were most pleasant in the desert. Frances and three other Gray Ladies were getting awards. Two of them had only been volunteering with the American Red Cross for six months and the other one not much longer. Frances didn't know them well, except as the lead for the library and working with them to maintain order with the loan program. She'd become strict after an instrument went missing that one of them failed to properly sign out. Luckily it wasn't on loan, it was donated, so she didn't have to account for it. She felt each instrument was her obligation to protect and return, like someone's child she was watching, so to these new girls she probably seemed like Edith, strict and cold, which she thought funny since she and Mary used to goof about Edith being so tightly wound.

Frances said hello to her parents, Nicholas and his mother who sat in the rows of chairs set up in the lobby for the ceremony, giving them hugs before taking her spot up front. Her mother had arranged for a photographer and reporter to be there from the paper, which Frances knew would lead to her being on the front page the next day, or inside the Torney Section. Her mother never missed an opportunity to get their family boasted about in the paper or a cause she cared about. It was expected that Frances would play along as she lived her life this way since a child, the papers documenting anything of note about her father and mother and now her.

Frances sat with the other honored guests off to the side of the podium, next to Edith who eagerly leaned over and said, "Your mother just told me your father would like to donate to our Red Cross Chapter again." Edith smiled, an unusual behavior for her. She added, "That is nice of them, after all they've done already."

Frances smiled and said, "Yes, it is." Because she knew why and how her mom did this. It would be announced in the paper. It made her father, the editor and her mother, a social leader in the community, look good, especially connecting it with their daughter's volunteer work and her award. She didn't think they were bad people and it was nice that they donated, but it wasn't purely just from the heart.

A local boy scout, not even ten years old, led the group in the Pledge of Allegiance and after, the National Anthem was sung by one of the Red Cross women who got pegged to do all the events because she had a strong solid voice that didn't crack on the high notes. When she finished, the Army Chaplain took his place behind the podium and began his talk about the meaning of selfless service and doing God's work helping the wounded, the lonely and suffering with compassion. He spoke about the true meaning of love for our fellow human beings being based in compassion and then he tied this back in, rather skillfully Frances thought, into how the Gray Ladies serve those they do not know, but who fought for the country against formidable odds and when coming back home to heal their wounded bodies and spirits, these women helped them get through their challenging days. The chaplain liked to pontificate and used every gathering to take as much time as he could to be center stage. Fifteen minutes in, the people were getting bored and Frances thought about how much she missed Mary. Signing up to be Gray Ladies was Mary's idea because she wanted to meet guys, but she'd stopped volunteering since getting pregnant and she had Frank now, so she didn't need to meet men.

Frances looked out into the crowd and waved to Nicholas who stood out because he was so tall, trying to get his attention, but he was so busy chatting with his mom, that he didn't notice.

After the chaplain finished, Edith came up to the podium and delivered the recognition to the other women first, leaving Frances for last.

"This next young lady has done an exceptional job for the past two years." She began. "In two years of service, where she not only helped provide companionship, conversation, letter writing, a laugh, filled up a water cup for a soldier who was thirsty, she also stood up to oversee the Red Cross Book Share Program where she made it her mission to fill all requests the soldiers made, making countless trips to the library, returning and checking out books for the men. She also took charge to expand the library to include musical instruments, first running a donation program to find a guitar or a flute not being used that would help pass the time here at Torney by a soldier recovering. You know, the days of recovery from rheumatic fever and all the various challenging injuries and illnesses men from the Pacific front sustained are many and hard for our boys in service and this is a burden this young lady has taken on, volunteering her time to raise the spirits of the soldiers who gave so much for our country. It is my great honor to call up Miss Frances Clark."

Frances went up to the podium to receive her certificate and pin and in the back of the crowd, a group of Torney patients clapped, hollered out her name and whistled. "We love you, Miss Frances." George yelled out, which made the audience laugh. Frances saw George, sitting in his wheelchair, wearing his army coat over his hospital clothes, having dressed up for the ceremony. He waved to her and she waved back, her face lighting up when she saw him. Nicholas looked back to see who she was so happy to see. The photographer took snaps of her at the podium, shaking Edith's hand and holding up her certificate of achievement. Frances blushed as she smiled and looked back at her cheering group, a bit embarrassed, as she sat back in her seat.

Edith gave her last bit of comment to the group, "The war is over, but there is still so much work to be done and one way each of you can easily make a difference is to donate blood as often as you can."

Edith called up the chaplain to conduct a closing prayer and she sat down next to Frances and whispered to her, "See? What you've done matters?"

The chaplain asked them to bow their heads to pray. Frances listened to the drone of the chaplain deliver another long-winded listless talk to God when she heard her own voice speak up. "God, please let me do more." And this surprised her because she said it out loud. It was a whisper, a faint whisper, but loud enough that Edith heard.

The ceremony over, Frances was pulled over by the photographer to George and his buddies. The reporter had already cornered them to stay for a photo op with Frances and had her pose sitting next to George and surrounded by the men.

Nicholas made his way over to Frances. "So proud of my girl!" he said and put his arm around her and pulled her close after the photo taking completed.

"Nicholas, this is George."

They shook hands. "How you doing George? Nice to meet you," Nicholas said enthusiastically, giving George all his focused attention.

"Fine. Fine. Thanks to Miss Frances here. She makes sure I've got my harmonica to play to pass the time."

"Nicholas, you should come play with us. You're good on the harmonica. George makes me play with him I think just to get a laugh out of how bad I am."

"Yep, yep Miss Frances. Ya got me."

"Would be an honor to spend time with you," Nicholas said warmly and shook his hand again. "Frances, you ready to go?"

"Yeah, give me a minute."

"Excuse me, my mother's waving me over," Nicholas said to

George and headed over to his mom who was waving from the other side of the group.

"You got a nice guy there."

"I do," Frances agreed as another patient came up to wheel him back to his room.

"I got him, Miss Frances," he said to her.

"Thanks, Chip," she said and looked at George, "See you day after next."

"Day after next," he repeated, agreeing to her that he was looking forward.

Frances walked over to Nicholas and her future mother-in-law for the drive to the tennis club for the post ceremony lunch her mom had planned.

"You were so nice to George," Frances said immediately as they headed out.

"He's a wounded soldier, Frances, nothing more respectable than having taken a hit for his country."

Frances felt honored to be with Nicholas in this moment. He was a man she respected and the way he cared for his fellow servicemen was something she admired. "Wasn't that sweet? That they came? Most are in a lot of pain, like George..."

"Think they're all in love with her," Mrs. Draper said to Nicholas, as they got into the car.

"They are in love with her, Ma."

"Why would you two think that?" Frances asked, annoyed at both for talking about her in front of her, like she wasn't a woman with her own thoughts. This was something they often did.

"What dear?" Her future mother-in-law said.

"That they're in love with me."

When they rode in the car together, Mrs. Draper insisted on being in the front as she always had to be at the top of the pecking order with Nicholas. This was something Frances would be dealing with during their entire marriage she was beginning to realize. Spending her days with Nicholas and Mrs. Draper, going to brunch at the club. Mrs. Draper gossiping about others with Nicholas and the two of them belittling her intellect and constitution.

She was acquiring, along with Nicholas, an opinionated and needy mother-in-law with Mrs. Draper.

"All of them are in love with you, Frances." Mrs. Draper said from the front passenger seat. But you know this," she said in that dismissive tone as if Frances should not be acting surprised to hear this.

"No. I don't know this," Frances replied.

"She doesn't mean it that way Frances," Nicholas stepped in. "She means it as a compliment. Look at you. You're gorgeous. If you were helping me out while in there, I'd be in love with you too. It's a compliment."

"Exactly. It was meant as a compliment, darling," Mrs. Draper added.

"It's not a compliment."

"Sure, it is," he said and both he and his mother started laughing. "Are you getting upset?"

"Dear, don't be so serious. Come on, you just got an award!" Mrs. Draper added.

Frances grabbed onto the handle and cranked open the window, suddenly feeling like she needed fresh air on her face. Nicholas and his mother continued with their blabbering in the front seat about the men at Torney and how lucky Nicholas was that not one of them stole her heart while he was away, like she was so gullible and without a backbone to decide who she'd become affectionate with in her life. She couldn't stand their placating and their demoralizing her like an object and this after being recognized for the important work she'd been doing at Torney. She looked out at the desert thinking, keeping quiet.

My heart was stolen and I walked away for you.

They went inside the tennis club which was filled with Sunday brunch guests, all of whom knew her family and Nicholas' mom as both families were prominent villagers and active at the club.

Nicholas with his arm around her shoulder, holding her like a toddler in a crowd. Her parents beat them there and were sitting at their usual circular table by the window looking out over the tennis courts. Mrs. Draper was having a hard time walking as she had a bunion on her right foot which she never stopped telling everyone was causing her such pain. As she waddled to the table, stopping to speak to everyone she knew, she laughed and smiled like a politician, until she got to their table and spoke underhandedly about someone she'd just spoke nicely to.

"There's our special girl." Her father grabbed Frances into a hug and shook her side to side like a stick figure she was trying to break in half. Then she planted a kiss on her forehead. "My girl," he said as she sat down at the table and gulped down a glass of ice water.

"A blabbermouth, that chaplain," Mrs. Draper said as she fanned her face. "It was too hot out there in the sun to go on like he did."

Frances' mother agreed and the two of them went on and on about the wedding, asking the young couple here and there their opinion on this or that and Frances kept saying, whatever you want, sounds good, I like pink. I like blue. No, I don't like yellow. It was a barrage of questions in between a comment here or there about Frances' award. "So proud of my girl," Nicholas would say and then her father would say it too, as if he couldn't come up with a fresh phrase to compliment her with because he was trying to one up his soon-to-be-son-in-law who was staking a claim on his daughter who'd always been his girl. "So proud of my girl!" her father would say and then "So proud of my girl!" Nicholas would say, in between the mothers asking ridiculous questions like did she have something old, something new, something blue?

"Can you both stop saying that I'm your girl. I'm a grown woman."

"Frances, it's endearing," said her mother.

"You'll always be your father's girl. It's sweet," Mrs. Draper added.

"I'm a grown woman," Frances snapped at Nicholas, raising her voice so that others having brunch looked over.

"You're not my girl, we got a problem," Nicholas answered egotistically.

"I am, but I'm not."

"You are, but you're not. What does that even mean? Are you feeling ill?" Nicholas leaned into her and quietly asked, "Are you having your cycle?" She rolled her eyes as she couldn't believe this was what he took from her statement.

"That's a stupid thing to say Nicholas,"

"You're just acting like you are?"

These head bumps between Nicholas and her had started showing up frequently now. They couldn't get along for more than a day without sniping at each other.

"Let's bring it down a notch," her father piped up to both.

"Sorry." Frances replied. She was being irritable again and she knew that she was the one who was being too sensitive, but she'd changed on the inside while Nicholas was away and they still treated her the same, even after getting the award today. She realized that who they were in this moment was who they would all be in the future. Sure, she'd have children come along that would join the brunch table at the club down the road, but this was who they'd be in the decades to come. Nicholas and her having dinners with her parents; Dad and Nicholas belittling her and her mom backing them up. She didn't know if she could take it.

After brunch, she and Nicholas went to the pool for a swim.

"Wish you'd show me more respect in front of your father. I was just paying you a compliment," he said while they placed their towels on lounge chairs.

"What's going on with us?" said Frances—though she had a pretty good idea.

"We're just getting to know each other again. I gotta say Franny, you're different than when I left. Not sure who I'm marrying."

"Yeah, you too. Nicholas, how about we start over, you know, and tell each other really what we're thinking and ask questions we want to know. Just get it all out on the table so we can go into this marriage with a clean slate."

"Snapping at me in front of you father makes me look weak."

"I know. I'm sorry. But that's not what I mean, like I wanna know what happened to you in the war. What did you go through? All of it, I want to know all of it so we can be close."

"It's war, Frances, what do you want me to talk about. Guys dying in front of my eyes?"

"Maybe? I don't know exactly, just knowing you and who you are is what I want. Nicholas, we're about to be married. We have to figure this out."

"Iwo Jima was hell most days. Lot of hard stuff to get through. You know. I mean Frances, you had to have talked to guys at Torney about what it was like."

"Yeah, but you're *my* guy," she said which made him laugh.

"And you're my *girl*." He leaned over to kiss her. "I can't wait until I can tear your clothes off," he said, passionately.

"Why's it every time I try to get close to you, you just wanna make out?"

"I'm happiest when my lips are on yours," he joked.

"Cut it out. I'm serious."

"Why you gotta be so serious Franny? I'm ready to have fun. I've been serious for too long, fighting and killing..." He stopped there when that word came out of his mouth and he stood up from the chair and put on his shirt and sliders.

"Where you going?"

"Somewhere I ain't gotta be serious."

"Nicholas?" He started walking away from her. "Nicholas, come back."

Nicholas turned around and walked back to her, with the look of a broken man on his face. "Why you gotta make me remember and say that word, Franny. Why? All I want is to come back and forget about Iwo Jima and that hell. Marry my girl and be happy. That's what I came back for and you just won't leave it."

Frances could see now what she was dealing with. "I know you want to, but I can feel it between us.

"Feel what?"

"Like this, you and me, we're in some sort of play, like not being real with each other."

"I'm being real."

"Not when you don't talk about anything from the last two years of your life.

It's like there's part of you locked up."

"You get an award for writing letters for guys and reading books to them and you think what you see here, their pain and suffering is the real war, well it's not. It's a fairy tale from what I went through so I don't wanna talk about it and remember it. I'm trying to forget, but you won't let me forget. Do you remember those months I didn't write you?" He looked distraught. "I couldn't because I didn't care about anything anymore, not even us. Me and some guys came across a village and some of the guys raped a girl there and I didn't do anything to help her and I didn't turn them in and I didn't say anything to anyone and when we left, there was a girl who'd been hurt and I figured I wasn't a good man, you know, didn't do the right thing and I just didn't know if I wanted to live anymore. I wished an enemy bullet would take me out and even thought about doing it to myself. But I'd think of you and think of my mom. So, I don't wanna talk about it. I'm not gonna talk about it. I just want to move on and be happy."

"You're right. You're right. I'm sorry." She said as she went over to him and hugged him. "I'm sorry." He hugged her back and forgave her. He was traumatized and didn't want to be reminded. She did feel that he was pretending to be this guy who was just fine, but he wasn't.

"I'm just so grateful I made it back whole, you know, when I see guys like George who didn't...." He stopped, unable to continue.

"I'm grateful you made it back too." Frances reached out and hugged him, but this was the girl who was a Gray Lady volunteer holding him, understanding his empathy, not a woman who felt the passion that comes with being in love. Her heart was not in it that way, she knew in that moment and she knew she had a problem she could no longer ignore. Their relationship didn't work together and they would not live happily ever after if they went through with the wedding.

They made the error of having become engaged before he left for the war. The night-before-proposal in his front yard, one four-word sentence, Will you marry me? That she answered with one word, yes. It altered their lives from that moment forward, bringing them to this place years later, in a story neither of them should still be a part of, but didn't know how to end.

The day after next, as promised, she was back in her seersucker uniform with her hair pinned up and blew into a harmonica playing a horrible rendition of "When the Saints Come Marching In" with George. On the table between them was the Desert Sun paper with their picture on the cover and the article about Frances working for the Gray Ladies with the headline that read *Local Gray Lady Volunteer Honored* with a sub-line that read, *Torney Patients Attend to Thank Her.*

After the last note, Frances made a displeased face and shook her head side to side. "Why on earth do you let me play along with you?"

"You keep showing up here with a harmonica!"

"I'm horrible." Her disbelief turned into a giggle.

"You are. Dogs within earshot got to be howling."

"Oohhh ohhh ohhh." She mocked a howling dog. "Like that." He laughed.

"Like this," he answered and began howling even louder. Frances joined in, after which they burst into belly-aching laughter and looked around at the people on the grounds who looked over at them. It wasn't many people as it was in the day she sat in the garden with Oklahoma or John or the many other men she'd helped.

"You gotta get 'cher self a better job that pays so you don't have to be out here with me howling for free."

"I'm about to be married. Can't do anything soon." She said rather snarky, as if her next commitment for life had some bumps, meaning a lifelong vow of marriage.

George looked at her, "Oh, come on, now, your Nicholas seemed real nice."

"Yeah, he is." Frances rubbed her forehead and took a deep breath. "I'm a lucky girl," repeating what she'd said more times that she could count since Nicholas returned home without emotion and to get herself looking at the positive about their upcoming marriage. "I got something to tell you." She shuffled her feet in the dirt, moving off a few rocks from under her sandals. "I got told yesterday that the Gray Ladies are over, since the war's over, which is so good, you know, but they're shutting this place down and you know… times are changing, for the better in 'all, so it's good."

"They're transferring me to the army hospital near my home. Seems this is our last hoorah together." He put his hands up to the side of his face and shook them like they were pom-poms.

"I guess." She shuffled her feet. "Can I give you my address? Would you write to me? I'd like to know how you are if that's not too forward. I just keep having everyone leave and I never hear from them again and I'd like to hear how you're doing."

"Yeah, people disappear, don't they, with this fighting stuff. Getting done with soon."

"Gotta hope so," she answered, knowing that there was one more who would disappear one day soon. Alessandro. She stopped seeing him when Nicholas returned, unable to keep a double life going, but it wasn't working. The double life lived inside her heart, feelings she couldn't get to stay away no matter how hard she tried to love Nicholas. "But back to what?"

"Don't think it's back at all. Just forward. Only way I can figure it at least."

"Sounds 'bout right."

"Last hoorah?" he said as she raised his harmonica up, a gesture for them to play.

"Last hoorah. It's true. I've been found out." The stress on her face lifted as she placed the harmonica to her mouth and played notes like a two-year-old, without structure and George joined in to play a disastrous mess of notes, loud and fast.

Chapter Fourteen

Going back in to finish the job, Frances drove her mother's car to Torney which was becoming more of a ghost town each day.

The Torney Forum, a discussion group of leaders at the hospital had led the communications about the closing soon to happen. Military personnel reassigned, patient numbers dwindling and civilian workers getting jobs elsewhere. The end of the war began a phase of villagers getting back to normal life despite rations being still in effect and the wounds of war hardening into scars. Trying to move forward when she knew how dark the world could be was getting to Frances. She found herself wallowing in the house, unmotivated.

She'd spent the last four days mostly in her room pondering the point of life. It worried her parents whose only advice was that she needed to "buck up" and "get on with it." That's "what people do" and what she'd "need to learn to do too" since she was an adult. It was how her family dealt with everything and in her mother's case meant covering everything with a smile pasted on her f Frances just couldn't do it.

German atrocities uncovered

horror of what happened blanketed everything. It persisted in her mind: images in the newspaper of liberated camps, emaciated prisoners had broken her ability to smile.

Yet her life seemed almost perfect. Nothing horrible had happened to her as she'd walked through the war years seemingly unscratched to the casual observer; a young girl with a love story and a high school sweetheart returning home to marry her. Pictures of her reality wouldn't haunt a person if they simply viewed pictures of her life, this favor from God she'd seemed to be granted. Frances Clark always gets what she wants. That was what she was known for, her brand amongst the town, the local princess. So perfect a life, anyone would want it! Her father reminded her of this when she'd had a crying fit the night before and proclaimed to her parents that they didn't understand her.

The storm of war had come into their town, eating away at lives and altering everything overnight and now that it was all done and she had time to reflect, to read the papers articles about the Final Solution and to understand that man was to be feared more than she'd ever thought possible. She'd bloomed during the trauma and now was crashing in its wake and as her wedding day grew closer, the regret for giving up on herself increased, but being selfish meant being brave. She wasn't brave for herself. She was only brave for others ⸻ng a lie.

⸻ishing boxing up the reading library to return the
⸻ The books had been so important to the men, a
⸻ could help take their mind off physical pain
⸻ to live with every day from the war. The
⸻king a guy away to another place had
⸻ouldn't image a world where she
⸻ Tale of Two Cities, Romeo and
⸻ was a detective.
⸻ve in a long time. It'd
⸻t was something

"Time heals all wounds," she said out loud as the pulled into the parking lot. This was the phrase her mother said to her all the time as a kid growing up and it was only now, at the age of twenty that she wasn't so sure this was right. Time had *changed* the wound of Oklahoma passing. It was still painful, but in a different way and served as a marker in her life of that time and of their friendship. It was a time she reflected on as being a young girl new to the Gray Lady role, too caring to protect herself and too involved to protect Oklahoma. That special time with him got her to this place where she was confident helping the men, but now there were few if any men to help.

She felt nostalgia for those earlier days when there was a city of men and women working together to help with the war effort. She always knew back then that it was temporary and now the end of that temporary time was happening with the war over for four months now. She didn't want war again, of course not, but she did want all the friends she'd made to stay there with her, but so many of them had left already, gone back home or moved on to some other job. She felt such loss from this. It hurt, like a constant stab to the heart and she wanted it to stop.

She carried three empty boxes into the lobby room where the library was off to the side. She'd already returned several boxes and today would be the remainder. She hadn't returned the musical instruments yet to their owners who donated them. Some were given on loan, others for good. She'd be giving those handed over for good to the high school for their music program and was to make this her last task after all the books had been handled because she'd been procrastinating about what to do with the violin.

As she packed books into a box, she read the spine and remember moments with a certain man reading that book: this book she'd read to PFC Pablo Rojas as he dried the rheumatic fever out of his lungs in the warm desert; and this one she handed over to a guarded soldier who didn't like to talk with anyone unless it was necessary; this book was never read at Torney by the soldier she chose it for name Liam as he passed away shortly after arriving. She set that book aside to read out loud in his honor so that he could hear it from heaven.

She noticed the box of musical instruments sitting off to the right of the bookshelf had been moved and on the other side of it she saw there was what looked to be an instrument case and panicked. She rushed over and picked up the case, then placed it on the table like she'd been given a bomb that was about to explode. She waited, breathed heavily, as she carefully unclipped the case latches and flipped back the top. *Scraggly instrument* she thought as she looked at what had been in his arms as he poured his heart into the old girl to make her stand out with fresh sounds. She rubbed her hand across the violin strings and neck, the places he'd touched, creating sounds so vivid and sweet and pure that it made people cry. She touched the edge of its scratched rosewood body and tears welled. She felt so torn again about what she was doing with Nicholas. Why did this all have to be so hard? She didn't ask for it. She didn't want to fall in love with another man. It happened naturally as true love should, she knew now, but it was too late.

Frances shut the case, closed the hinges and hurried out of the room with it in her hand. She rushed out of the main building and went to the Red Cross tent, looking for Edith inside. There were only three women there, none of whom she knew as they were brought in from other chapters to help their Red Cross chapter move into a small office in the village where blood donations could continue and people might donate money and other items the Red Cross still needed, especially overseas, providing care in war-torn areas. A shortage of food and medical care were still needed by so many in Europe as the aftermath of the war was as brutal. There would be long lasting trauma and devastation. Homes demolished, livelihoods gone and permanent injuries.

"Is Edith here today?" Frances asked, desperation in her voice.

"Haven't seen her," the red-haired one responded and the other two confirmed by shaking their heads.

"Did one of you return this instrument to the library?"

"I did," the dark-haired-one answered. "It was dropped off by the sergeant who works with the prisoners. They're moving them out tomorrow to Camp Haan."

The moment she didn't want to have happen would happen. Alessandro was leaving. She'd lived the last year content, knowing that even though she couldn't have him, at least she knew that he was close and in a situation where no other woman could have him either. She hadn't realized this was what had been sustaining her until now. She didn't want to go back to life before she met him, where he was nonexistent in her world. But she knew in this moment when she wanted to scream "NO!" when she heard he was going away, like one of her limbs getting pulled out of its socket then severed from her body, but she'd always feel it there as a phantom pain for the rest of her life just like John did.

"Girl, are you all right?"

Frances sat into the chair and the three women came to her.

"You're pale," one said.

"A ghost," said the other and brought her a glass of water which Frances accepted with a shaky hand and took a sip.

Another grabbed her free wrist and took her pulse, pressing fingers on her veins and looking at her wristwatch, silently counting her vital.

"Should I get a doctor?" another asked.

"Her pulse is high but normal."

Tears fell from Frances' eyes. "I'm fine." Frances wiped them away, unable to explain the breakdown she was having in front of them, the unexpected collapse she'd been trying to avoid for so long, since that day when they kissed and she knew then that he loved her and she loved him. The forbidden path she'd strayed onto, where she loved the man she loved, destroying the man she'd committed herself too and destroying her family's name in town and the dreams they had for her. This was the moment she'd staved off because it was wrong—or so she thought. Until this moment when it hit her that true love was more than asking a four-word sentence said out of fear like

Nicholas did when he asked her to get married. And for her, saying yes because it seemed the right thing to do and now still agreeing to marry him because she was too fearful to say no. The way she felt about Alessandro was true love because it was a natural bond that endured even when they were apart and grew, despite their circumstances. Love was more than just words, or a kiss, or a vow, love was mystical and unexplainable and what she felt for Alessandro was exactly that.

The Red Cross women placed a cool towel over her forehead and formed some kind of protective ring around her as if bracing Frances from a fall if she fainted. She felt fractured as she cried for the first time over the loss and suffering, she'd seen for the past two years at Torney, working with the men, for the loss of Oklahoma, for the pain she shared with John and the fear she'd seen in George. These were only three of so many she'd gotten to know and cared about. Even Alessandro. But in the end the truth was, like Nicholas and his mother said, these soldiers probably were in love with her, or the hope of having a woman like her there beside them.

But there was only one of them, Alessandro, who she ended up loving back.

"I'm better," Frances told them as she blew her nose and stanched the tears. "Thank you. It's just been a hard... week." She almost said *It's been a hard WAR*—but caught herself.

Grabbing the fiddle case, she stood.

"Congratulations on your award last week," one of them said cheerfully. "Remember, we have positions at the Red Cross open if you want to continue helping out."

"Yes," another one affirmed. "There's still so much work to be done."

"I'll remember that."

Frances walked out of the tent and toward the prisoner housing building like a person who's had a spell cast on them and can't not walk in that direction, walking quickly across the hospital grounds, back to the scene of her crime a year ago, the Italian barracks. A few people passed her and noticed her determination to get where she was going, filled with a purpose so strong that no one dare get in her way. The fiddle case swung forward and back as her arms moved forward and back to propel her faster—when suddenly the handle broke and the case fell to the ground.

She stopped and wondered, was this was a sign for her to not go? She looked at the broken handle in her hand. The leather and stitches were frayed from years of use and would've broken any day she decided. She pushed off any thoughts in her mind that this had any meaning other than that she should move forward. She flipped open the case buckle and placed the broken case handle inside. Closed and locked it. Tucked the case under one arm and continued to the POW barracks.

Outside the door, she could hear men speaking in Italian inside and could see blurred views of the men in the room, some walking around, others sitting or lying on their bed. She knocked on the door. No one answered. She knocked again.

"Alessandro Reggio," she called out. "I need to speak with Alessandro."

The men got quiet inside the room, but no one opened the door. It was an American woman asking to come inside and they'd been warned to be careful with any of the American women they met since their first day at the hospital. No good can come from fraternizing with the ladies here. Can only lead to problems for you, was what their handlers in the army repeated, no matter which one was overseeing them that day. They'd all been trained to remind the POWs that they are not to be around women there alone. Any inappropriate contact could land them in a military jail and all privileges taken away.

"Alessandro Reggio!" she called out again and knocked again, hard, with her fist so there could be no doubt to the men inside that she was there.

Frances opened the door but didn't cross the threshold. Inside the large room, bunk beds lined the left and right side of the room, so many she couldn't count and so many Italian male faces stared as if a madwoman had just entered their private lair. Their duffle bags stuffed like sausages, walls bare, all the signs that they were preparing to leave soon.

"Alessandro Reggio?" she repeated. "I need to speak to Alessandro Reggio."

To the right, three bunk beds down, Alessandro sat on the lower bunk, like he'd been wakened from a nap, barefoot, with his shirt off, wearing khaki pants. He stood up, walked forward a few steps.

"Frances?" he said in a deep trombone voice. Hearing him say her name in that concerned, confused manner, that alone was enough to last her another year if she had to go on without him—but not a lifetime. Of that she was certain.

She took a step forward. The men around the room looked concerned seeing her in their barracks. This could go badly for them if she reported any type of bad behavior like rape. She would be believed and none of them would stand a chance. Frances took two steps across the threshold. The men started talking in Italian at Alessandro, angry, concerned, to get her out of the room immediately. Frances did not understand what they were saying, but she could feel the tension in the air. The angry looks on the men's faces scared her.

Alessandro walked hurriedly towards her, his large chest, muscular and broad, his chiseled jawline, his deep brown almond shaped eyes, having become even more handsome since he left the hospital room with his injury so long ago. "Frances? What are you here for?" He asked as he took her arm and directed her back outside to the deck landing in front of the door. Behind them, one of the prisoners inside shut the door.

"Why did you return this?" she asked as she held out the case.

"They send us away."

"Tomorrow?"

"*Si*. We go."

Frances looked off to her left, as if she needed to get away to take this news in, but didn't want to leave his presence, allowing only her eyes to disengage as she thought of how her love was leaving.

"It's yours. Take it with you." She looked back to him with pleading eyes.

He didn't take it from her, instead he looked at her as if undressing her with his eyes. He had since they last saw each other, become the strong and healthy man he was before she met him that day in the hospital room so long ago. He was healed and confident. She'd never felt more for him than she did now and she wanted to scream about this because she'd wished with Nicholas back that she might feel less for him, even forget about him.

"I cannot. It is not mine."

"Take it so you can play."

"Only if you find me and take it back. Only if you'll promise that to me. That you will find me and take it back one day."

She knew what he was asking, that she come to Italy so they could be together. A dare. Challenge. And while she couldn't promise this, she was happy he'd asked.

Because it meant he still loved her.

"I can't promise that Alessandro. I'm marrying Nicholas."

"Frances?" he said it as if he were begging her not to.

"It's settled. The wedding is in a few weeks."

He stepped back, as if his heart had stopped. He breathed heavily as if trying to get himself together from the blow of hearing his one true love is about to marry another man and can't be swayed otherwise.

"Then I can't take it."

They stood together in silence for a full minute, both understanding what this meant.

"Please, don't hate me."

Alessandro looked like he wanted to say so much. He leaned back into her as if he were going to kiss her again but pulled back.

"You asked me what Oklahoma said to me his last day."

Now she was the one who looked tortured, remembering Oklahoma and those days with the three of them in the hospital room.

"Do you want to know?"

"Yes."

"'Take care of my Franny. She loves you and I know you love her.'"

Frances lowered her face, still clutching the instrument case. She looked up.

"I do."

She did, but she was marrying another man. What was he to do with this information now? Nothing.

"Go, Frances."

He turned around and went back to his bunk.

"Bye Alessandro Reggio," she whispered as she stood alone on the porch, hugging the fiddle case, not moving for minutes, not wanting this to be how it ended between them.

She shifted the case under her left arm and walked down the deck stairs and towards the main building when she heard his voice.

"Frances!" he yelled out from the deck, having come back outside. They stared at each other, each wanting to run into the other's arms, but neither could do this.

"Everything all right here?" Sergeant Hamlin called to her as he was coming back to the barracks from the other side of the building.

"Yes," Frances said. "I was just getting the fiddle before he left."

"You shouldn't be coming here on your own," he said with a frown, then looked at Alessandro. "Get back inside."

Alessandro turned and left.

The Sergeant came towards her. She pivoted on one heel and started to walk smartly back to the hospital. He kept up with her. "Aren't you engaged to that Marine just come back home? I saw the announcement in the paper."

"Why?" she said, nervous he might be the one who saw them

kissing and could in an instant, with one call, ruin her life.

"The ring you had on in the photo... you're not wearing it?"

She looked down at her left hand.

"I, um, I'm closing down the library and didn't want to damage it, so I put it in my pocket. She took the ring out and placed it back on her engagement finger.

He didn't believe her. He sensed the truth, that she'd taken it off so Alessandro wouldn't see it. "Your marine know you snuck into the POW barrack without permission? You'd be smart to be careful of such behavior. These men may seem safe, but they're fascist. Luckily tomorrow we're gettin' rid of 'em, so it'll be even safer around here. But I suspect you knew that and that's why you showed up here to see that greasy wop."

She stayed quiet. He circled her, a tactic he used to make her feel trapped. Intimidated.

"Who's the marine you're marrying? Nicholas Draper? Do I recall correctly?"

He was poking at her, teasing, as if she were a green recruit.

"What do you want?" Frances asked him, trying to get to the meaning of his intentions.

"Thing is... ain't it odd that you came here today to get that fiddle when I turned it over to Edith yesterday. Figured wouldn't be right to have it leave here with him and maybe get taken all the way back to Italy, when some nice person donated it for our injured American soldiers to play."

"Yes. I knew that."

"You did?"

"Yes."

"So how come you came here to pick it up, when it was already back in the library?"

She held back.

"Could it be so you could see him again? Alessandro Reggio?"

She laughed, summoned every ounce of false bravado: "You caught me."

He looked curious. How could this engaged young woman agree that he'd caught her trying to see an Italian prisoner of war?

"I did want to see Alessandro again. Not for what you are insinuating. I am engaged to be married."

"You said that."

"When I explained to Miss Edith that the owner doesn't want the fiddle anymore, we decided to offer it to Alessandro to take as a thank you for playing for everyone here."

"So why are you leaving with it?"

"He refused it." She turned and walked away, not waiting for him to respond, calling over her shoulder: "I'd be careful starting any rumors of that sort. My fiancé won't appreciate you spreading lies neither would Miss Edith.

The battle line drawn, he moved to block her path, smirk on his face, understanding he'd barked up a tree he didn't want to climb, but she would see he still wasn't buying any of it.

"Can you step aside?" she said.

He stepped aside and she walked away.

Terribly shaken by what had just happened, Frances walked slowly back to the main building thinking of Alessandro and replaying every moment of their encounter. The way his hair flipped back, the way his pants rode low on his hips and the way his eyes watered up when she said she was marrying Nicholas. The connection was real between them. She wasn't just making it up, something she'd worried over many times. The chemistry was undeniable.

She arrived back at the library and found Nicholas flipping through a book he'd taken off the shelf. "Nicholas? What are you doing here?"

"You said you were loading up books and taking the boxes back to the library. Figured you could use a hand. Where 'ya been? I've been here awhile and nobody could find you."

"I was getting this instrument back from a patient." She set the case next to the box of instruments.

"You feeling okay?

"Yeah, why?"

"You look pale, like you saw a ghost."

"Ghosts aren't real Nicholas."

"Fran, I'm just checking on you. You don't seem right. Something bothering you?

"No. I'm just being a jerk. It's real nice of you to come help me."

"Truth be told, Frances, I'm getting a little bored here in this sleepy town. Kinda hard switching back to my old life." He leaned over and kissed her on her cheek. "Lucky I got you though. You're about the best thing goin' right now."

"Here, these books on this shelf need to go into a box. Keep them in order or Phyllis the librarian will have a heart attack." She pointed to the shelf.

He moved the books off the shelf and into a box.

"You miss the war?"

"Nah, not the war, just my buddies, the life."

"I get it. I'm starting to miss how things used to be around here, you know, lotsa fellas

to help and now there's hardly anyone. Pretty soon they'll be no one and they'll shut down the hospital, I guess."

"But you're a woman. It's different for you."

"How?"

"You're not supposed to work like this. That was only because of the war. When you're

my wife, working's not an option."

"I'll be your wife, but you won't own me."

"I don't mean it like that, but getting married and having kids is what you need and

you're gonna get all that. But bein' out of the Corps? It's hard to let go."

"What if I *want* to work? I've been thinking of going to school, becoming a nurse."

"Why'd you wanna do that?"

"Because I'm good at it. I like helping."

He went over to the music instrument box, picked up the fiddle, opened it.

"Be careful." She didn't want him touching Alessandro's violin.

"Of what? Scratching this beat up fiddle?"

She didn't know what to say, but she watched him handle it and her distaste for his hands all over it was palpable. She went over to try and get it from him, but he saw it as a game and laughed her off and started dodging her advances.

"Tried to play the fiddle a few times." he put the bow to the instrument and scraped it back and forth. Sounded like nails on a chalkboard.

"Stop it!" She moved after him.

He dodged her. "Why? You don't like my playing?"

"I'm serious!" This got his attention.

"Ah Franny, I'm just kiddin' with ya. Just trying to have fun." He said as he turned over the instrument and bow to her.

"It's on loan!"

"Yeah, I know, I know. You run the music instruments for the fellas here and that's real *good* of you."

She placed the fiddle and bow back in the case.

"Many guys requisition a fiddle? I mean, hell Franny, I don't know anyone who plays a fiddle."

"One."

"One," he repeated as he went back to putting the books into the boxes. "Guess one's enough."

"Yeah," she answered.

He could tell he'd made her mad, so he stood up and walked over and gave her a hug. "Too much rough housin'," he said.

As she was in his arms, she looked over his shoulder at the violin case and thought about how Alessandro was leaving the country the next morning and there was nothing she could do to stop him from leaving.

Chapter Fifteen

She lay in bed awake. It was now well past midnight. Wind blew the palm trees outside mimicking the sound of ocean waves.

She sat up, rested her back against her headboard and pulled her knees up and wrapped her arms around them. The swishes of the palms outside her window played shadow dances on the walls of her room from the porch light being blocked and unblocked as the palms swayed in the sharp wind. The hour hand passed midnight nearly an hour ago. Now she was living in the day he would leave her forever. Alessandro would soon be gone. It felt as if another death were happening. Like Oklahoma, he'd be gone. Forever.

Frances put her head down on her forearms. Desperate feelings so intense made her so limp her head fell forward like a dying rose. If the feelings would stop, she'd lay back down and try to sleep the hours away until he was gone, but the pain only grew stronger. She stayed in this painful contemplative state until time moved on: 1:00 a.m., 2:00 a.m....

"Don't go. Please don't go!" she whispered out loud and repeated in her mind over and over to herself. It was a thought for him, but also for herself. Like she'd been taken with rage, emotion, heartbreak. Frances wanted to scream, throw a fit, cry out so someone might understand how much she wanted, how much she seemed to need Alessandro next to her. That this could never be, had her unhinged.

When he left, just hours away, on this day, he wouldn't be just hers anymore. A prisoner in her small town, kept under her control so she couldn't lose him to another woman, not yet. No, today that was all over. The secret world in which she lived, where she thought of him, listened to him play the violin in the soft, distant night and wished to be beside him every day of her life—was over. Sending him back to Italy was setting him free. She'd lose him, truly, forever. Floating away like feathers falling from a bird in flight, all attachment lost, the detachment final and this fact alone had her thinking about doing something that she'd never be able to erase. But as the clock ticked down the night, the longer she sat up against the headboard, Frances knew she was going to risk it all. She would go, she knew. She had to summon the courage to get out of bed and get going—but she delayed a half an hour more, paralyzed with fear, acutely aware that when she crossed the line she'd decided to cross, the person she was now would no longer exist, killing the self she was today not easily done.

I am not who I thought I was. She accepted this fact as she moved to the edge of the bed, contemplating further as she placed her feet firmly on the floor. *If I stand*, she thought, *I go.*

She stood.

Fear on her face highlighted by shadows cast by the porch light so that when she looked in the mirror on her desk, she was faced with a whole new reflection of the real woman she was, ready to take a chance, but still so scared. The mirror only telling one story of her, the façade, what others saw. The truth still hidden. She'd known who she was for almost a year now and had been fighting it, postponing it, pretending she wasn't this. But with time running out, she could ignore it no longer. Who she was, she accepted, was the girl she saw in the mirror, scared but real and released from the facade.

Only hours before the sun came up. Then, once the men filed into the transports and the wheels rolled, he'd be gone forever. She had only hours left for a chance to be with him now and this scared her more than getting in trouble. Frances pulled out pants and a shirt from her dresser and shoes from her closet. Discarding her nightgown onto the floor, she looked at her naked body in the dark light as if taking a last view of her innocent body. Putting on her pants and a sweater first, she slipped on her shoes, then brushed out her hair. She saw herself as quite possibly gorgeous in her natural way without lipstick and rouge and this fortified her. Quietly, she slipped out, taking the keys of her mom's car out of her purse which was on the kitchen counter and quietly moved past furniture blocking her path towards the front door, gently opening and closing the front door carefully, taking care to keep the metal screen door from slamming shut, then she pushed through the windy air to the driveway.

In the car, turning the ignition, she looked to the house to see if the engine starting was heard by her mother and father. No sign of them being disturbed yet. Their silence signaling her to go, as if they were giving her permission. She breathed in, then put the car in reverse and drove away with the headlights off, down the quiet neighborhood, her neighbors all asleep. She passed the lawn where Nicholas proposed and reflected on that night years ago without a shred of nostalgia. It was just something that happened. She felt no emotion about it, not a reason to turn the car around and call this off. She drove to a main road outside of the housing development, turned on her lights, rolled down the window. As the car picked up speed, her hair flew about in the wind. Determined, she moved down the dark road, only the beam of her headlights visible in front of her. The night was silent except for the sound of the wind, hum of the engine and the traction of the tires on the asphalt road. She noticed these uneventful sounds in a way that, on a normal day, she wouldn't have noticed, because these were the sounds of the quiet night on which she'd chosen to change herself forever. Her senses fully engaged.

Crossing over the last mile to the hospital, her heart pounded as she grew closer. She drove past the El Mirador Tower. The pointed shadow in the dark sky, where she'd watched the convoy of prisoners being brought in and where she heard Alessandro play for the first time on New Year's Eve. It seemed a hollow space now, where she'd hid so many times, waiting, her life on pause, but not tonight. She drove by the tower, past the main building, towards him on a road that ran along the south side of the grounds. She turned off her headlights and drove slowly down the darkened landscape by the end, beyond the laundry, beyond the Red Cross tent and stopped not far from the prisoner barracks. Frances parked on the side of the road, in a dirt landing behind a large grouping of Joshua trees and Oleander bushes so that her car remained partially hidden from view.

"Do you go?" she asked the darkness before her. Fuzzy lines of limbs moved in the wind like orchestra conductors. "I have to go," she answered herself as she gripped the steering wheel.

If she went, she'd be different and her life would henceforth contain a secret or maybe even a scandal. She wouldn't know until the night was over. Would they get caught? That was the risk that would determine the outcome, but she'd have nothing of him if she didn't go.

She'd asked herself a question to which she knew the answer. She *would* go. Where she got the courage to get out of the car was unknown. Ten minutes more clicked down. Click. She pulled on the door handle, stepped out of the car, closed the door behind her and stood in the dark facing the back side of the Torney hospital grounds. Temporary army buildings created a skyline view against a sky of stars, clouds and the moon, with the mountains to the left etching their grandness with palm trees and desert weeds swaying in the breeze. The world seemed vacant as she waited on herself to go forward, her mind blank. She thought of nothing as if the past never existed and the future would never be created. Car headlights approached from the direction she arrived stopping her daze, snapping her back to the knowledge that time was short.

Frances ran across the road towards the Torney grounds, having to pass through a field of dirt and rocks and indigenous plants of cactus and weeds. It was a few hundred yards before she stood on the edge of the hospital grounds, at the very back end of the lot. Frances passed storage buildings used by maintenance, keeping close to the sides of building walls, snaking against them like a burglar trying not to be seen until she reached the side of the barracks where the prisoners were held.

She gently stepped onto the wood landing and carefully opened the screen door and stepped into the barracks where the men were sleeping. She moved over to the third bunk on the right to Alessandro and tapped him gently and as he startled awake to see her, she placed her hand over his mouth so that he didn't say anything and signaled with her free hand for him to be quiet by placing her index finger in front of her lips. She took his hand and pulled him up. He grabbed his shoes under his bunk and together they moved silently towards the door.

"*Non andare,*" one of the Italian's who woke said as they passed. "*Arrestato!*"

Alessandro paused. "*Devo.*" He replied in a whisper, then looked to Frances and nodded to signal, let's go.

Outside the barracks, Alessandro hurriedly slipped on his shoes, then Frances led him across the field toward her car. What was a slow and thoughtful night for her until now had become fast-paced and headlong as the reality of what she'd started could get them both in serious trouble. They stopped and ducked low as a car pass on the road. When far enough away, she took his hand and led him to the car. Once inside, she turned the ignition and pulled onto the road and accelerated to a high speed while looking in the rear-view mirror to see if anyone was following. Adrenalin from what she just did lit her up so that she couldn't not look at him. She kept looking to see if they were being chased, scanning the side mirrors and rearview again, locked onto them only until safe.

"Frances?" Alessandro didn't look behind the car. He only looked to her for answers as to the reality of what they'd done.

"Yes."

"Where are we going?" he asked in perfect English with his heavy Italian accent.

"Someplace safe." She looked at him in the dim light, unsure if he was angry at her. Insecurity left her worried for a second that she misread his feelings for her. "I had to see you one last time."

"I have to go back," he told her.

"I know."

Frances drove to the outskirts of town to a date palm forest in the Coachella Valley that she and her friends would sneak off to late at night to hang out. Rows of mature date palm trees poked out of the earth in an otherwise flat desert. A surviving crop planted decades before. She parked the car between the rows, turned off the engine and headlights so that the place became dark down below by the ground, but the bush tops stayed lit by moonlight. Like waving to the world hello, they swayed in the breeze.

She turned to him. "Come on."

She opened her car door and stepped out. He followed on his side of the car and both met in front of the hood. Frances stood before him, head tilted up with confidence, then held out her hand to him. "Let's walk," she said as he placed his hand in hers and they moved between majestic rows of date palms.

"Frances?" He stopped. "Why am I here?"

"Because I love you. I've tried not to love you, but it's not possible."

"*Non so che dire,*" he answered, quickly, then realized he was speaking in Italian. "I don't know what to say."

"You don't have to say anything," she answered, matter of fact, stating without reservation. "Still, I love you."

"Your fiancé?" Perplexed, he stepped back and looked around as if grounding himself, as if Nicholas might appear out of the shadows at any moment.

She stepped closer to him and took his hands. "Alessandro, no matter where you go, no matter where I am for the rest of my life, I will love you and I need you to know before you leave tomorrow. Before you leave my life forever."

"I love you," he admitted.

Happy to know now that he loved her too, she rushed into his arms and they hugged each other as if they'd been starving and each was food. She rested her head on his chest and he wrapped her body with his large arms. The smell of him she recognized from before, a musky odor from the soap the prisoners used. She looked up at him and moved the hair away from his eyes that the wind blew onto his face and she rose onto her toes to reach his lips with hers. He lifted her inches high off the ground, neither of them noticing, as their kiss moved on to more. So tall and broad were his shoulders, he placed his hands on hers and pulled her up to him as if she were feather light.

She ran her hands under his shirt and over his back and shoulders as they kissed, then raised the cloth up to get to him and he pulled his shirt over his head. She took her shirt off and he kissed her bare chest standing in the moonlight as her hair moved above him in the breeze. He set his shirt down on the ground, took her hand, pulled her down together as they kissed and touched passionately and made love on the floor of the date palm forest.

After, they held each other quietly, tightly, the wind brushing against their naked bodies.

"Must go, Frances."

She knew he was right. "*Si*," she said as they both sat up and gathered their clothing and got dressed. "I'll never be sorry." She told him as she placed her hand on his cheek and caressed his face. "I am yours forever now."

"I am yours," he answered, then kissed her again.

They were silent on the drive back as the sky went from black to dark blue. The tension of getting him back into the barracks before being found out excited each of them so that the sweetness of their time together now was filled with urgency and danger.

It somehow only mattered that they got him back.

Frances sped, scanning the side and rearview mirrors for other cars and Alessandro ducking down when one approached. It would be a police officer who might pull her over and wonder why a young woman was in the desert alone in the middle of the night. It could be a police officer searching for a POW who'd been found missing in the last few hours. Alessandro's right leg tapped with nervous energy and Frances felt sorry for the first time that she'd put him in danger. All she wanted now was to make sure he returned and they weren't found out. The closer she came to the hospital grounds, her muscles tensed and her mind raced through all the possibilities of what might await them. Until he was back inside, until he was returned safely and unknowingly, neither could breathe normally.

Back at the spot she was at before, she pulled over to the side of the road. "Quickly," she said and turned to him. "Go." Her eyes full of tears, she raised a hand to his face and he leaned in and kissed her one last time, so sweetly, then stayed with his face next to hers, not wanting to leave. "Alessandro. Go."

He pulled back and looked at her one last time before he got out of the car and faded into a silhouetted figure running back through the field to the barracks. She watched for lights or disturbances to show in the distance, waiting to see if he was found out, but he was not as she did not see anything happening out of the ordinary in the distance. No lights, no voices, nothing to make her think he didn't get back to his bunk without being noticed. Frances noticed a car approaching, so she pulled onto the road and headed to the front side of Torney where she parked on the other side of the hospital grounds to see if it had remained quiet at the barracks. No movement. Nothing stirring. Ten minutes more she waited, not believing it was so easy despite the risk and began to feel the surge of excitement of what had taken place between her and him, so perfect she'd wonder if she'd been in a fairy tale.

Cars approached Torney as the day staff arrived, so Frances left the area and drove around the edge of town, not wanting to go home yet. The night's events played out in her mind like a movie, each moment of their hands on each other, the feeling of his body next to hers, but mostly the amazing feeling of being in love, *truly* in love, had taken her to an understanding that life was more than what you saw on the surface. Life was about love and love was a feeling she had for Alessandro, but not for Nicholas. She'd never felt this way about Nicholas and the thought of going forward with the wedding felt untenable.

Frances drove out to Highway One where the convoy that came in would be going back out to take away the prisoners. There was only one main paved road into Palm Springs and this would be the road upon which the convoy would travel back to Camp Haan in Riverside which is where Alessandro had been before being moved to Torney. It was now one of five designated separation Army centers for prisoners being processed to go home in the states and Americans returning from abroad before their final journey home due to its proximity to the Los Angeles port.

She pulled over, got out of the car and sat on the hood. She had an hour still before her parents would wake and discover that she and the car were gone and hoped the convoy drove past by then. She picked up rocks and threw them out to the desert and watched as the sun rose not long after.

Within the next hour, she saw the convoy approach in the distance. Eight military transit vehicles moving down the road towards her. She watched the trucks come closer, not taking her eyes off them as they passed and searched the faces of the men for Alessandro. For one last look at him. And then there he was, in the third truck, looking at her as the truck passed and they saw each other for the last time.

She watched the convoy until it was far away. After a curve in the road she could no longer see them. She then got in her mom's car and broke down in tears as she had in the Red Cross tent. What she feared then was now done. He was gone.

It was day now. No longer hazy, no longer covered by dark skies and Frances saw so clearly what she needed to do. She wiped her eyes so she could see well enough to drive and turned the car around on Highway 1 and headed back towards town, pulling up to Mary's house. She needed to talk. She needed her friend.

She knocked on the door. "Mary? It's Frances. I have to come in." While daylight, it was early and Frances could tell they were still sleeping. She saw a light turn on inside and some rumbling voices.

Frank and Mary opened the door to see Frances in tears. "Oh, dear God," Mary said and she reached her arm around her and brought her into the house. "Frank, give us a minute."

"I'll be in the room if you need me," Frank said and went back to bed.

Mary led Frances into the kitchen and pulled out a chair for her at the table.

"What is it? What's happened?" Mary asked.

"I don't know what to do," Frances admitted, her hands shaking as she took the cup of water Mary brought to her and lifted it up to her lips like she was outside in the cold sipping a hot drink, but the shaking was from nerves. She was in an elevated state, full of indecision, at a crossroad. Scared but thrilled.

"What do you mean?"

"I was with Alessandro last night."

Mary looked like Frances had slapped her across the face.

Frances reached out to her. "Mary."

Mary stood up and stepped back, turning her back to Frances.

"I need a minute."

"It was all me. I love him, Mary. I've loved him since I met him and I can't stand that he's left and I'll never see him again. I don't know what to do."

Mary turned around, anger on her face like her best friend had betrayed her and not Nicholas. "Yes, you do. You're going to marry Nicholas and forget all this nonsense about Alessandro. He's not one of us."

"Don't say that." Frances snapped back at her and shook her head in disgust. It was one thing to hear people in town talk about the POWs like they were traitors, but she couldn't hear it from Mary.

"Those Italian Service Units are just a way America could pretend that these men aren't traitors. They fought our men, the same men you and I helped get the pieces of their lives at Torney back together." Mary slammed her palm down on the table, causing Frances to jump. "Why do we keep having to come back to him, especially now that Nicholas is back? You're about to be married, Frances, I mean my God, what is so wrong with Nicholas that you'd throw your whole life away for this... foreigner?!"

"I love him."

Mary stood, placed both hands over her stomach like Frances had just kicked her there and turned away, leaned against the kitchen counter like she was about knocked down from hearing this come out of Frances mouth.

"You don't," she said, her back to Frances still, she said it again. "You don't."

"Look at me!"

Mary turned around, her face full of hate and anguish.

"I love him, Mary. And I can't not love him."

Mary sat back down at the table. "It's not you, Franny. You don't know what you're doing."

"I've tried this whole year not to love him. I've done what I'm supposed to do. I've been who I'm supposed to be and I'm so unhappy. I'm locked into marrying a man I hardly know anymore. Don't you see? You're my best friend, don't you see how much I'm hurting inside?! Don't you care?!"

"I care so much that I'm trying to stop you from making the biggest mistake of your life. I've been trying to stop you ever since you told me you kissed him."

Frances looked at her, angry. "How have you tried? Tell me. How?"

"I did it for you."

"You told Edith, didn't you? No one saw us kissing! It was you who told my secret."

"I did and I'd do it again if I was in the same situation. I had to tell her to keep you away from him. You were about to ruin your life for some Italian fascist who'd end up tossing you aside once he was free."

"You don't know that. You don't know him."

"You're just confused now. I know what's right for you. I know you didn't mean to have feelings for Alessandro, but you're not strong Franny. It's always been your problem and I think he took advantage of you."

"How could you?!"

"I've been trying to protect you and now you're angry at me?"

'That's not how it is. You're wrong!"

"If you choose him over Nicholas, I can't stand by you. No one will stand by you in this town. You'll always be known as that girl in the village who fell for a POW and humiliated Nicholas, who is a hero. I hear the way they treat American prisoners in Italy has been downright awful and here we are paying them to work, treating them with kindness and this, you give yourself to one of them when you have Nicholas? It turns my stomach."

"When did you become this person?"

"I've always been this person. I've always looked out for you, Frances and you don't even thank me. I could have told your parents what happened. I could have told Nicholas. I could tell people what you're telling me here today and ruin you in seconds, but I wouldn't. Never. I did the best path I could see to scare you into getting yourself straight without any of that. That's what a best friend does. Don't you understand that?"

Frances stood up. "Maybe you're right, you've always been this person and I just couldn't see how you really are."

Frances headed out of her house and Mary followed her. "One day you'll thank me. One day you'll understand I told her to protect you. That's what best friends do."

Frances turned around. "No. Best friends don't betray each other. I trusted you. Now I can't ever again."

"Frances, don't go," Mary called out as Frances got in the car.

Mary went to the side of the window. "Come back inside. Let's talk about this. I'm sorry."

"You're pregnant. I shouldn't be upsetting you."

"Everything okay?" Frank called from the porch.

"Yeah," Mary called back to him.

"I have to get home."

"It'll work out, Fran. Just marry Nicholas like you've always planned and it'll work out."

Frances said, "Go back inside."

Mary stepped away from the window. Frances pulled out onto the road, looking at her former best friend in the rearview mirror. A friend she'd known since grade school and now she felt like she didn't know at all. Of all the people in her life, Mary stood above all others. Now she was small, petty and practically dead.

As Frances drove away, she couldn't even look back in the rearview mirror. Mary felt like a distant acquaintance, if not a stranger. Every shortcoming Mary ever had now seemed magnified, a huge clue that Frances had failed to notice.

A clean break. Now she had to deal with Nicholas.

Chapter Sixteen

It'd been a rough morning already after having met with the Baxter family to return the harmonica they loaned to Torney. Charlie Baxter survived the war, but with significant burns to his body that doctors declared would leave him permanently disabled. His injuries were so severe that doctors didn't allow him to leave Europe yet as the travel would be too dangerous and painful for his health. When Frances met with his parents, she remained stoic. As a Red Cross volunteer, it wasn't her place to get emotional, so as Mrs. Baxter talked with Frances about Charlie's recovery, breaking down a few times over the pain he was suffering and how worried she was about her son, Frances listened yet remained reserved with her emotions, which was hard.

Now she parked her car in front of Mr. and Mrs. Keller's home. She grabbed the violin and tucked it under her arm as she walked to the front door of the large home the Keller's owned. She'd driven past the house many times in her life, but until this day, there'd never been a reason for her to interact with the well-known couple personally. It was unusually hot still for being this deep into fall and knocking on winter. The sun shone harshly on the Keller's front porch so there was no escaping the heat. Sweat on her forearm caused the case to slip as she rang the doorbell again.

She thought of Alessandro as she held the violin. He was back in Italy by now. She knew this from reading her father's paper every morning. There were several articles about how brokenhearted American women in love with POWs stormed the Long Beach harbor when thousands of them were boarding a transport ship for return. *Weeping Women Slow Italians' Embarkation. Women Crash Docks to see War Prisoners.* The articles talked of 100 women who stormed the doc and disrupted their boarding the ship. Weeping women clung to the pier fence, some got past military police and a few Italians were found in the cars with women. I can't believe what I'm reading, she accidentally said out loud in disbelief that she wasn't alone with her situation. Her father looked to her for more details and she brushed him off. Never mind, she said and in disbelief which got her father interested for a second, lifting his eyes over his paper. To know she wasn't the only American woman who had fallen in love with a POW was amazing, but Frances would never be the women at the harbor making a scene. Frances was practical and accepted Alessandro would go on with his life, marry, start a family, but at least they'd had their one night together that she would never regret.

Burning up in the sun, she knocked on the door again, then turned to go back to her car when the door opened.

"Dear? How may I help you?" Mrs. Keller was in a house dress still in the middle of the day. Frances worried she'd gotten her out of bed.

"Mrs. Keller, it's Frances Clark from Torney and I'm here to return Mr. Keller's fiddle."

"Oh, come here please, in, in."

"Is it a good time?"

"He'll be so excited to see Maisey Baby."

Frances followed the little round woman into the living room. "How is Mr. Keller doing?" she asked as she stepped into the entry hallway that was lined with photos of a life between the two, from young to old, with kids and grandkids, all the pieces of a well-lived life with each other.

"He's about to get himself a stern warning from me to perk up or it's curtains for him."

"Excuse me?" Frances answered, surprised to hear this coming from her mouth.

"It's what we say to each other in hard times. You gotta perk your-self up. No one else can do it for you."

"Right," Frances said as she stood in the living room holding the instrument case.

"Can I get you something to drink?"

"No. I'm fine, thank you."

Mrs. Keller continued walking down the hall, then stopped and looked back at her. "Dear, come on. He's not been out of bed for months now."

"Are you sure I should go into his bedroom?" Frances asked.

"Come on." Mrs. Keller waived her to follow. "It'll perk him up to see a young lady."

Frances walked through the living room towards the hallway, viewing the hold of a long life decorated with pictures and statues from trips taken over the years, a Statue of Liberty, a Niagara Falls snowmobile, mementos put on display of their life together.

"Dear, you have a visitor," Mrs. Keller called out as she stood in the doorway of a bedroom and waited for Frances.

"Huh?" Mr. Keller called back.

"A visitor." Mrs. Keller told him just as Frances made it to the entryway.

They stepped inside. The air was stale and sick. Mr. Keller was propped up with pillows behind him in a large king-sized bed which made him look even littler. He looked far worse than he had the year before when she saw him, bent forward more, having a hard time breathing, pale, but a hint of sparkle remained in his eyes.

"Is that my Maisey Baby?" he asked.

Frances smiled. "It is, Mr. Keller." She stood back, uncomfortable in his private bedroom.

"Bring her over." He said and patted a spot on the bed next to him.

"Dear, sit here." Mrs. Keller pointed to the sitting chair next to the bed. Frances placed the instrument case onto the bed and stepped back, sitting in the chair. He fumbled with the locks, excited to see his girl again after being apart for so long.

"Here." Mrs. Keller took charge of unlocking the buckles and opening the instrument case.

"There's my beauty," he said and laughed.

"I'm glad you've perked up," said Mrs. Keller.

"Give me her. Gotta feel my baby in my arms." He placed the instrument on his shoulder and grabbed the bow and started doing some fast picking that stopped after thirty seconds as he coughed and caught his breath.

"Tell me, lots of soldier's get their hands on this girl?" he asked as he placed the instrument on his lap and rubbed his fingers over the scratched wood.

"Watch your mouth there, dear."

"One." Frances answered because it had been only one who played the instrument.

"Did he treat you right?" Mr. Keller asked the instrument as if he were speaking to a daughter. "Tell me, what'cha know about him, this one fiddle player?"

"I don't know much about him." She answered, wondering if she should tell the truth about the one soldier at Torney who played the violin.

"What was his name at least?"

"His name?"

"Yes."

"Henry." Alessandro Reggio would be a dead giveaway that the soldier was Italian, so she lied.

"What do ya know about him?"

"He was from a small town in south Oklahoma."

"Ah," he raised up the instrument to his shoulder and played again, only to stop soon after as his strength wasn't there to play for long. "Oh, that winded me. Out of practice, Maisey Baby," he said to the fiddle like they shared a common language. "Tell me about Henry."

"Oh, okay. I don't know much."

"Just a little."

"He fought in the Pacific. Was fresh out of high school when he was drafted. He got badly injured in his right arm. Doctors were afraid he would lose his arm from the injury for a while, but he started healing so that's when the fiddle was given to him to play and he started playing every day and this helped his arm get better. Dark hair and deep brown eyes. He liked to read silly books like *Freddy the Detective* that was about a pig who worked as a detective on a farm solving crimes, like who stole the chicken eggs. He was from Oklahoma and had a funny personality. He's back home now in Oklahoma. He was a real nice guy, but like I said, he's gone home." Frances stood, suddenly uncomfortable and feeling she wanted to flee immediately. "I should get going."

"Dear, let the young girl go on. She's got places to go."

"I know. I know," Mr. Keller said. "Just was thinking maybe I'd give this fiddle to Henry." He put the fiddle back in the case and became slightly sad. "I'm not gonna be able to play much longer."

"Sure, you will, Mr. Keller."

"When you get to be my age, you know things'll happen, you just may not be smart enough to pick the exact day, but you're close when it's all said and done and I'm close, you know. The future is less a mystery at my age."

Mrs. Keller looked emotional. "Now you, perk it up mister. No sallow talk."

He smiled at Frances, "This one." He reached out and took Mrs. Keller's hand and patted it. "She's my real baby, fifty-two years in love." He held up the instrument case to her. "Can you get this to Henry for me? I want him to have it. It'd mean a lot to me."

"Mr. Keller, I..." Frances answered, suddenly feeling the weight of her lie.

"You think you could try to find him? Maybe the Army could get his address for you so he could play her again since I don't have the strength anymore. Would you do that for me, please?"

"I can try."

"It's settled then," Mrs. Baxter added.

"Thank you, Frances," he said, knowing he'd never see her again as he wouldn't be alive for long.

Frances left the Keller's home with the fiddle, the one instrument she wanted to get away from, but it wasn't possible. As she set the fiddle in the passenger seat, she broke down, tears so hard she didn't know if they'd ever stop.

Exhausted, she didn't move. Frozen, she looked ahead at a little boy playing ball in the yard a few houses down, kicking it with his foot up against a chain link fence. The ball rolled into the road and the kid ran after it without looking for cars, picked up the ball and ran back to the yard as if he'd done that a hundred times and always knew if a car were coming, probably by the sound of the engine or tires on the asphalt, all those sounds she keyed into the night she drove to meet up with Alessandro. She moved finally, turning on the car ignition and putting it in gear, heading toward the kid playing with the ball and before she got one house away, he grabbed hold of his ball and looked at her as she drove past. *He can hear when the cars are coming,* she thought. *He doesn't need to look to know. He can sense it. The boy knows.*

Frances pulled the car over. "Hey kid!" she hollered out the window. He looked at her like he'd done something wrong. "You better be careful running across the street. Look both ways." He didn't answer her. She was a stranger. "You hear me?" She waved at him to come closer. Timidly, he stepped to the passenger side door. "I said you need to look both ways before crossing the street."

The kid was fixated on the case on the seat, not what she said. "What's in there," he said, holding his ball like a security blanket.

"Well, that depends." She unsnapped the clips and opened the instrument case. "Some people call it a violin. Some call it a fiddle. Depends on how you play it."

"That's neat." He looked back as his mom came out the front door to see what was going on. "I gotta go do something."

The boy ran off and she started crying again.

"I gotta go do something, too," she said to herself, finally accepting what she knew all along. "It's time."

She pushed down on the gas pedal, and headed out to handle what couldn't wait anymore. She didn't love the man she was about to marry. She should have ended it the day Nicholas returned home, but she'd been a coward. She and Nicholas never fit together like Mr. and Mrs. Keller—and they never would.

Frances drove to the village when Nicholas was hanging out with the guys in town and found him playing handball against the wall. She parked the car and went over to him.

"Hey darlin'," He said to her when she approached, "The soon to be Mrs. Nicholas Draper," he added, then kissed her on the lips. He was showing off for his buddies who hooted and hollered to egg on his ego.

"Nicholas, can I talk to you?" Frances asked. "Away from the guys?"

"Something wrong?"

"Yes."

"Fellas, I'm out. Goin' off with my gal. She's prettier than all of you." The young men whistled and sneered as he walked off with Frances behind a building. *Can't blame 'ya. You the boss, Nick. Kiss her on the lips.*

"What's wrong, Franny?" He could see it in her eyes that she'd been crying and now she cried again as she looked at him. He pulled out a handkerchief and handed it to her.

"You're so sweet, Nicholas, but I can't marry you."

Shellshocked, the enormity of what she just said hit him like a slap to his face.

"I don't understand."

"It's not you or me or either of us, we just don't fit together anymore."

"This isn't happening," he said angrily, like he knew it might and was just trying to get to the altar to secure she was his and now he was losing.

"Don't be angry with me, please."

"How should I be then?"

"I don't see how we're gonna get through a lifetime together when we can barely get through each day on the same page."

He was silent, taking in what she was saying to him like he knew it was coming and now that it had, he wasn't surprised.

"Say something. Please. Nicholas."

"I don't know what to say to you, Franny. I mean, we're getting married next week and

I don't know what to say."

"Say you know I'm right, because you know I'm right." She grabbed his hands in hers. "I know I'm right and while you're gonna hate me now, you won't later. You'll only hate me for a little while, but I'm doing this for both of us. You deserve someone who's going to love you like they would die if they had to spend a day on this earth without you."

"I've tried. What do you want me to do?"

"Accept it. I want you to be happy. I want to be happy and us together, we don't make each other happy like we should. It's a dangerous game we're playing, this pretending and it's going to ruin us so I'm saying finally what neither of us has been willing to admit."

"When I'm around people here in town, I'm treated like a hero by everyone but you. I don't know what you want from me, but it seems like it's never enough and that you're always so angry at me."

"I'm not angry with you. I'm angry at myself for being too scared to say what I really want in life, to go after it and I just let everyone else tell me what to do and what to decide and I hate myself because of it. I hate myself, not you. You're everything a girl could want, if that girl just wanted to be a wife and stay home and have kids, but I don't think I'm that girl anymore. I've changed. What I want isn't that anymore, but I've been steered into this life that I agreed to and meant it at the time, but it's years later and we're older and neither of us feel about each other like we should and nothing anyone says can make that right. It's just a fact that it is. I love you, I do, but not to be my husband for life. I don't think we agree on much, if anything and I've been too weak, just too weak to say it and look at what I've let go on, all of this, the wedding plans, the deception that I'm not being honest with you because I'm too scared to speak up."

He leaned against the side of the building like he needed a brace to hold him up. "What'll I do now?" he said as he shook his head from side to side, trying to figure out what the hell was going on.

Frances walked close to him. "Whatever you want. You have your whole life ahead of you."

"I waited to get back here for us to begin and Frances..." His voice cracked as he held back emotion.

"You made it back here, Nicholas. And that's good."

"Frances, please don't do this."

"I have to."

"I made it back here for you."

"It got you back here. And I'm so glad. But it's a different world. Different and a different you. That doesn't change the fact you made it back. You are a hero."

It was the end of their beginning finally. It should've happened days after he returned, Frances knew, but she didn't have the courage.

What followed was the beginning of the end of them which, now, like the winding down of the war, the closing of their wedding plans, began after their heartbroken mothers got over the end of their match. The dismantling of the planned event, piece by piece, was brought down, but much faster than building out the plan. The wedding cake that was chosen after tasting three different types, was cancelled with one visit to the baker by her mother. The wedding gown that was being altered for the day, was placed in the hall storage closet in a beautiful box Frances mother had purchased for the dress to be used after the wedding. On and on, each piece of the day set up so carefully at first, now cancelled swiftly and as Frances stood by, as her mother handled this unexpected change in her master plan for her daughter, Frances knew her decision was the right choice. No regrets except she wished she'd ended it sooner.

On the morning of their wedding day, Frances stayed in bed for a while, pretending to be sleeping the first two times she heard the door creak open, which she knew was her mother checking to see if she was awake. On the third door opening, she spoke:

"You can come in. I'm up."

Her mother stepped inside carefully, like Frances might break if she didn't.

Frances said, "You don't have to worry."

"Your father and I, we're worried."

"Don't worry."

"What will you do today?"

"Stay in my room."

"We should go out, maybe?"

"I don't want to go out. Everyone will stare at me."

"It's big news."

"How big?"

"Everyone's talking about it."

"So embarrassing." Frances burrowed under the covers. "I'm staying in bed."

"Don't do that. It won't help."

"You know I'm sorry, Mom. You and Dad having to go through this."

"It's not about us, Frances."

"We wouldn't have worked. Nicholas and me, we're not the same as we were in high school. He's changed. I've changed. We would have fought..." Frances began to tear up. "We would've destroyed each other."

Mom went to her bed, sat down next to her and took her in her arms. "Frances, you are my only child. I just want what's best for you."

"This is best. Trust me, Mom."

Frances stayed in bed for the rest of her wedding day and read the novel she'd set aside to read out loud for the soldier named Liam. She never knew his last name. The day he was brought in, he was one of so many who'd been seriously wounded in North Africa and were finally getting to the states for medical care.

They'd been told a plane was arriving with badly injured men. All Torney staff were made aware with an announcement on the PA system. When the military plane arrived at the airfield, several ambulances were waiting to transport the men quickly to the hospital, but it was more men than they had expected. Eighteen with life threatening injuries and illness were brought in and staged in the lobby for evaluation. The most critical sent straight to surgery, the ones most in pain tended to first. This soldier was off to the side, waiting for the doctor when Frances offered him a glass of water which he drank quickly so she poured him a second glass. Carrot-colored hair, pale skin, he didn't seem to be near death which was why she always struggled with his loss as she wondered, *What did I miss?* He laid his head back after he drank the water and closed his eyes so she moved on, knowing not to disturb a soldier resting, but selected The Great Gatsby by F. Scott Fitzgerald for him later while at the library returning books and checking out new books to fill soldier requests.

When she arrived in his room to give him the book the next day, he was still and the room seemed different, like time had stopped as she took a few steps forward and saw that he had passed and ran out of the room for help. She flipped open the cover and past the title page to begin chapter one in a whisper so he could hear the words from heaven.

She read the book the entire day she was to be married, fending off her parents who tried to get her to come out and sit by the pool and talk. Their shock had gone from upset to settled with the outcome and now they just wanted their daughter to find her way again, but they didn't realize that her not standing at the altar on this day was her beginning to truly find herself.

The wedding day passed and weeks clicked away until it was the day Mary was getting in a car to move to San Francisco. They'd talked briefly since the morning Frances came to her house in tears and the tension between them hadn't settled yet as Frances refused to talk to her about canceling the wedding or Alessandro. Frances was too angry still, having refused to see her. So as the day arrived for Mary to move away, they still hadn't patched up their friendship.

But at the last minute, Frances found herself driving to Mary's house, speeding down the road to get there before she drove away, her heart damaged by their fight. As she turned onto her street, Frank's car was pulling away from the house. Frances honked and sped up to catch their attention. Their cars pulled over to the side of the road and the girls rushed to each other and hugged.

"Frances, I'm sorry," Mary said as she grabbed onto her childhood friend like she knew this was the last moment they'd ever be these girls.

"Don't be. Nothing to be sorry about. You were just trying to protect me." Frances gripped her close.

"Always," Mary said as she pulled away. "I didn't mean to hurt you."

"I know." Frances placed her arm around Mary's shoulder and walked her back to Frank's car. "How's the baby?"

"Buggers got me sick every morning lately," Mary said as she stopped walking and turned to Frances, taking her hands. "Frances, you won't be angry with me forever?"

"No."

"Because I couldn't stand it if you were." She placed Frances' hand on her belly. "You're her godmother, you know, so we need you to be here."

Frances hesitated. "I'm not going anywhere, Mary," she said feeling again how she'd no hope now for her life with Alessandro gone and her marriage over. "I've got nowhere to go."

"Mary, come on!" Frank hollered out to her from by the car. "Got to get on the road. Long drive."

Mary turned to Frances with tears in her eyes. "Please don't be mad at me. I can't do all this without you. I'm scared to have this baby, Franny and you're the only one I can tell this secret to. Please don't cut me out for too much longer."

"You're going to be a wonderful mom." Frances grabbed Mary into an embrace where the two friends hugged each other like they were never going to see each other again.

Frank and Mary got in the car and Mary waved out the window as their car drove away and she yelled out, "I love you!"

Frances waved back with a smile on her face, then stopped when the car was far away and her smile retracted. It was the second time in recent memory that she'd stood on the side of the road and watched someone she loved leave, both equally painful for different reasons and yet she felt so tired from it all, like she could just lay down and sleep for years.

Part Three

Surrender

Chapter Seventeen

Alone now, by circumstance and by choice, Frances paused her life, looking at her existence as if it were a reflecting pool. Spiraling down, she was in crisis, more unsure of herself now than during any other time of her twenty years. No understanding of where her life was headed overwhelmed her and trying to accept who she'd become consumed her.

She retreated, staying day after day in her bedroom, searching for peace, clarity, direction, but didn't find it. Each day was the same. She was confused, bitter, unhappy, numb, yet still not clear. Days turned into months and the passing of time made her lose hope that she'd ever get better. Waiting it out wasn't working. Frances knew she had to get stronger and force herself to live again, despite it feeling pointless. Solitude was a punishment she'd given herself and only she could decide to end it.

Early one Saturday morning she rode her bike to the club as she had for years to play tennis with Mary, but this time she wasn't meeting anyone. She parked her bike at the club entrance and went inside, saying hello to the staff she'd known her whole life. They greeted her yet seemed shocked to see her. This confirmed she'd been the subject of gossip since calling off the wedding. *What if they knew I'd spent the night in the arms of an Italian POW?* she thought, as she took in their innuendos about her from the looks on their faces, wide eyes, open mouths, raised eyebrows.

"Their jaws would be on the floor," she mumbled to herself.

She had suspected the sudden cancellation of her wedding was news yet didn't understand it was the biggest gossip tidbit in town. Because Nicholas was free, thanks to Frances backing out of the wedding, he was available for the single girls. Her loss was their gain. Then there was her disappearance that added juiciness to the story and a mystery to be solved. What is wrong with her? Has she gone mad? What really happened between them? Most versions of their relationship demise painted Frances in bad light, perpetuated by Mrs. Draper who hinted to anyone who would listen, that it had been Frances' obstinate personality that caused Nicholas to end it.

Her parents were crushed by her transformation into a hermit. Helen knew, as a mother does, that there was more going on with Frances than just the ending of her engagement, but Frances wouldn't talk. Physically present, yet nothing about their little girl was the same and nothing they tried helped. Frances understood that she'd disappointed her parents, Nicholas, Mary, Mrs. Draper, all of them. Even Alessandro, by taking him that night to be with her while telling him she was marrying another man.

But of all those she'd disappointed, how it hurt her relationship with Mary devastated Frances the most. She thought Mary was the one person who wouldn't judge her. She was wrong. Sitting in the mess she'd made that the passing of time wasn't fixing, she hid out from the world. Working at Torney made her feel like something of a hero. Now she felt like a terrible person, a traitor, who'd let everyone down. Falling this far was humiliating. She had only one thing on her side: she'd been brave. All this fallout was the aftermath of this bravery. Henry had failed to mention that being brave was hard, something she'd tell him when alone in her room.

You didn't tell me the bad side, Oklahoma. You left a lot out, Oklahoma. I know you hear me up there, Oklahoma...

Frances walked into the tennis store and purchased four cans of tennis balls. They were back to cans now that the war was over. She'd thrown out her old ones that morning after testing them as she'd last played with Mary before she got pregnant. She'd attempted to bounce a ball—flat. She'd toss it in the trash, try another ball—flat. Toss it in the trash. She did this to five bags of balls, each held four. Tossing them into the trash was surprisingly cathartic, helping more than anything she'd done to try and get it together. A symbolic ritual for healing.

She'd been stuck, reliving her life the past two years, trying to understand who she was after saying goodbye to Mary, Nicholas, Alessandro, Oklahoma and all the men and women she worked with at Torney. The simple act of bouncing the old tennis balls to see if they'd gone flat, then learning that they had and tossing them into the disposal bin helped her accept what was now. *I'm done living dead,* she told herself as she put the lid on the trash can.

Stepping on to court #4, she opened the three cans of new balls, using the sardine-can key, savoring the satisfying whoosh. She placed them into a basket on the serve line. One by one, as she tossed the ball up and whipped her right arm around to slice a serve into the opposing square. She knew she'd be okay. She hadn't been sure she would in her months of solitude, hiding out from life as her parents worried. They saw her transformation from a vibrant young woman into a zombie. Scared, they had talks about going to a hospital for care which Frances refused. There was nothing wrong that medicine could fix. "Time heals all wounds," her mother would go to when nothing else worked and hoped that her daughter would come out of it when she'd had enough time. Frances pushed back every time. She wasn't ready until today. It finally clicked that she needed to live life, not just exist She was ready now.

Ned walked by the court, surprised to see her. "Playing against yourself, I see."

"Yeah. But you're here now. Wanna volley?"

He came onto the court and took his racket out of the backpack swung off his shoulder. "I like to win so don't expect me to go easy on you."

"I'm not worried about it. You won't win. I've seen you play."

"That hurt." His chest caved in like she'd socked him and he grabbed at his heart.

Frances giggled. "Ned, get back to the serve line. Time to eat the ball."

"Ha. You got a lotta gumption, girlie," he said as he took a position on the opposite side of the net.

"I'm known for it. I hear I've got quite a reputation now for my gumption."

"Eh, it's dying down lately."

"The talk about me?"

"Yeah."

"Good."

When she arrived at the serve line, she looked at him seriously, whipped her right arm back, tossed the ball up high and smacked it down hard, slicing to the left and just at the back line corner. Ned reached for it hard, lunging to the side as if his honor depended on him returning her serve and landed on the court in defeat as the ball sliced just underneath his racket.

Frances rushed over when he made a moan sound and grabbed his knee like it was injured. "Ned? You hurt?"

"No. I think my leg is broken!"

"Really?"

"And my arm." He continued which laying on the court and not getting up seemingly because he couldn't.

"Should I call someone? What should I do?" she answered, scared and kneeling beside him.

"And my toes are broken."

"What?"

"And my nose."

She rolled her eyes, aware that she was being played. "Your nose isn't broken, you pretender." She pushed his nose with her racquet to make her point.

"Ouch, ouch."

"Stop lying Pinocchio!"

He sat up, cracking up at the prank. "You may beat me at tennis, but I'll always beat you in pranks!"

He stood up and held out his hand to help her up and she resisted taking it.

"How do I know I can trust you?"

"You don't."

She pushed his hand away with her racket. "Not gonna chance it." Laughing too hard now as she pushed herself up to a stand. "Ah, you got me to laugh, Ned."

"I'm good for a laugh."

"How's Mary?"

"Still a brat."

"Stop it!"

"She's my baby sister so I can call her a brat."

"Wish long distance calls didn't cost so much so I could talk to her more. I miss her."

"Me too."

"No!"

"It true. I miss my bratty sister."

Frances tapped him on the shoulder. "Come on. Volley with me. It's been a while since I've played."

Ned nodded, "Right. No more joking around."

Each returned to their sides of the court and volleyed for a while before taking a break for water. They stood under the awning for shade wiping off sweat with their athletic towels.

"You've gotten better," said Frances.

"You've gotten worse."

"Yeah, can't argue with that."

"I gotta get going. My dad needs me to help him figure out why his car won't start."

"Does it have gas?" They giggled at this.

"It has gas."

"Well..." She said, unsure of where to take this. "You're not such a jerk after all."

"Never was."

"Well, as my best friend's older brother, this made you the easy target."

"Who'd a thought you and me could actually get along?"

"Yeah."

"Wanna see a move some night?"

"Ned, are you asking me out?"

"I'm not sure. Yes? Maybe I am." He answered charismatically, both understanding the awkwardness of the moment.

She thought about it. Was Ned someone she should've loved her whole life but missed it? "Maybe. I'm still sorting myself out."

"Let's go as friends. See if anything comes from that—sound good?"

"Could use a tennis partner for Saturday mornings. You available?"

"Next week?"

"Eight a.m."

"Deal."

Frances practiced her serve a while longer before going into the café to get a lemonade at the counter. She could only stand being there for ten minutes because all eyes were on her. This kind of local celebrity wasn't what she wanted and remembered when she was with Nicholas and all the women looked at her with envy. No young girl wanted to be her now.

Four Saturdays later, after playing Ned week after week, she no longer felt awkward being out in the world. She'd practiced being human again, repeat exposures so she could return from a wounded, timid creature stuck in her room, to a functioning member of society. She worked at the library reading to kids for story time, becoming a star in their eyes, acting out the characters, roaring if there was a lion, meowing if there was a kitten. She began to feel like herself again. She'd even gone to see a movie with Ned and instead of becoming his love interest, she'd become his sounding board for a girl he was dating. Yet when he'd get frustrated with his girl, he'd ask Frances to marry him and she'd tell him that she can't marry her brother. He'd remind her that they weren't blood relatives. What she thought, yet could not say, is that Alessandro was the only man she wanted, still. She belonged to him for now at least, until she didn't. It was just this way despite the space between them. Alessandro held her heart and had since the day she clasped his hand for the first time. She was devoted to him and didn't want to let it go, not yet at least.

Many months later, she rode her bike down Palm Canyon Drive, heading to the Red Cross office that was set up at the edge of the popular part of the street, where the stylish restaurants and clothing stores weaned down to the less attractive businesses for tourists such as insurance agents and plumbers. In the notable area of the paper that morning, there was a blurb about a woman working with the Red Cross in Italy who'd visited a friend in Palm Springs. Frances wanted to know about this program.

Miss McClung, Enroute to Italy, Visits Miss Harrod here. As food administrator for southern Italy with the American Red Cross, she visited several days last week with Miss Neva Belle Harrod while on a month's furlough, is returning to Italy. While here, she spoke to a group of Roosevelt school children. (Source: The Desert Sun Newspaper).

. . .

She got off her bike and walked up to the window that had all the messages she used to be bombarded with while a Gray Lady. Blood donations needed. Money donations needed. First aide donations needed. Volunteers needed. The messages were plastered all over the window so anyone going by would see the need to help. She peered inside the window, hoping she'd see Edith, but it was Carla sitting behind the desk.

"Frances!" Carla yelled out, startled.

"Look like you saw a ghost."

"Been a while. Heard you...".

"Lost my mind?"

"Well," Carla answered, "you said it."

"Everyone's been saying it and if they don't say it, they're thinking it."

"Gossips."

"Town's full of 'em. Always has been and always will be." Frances read some of the volunteer adds put up on the wall for patrons to read.

Carla looked down at some papers on her desk. "I'll say it then. Can't believe you let Nicholas get away. That boy, if I was back at your age, I'd scoop him up and I'd be living it right."

"I got away. Had to."

Carla folded her arms and eyed her with her lips pursed. Frances felt her disapproval.

"Carla, you can stop."

"What?"

"Acting like my life is yours."

Carla stopped a second, "Well..."

"Don't be offended. Everyone does it. I should have married Nicholas – that's what everyone says, like my life is theirs."

"Was hoping to see Edith Marshall here."

"She went back home to Ohio where she grew up. Her mom passed and she inherited the house."

Frances remembered the story about Clarence and thought how

lovely it would be if Edith found Clarence and they finished their love story from so long ago. With mixed marriages illegal and how lives change with the flowing years, she knew it wasn't likely. But one could dream.

"You come by just to reminisce?"

"And donate blood."

Carla laughed. "Then let's do this. Can you fill this out for me please?" She handed a clipboard to Frances with all the same questions she used to get asked when she donated at Torney. "Not many donating these days."

Frances quickly filled out the form, check, check, check, then her signature. She handed over the clipboard.

"Frances Clark!" Carla looked like she saw something horrible. "These answers…"

"Yes?"

"Well, you've lied on your form."

"Says who?"

"You do get lightheaded after donating. You do faint after donating."

"Nope."

Carla gestured to the lab area.

"I am not sure what is going on."

"I'm different now." Frances smiled. "I'm stronger, Carla. I don't faint anymore."

"We'll see."

Carla inserted a needle into her arm. Frances watched, not wincing even when the needle punctured her skin and went to speak, getting cut off.

"Sitting back and relaxing now. No need to tell me."

Carla smiled. "World's gone crazy."

Frances closed her eyes. *Oklahoma, being brave is hard,* she thought, talking to him in her head as she did often. *The truth is that I miss you.* The *you* she meant to be all of them, Mary, Alessandro, Oklahoma, even the girl she used to be. She had conversations with him, with Alessandro and even at times with Mary. All three gone from her life. She would answer for them with what she thought they would say. It was ridiculous, she knew, but it was Frances' way of coping during her solitude and helped her to reflect and contemplate. This led to her deciding, despite all that had happened, that she liked herself again. She liked who she'd become and enjoyed her own company. She wasn't afraid anymore and she wasn't waiting for anything anymore. Not for Nicholas to return, not for Oklahoma to die, not for the war to end, not even for Alessandro to come back into her life. Nicholas returned. Oklahoma died. Alessandro left and would never come back. And Mary was gone too, but she had herself back and this was, it turns out, the person she needed most of all.

Frances opened her eyes when she felt Carla taking the needle out. "All done?"

She placed a bandage over the insertion site. "One second. Don't get up." Carla warned.

Frances waited, looking around the office.

Carla returned with a glass of juice and crackers for her to eat. "Here, have this and you're staying here 15 minutes. Don't care what you put down on that form 'cause I know you lied."

"I haven't fainted so no lie." Frances added with a snarky bent.

"Carla, you know that woman, Miss McClung, who was just visiting here and works with the American Red Cross in Italy?"

"What about her?"

"How do I apply to work for that program?"

"You wanna go to Italy?" Carla seemed baffled, then as if she got clarity, as if she put it all together.

"You know the gossips in town..." she paused, knowing she was lighting a flame with her next words.

"Go on." Frances taunted her, unafraid of what might be said.

"They speculate there was a POW, the one that played the violin and that you know him."

"Who speculates?"

"An officer. Told us you came around the barracks to see the dago more than once."

Frances raised her chin up. "Work related, that's why and only why. You're not suggesting I've done anything inappropriate, Carla?"

"Not for me to say. Just saying he said it and some others wondered.

"You wonder?"

"No, of course not. A nice girl like you would never make such a mistake." She said, as if telling Frances not to make the mistake of going after Alessandro.

"Of course not." Frances answered. "Nice girls like me do what's right. Always."

"That's what I said to him, of course."

"Of course." Frances agreed, as a threat. "Now, the program?"

Frances walked out of the office holding a stack of instructions and application for the Red Cross overseas program when, across the street, she saw Nicholas walking with a young lady she'd never seen. They saw each other and he stopped, staring at her from across the street. Nicholas said something to the girl, kissed her on the cheek and rushed across the street to Frances while the girl sat on a planter waiting for him.

"Nicholas," she said, surprised.

"Hello Franny." He looked uncomfortable.

She said, "I hear you're doing well."

"Yeah, you hear that?"

"My mom tells me all the gossip."

"What gossip?"

"That you're the catch of the town and every girl wants to date you, which is obviously true." Frances nodded to the pretty girl across the street waiting for him to return.

He laughed and they both smiled at each other for the first time since he'd returned home, a genuine smile. "All but one," he answered.

"Well, rumor has it, she's gone crazy." Frances made a circle by the side of her head with her index finger and crossed her eyes.

"Eh, don't know about that."

"Your mom still hate me?"

"That I do know about. Possibly, but she'll get over it one day."

They were silent for a moment, not sure how to end the encounter. He looked at the bandage on her arm. "You give blood? Thought you hated needles."

"That was the old me."

"Ah, right. You're not the girl I left all those years ago."

"And you're not the boy who went away all those years ago," Frances fought back a tear. "Look at me."

"Cause your realizing you let a good catch go," he said and smiled slyly, giving her a sweet jab because she set him up perfectly.

"I'm sorry, Nicholas."

"I'm sorry too, Frances."

And she reached over and embraced him in a long hug.

"Will you invite me to your wedding when you—"

"Definitely not," he said almost too quickly, which made them both laugh.

They pulled out of their embrace. "You were right, Fran." He told her as he wiped a tear off her cheek.

"Hearing you say that... it's everything..."

"But you still can't come to my wedding. Unless..."

"Unless?"

"Unless you're the one I marry after all." And now he was the one choked up.

"We tried our best. But you made it home, Nicholas and that's all I ever wanted."

"Yeah."

"See you later sometime?"

"Countin' on it."

Frances stuffed the Red Cross application into her backpack with her tennis racket, swung it over her shoulders and kicked up the bike's kick stand.

"It's good to see you, Franny."

"It's good to see you, Nicholas."

Frances rode down the street, slowly, listening to the sound of her tires on the asphalt, the spin of her chain around the gears as the wind dried her tears into dry desert air and she whistled like she had before the war, when she was young and free of all she'd been through.

Upon arriving home, she checked the mailbox to find a letter from George and opened it quickly, so excited to hear from him.

Dear Frances,

Sorry it's taken me so long to write. Coming home I got myself real tied up with getting back into the swing of things here in town. I'm doing fine now. My leg is all better and I'm working at the lumberyard in town and I even got a gal who is real sweet. She reminds me of you. I've told her all about you and how you helped me when at Torney. How are you doing? I imagine you're married now. Maybe a little one on the way? Well, whatever you are doing these days, I hope you're happy and I hope you write me back. I'd like to stay in touch and want to thank you for all your help.

Your friend,

George

Frances folded the letter up and put it back in the envelope, parked her bike and went inside the house and hollered, "Mom, I got a letter from George finally."

She rushed to her room and sat at her desk.

Dear George,

I'm so happy to hear from you. It sounds as if life is going well for you. It's great that you are feeling better and that you have found some-one. I didn't marry Nicholas after all. He's a swell guy, but we didn't seem to get along as well as we did before he joined the marines. It was hard to walk away, but it was for the best. I've been busy working at the library, reading to the kids for story time and I'm thinking of maybe joining the Red Cross and maybe even one day going to school to be a nurse. Please keep in touch. I like hearing how well you are doing.

Your friend,

Frances

Frances mailed her application for the Red Cross that same day, along with her return letter to George and waited. Only Mary knew she applied. They'd talk on the phone quickly every few weeks where Mary would complain about getting to be the size of a whale, how much she missed home and how exciting it would be if Frances got to go to Italy. Frances wouldn't complain about anything, repaired by solitude and living life brave. Her life felt right, just like the night she spent in Alessandro's arms. No regrets, only possibility.

Chapter Eighteen

Walking up the loading ramp holding her luggage, she felt the pitch of the ocean underneath her for the first time. She'd never been at sea, only on the beach where she felt the power of the ocean against her body as she surfed waves, but still with the comfort of her feet being able to touch the ocean floor.

With high anxiety, she stepped onto the ship and was greeted by a Navy sailor checking names off a boarding list.

"Name?" he asked, nearly without looking up.

"Frances Clark, American Red Cross."

He scanned the list, flipped the page to the next page, finding her there. He waved to a deck cadet waiting for instructions. "Compartment 10," he told him, then looked to Frances. "Welcome aboard. Follow this cadet to your sleeping quarters." He gestured to the young sailor waiting online for his assignment.

The deck cadet waved at her to follow him after introducing himself, grabbing the larger pieces of luggage. She noticed immediately that all personnel moved quickly on the ship, not taking any time for idle chatter. It reminded her of Torney during the month they took casualties from all fronts, everyone with a purpose and every second valuable. It felt strangely reassuring.

The Navy cadet led her down the side of the vessel, through a metal door and down a metal staircase, which led to narrow hallway with rooms on each side. He opened a metal door to compartment 10. The narrow space had two bunks, one to the left and right.

"Miss, this is the berthing area, just another name the Navy likes to give to your living quarters. First to arrive, you get to choose your rack." She looked at him confused. "Ah, sorry Miss, that's just another name we call your bunk."

"Oh. Got it."

"We have all sorts of names for things here in the Navy, ma'am." They placed her luggage inside. "I need you to come with me. A quick tour for the essentials."

She followed him to the washroom, which they call the head on a navy ship he explained. Everything was so small, built only for function and with as minimal of space as possible on the ship, even the halls where they'd have to turn sideways to pass someone coming from the opposite way. Moving on to the mess, he explained chow was three hours a day at 0600, 1200, 1700. Nothing would be served outside these hours, so she'd need to make chow times a priority. Safety was essential and that she needed to be on deck at 1300 for safety instruction.

They returned to her compartment. He asked her to show the other women in her room the same tour when they arrived, then emphasized attending the required safety training which would also be announced over the 1MC, which is what they called their communication channel on the ship. He ended his fast-paced tour with "Welcome aboard!" and left quickly, closing the door behind him, leaving Frances standing alone in the metal room.

Everything was metal on the ship and it felt hollow and echoed with tin sounds. Frances stood still, as if stuck in the spot, only her eyes moving left, right, up and down. It was cold and sounds outside the room echoed inside hers, like they were all inside the same metal beast that reverberated everywhere when steps and noise were made elsewhere. She listened to the new sounds, the moans and pings and claps in the walls. She was scared, she realized, when she saw her hand shaking. This wouldn't do, being scared and behaving like a chicken. *Always be brave.* Oklahoma popped into her mind so clearly, hearing his midwestern drawl as if he were standing next to her, snapping Frances out of it.

Frances placed her suitcase on a lower bunk and opened it. Half of the space was taken by the violin case, the other half with her clothes. Frances raised the instrument up. Her fingers moved across the strings, plucking a few so they chirped and pinged, then placed the instrument under her chin and the bow against the strings, then moved it across them, back and forth as she attempted to get her fingers in place of a D Major chord, the first one she'd learned from a book she got at the library. A gentle sound reverberated around the steel walls and she softly swayed as she stood, making the violin—not exactly sing, but speak. Back and forth, she moved the bow across the strings and moved her fingers into the few chords she'd learned before hitting an off-key sound which made her smile. Alessandro never hit an off-key note with this old beast of a fiddle. That was why she smiled. She thought of him again and peered into the body of the instrument.

Underneath the circular hole under the strings, faintly carved into the wood was a heart shape and inside the heart was A + F.

"Alessandro loves Frances," she whispered faintly as she reached her finger under the strings and touched the etching on the interior of the violin body.

She'd noticed this carving only a month before, after she got the offer to go to Naples and she saw it as a sign that she should go, despite her fears. Maybe they'd meet again and she'd give him back the violin that should be his. *Find me,* he'd asked her outside the barracks when she tried to give it to him before. She answered him with crushing words. *I can't. I'm marrying Nicholas.*

Now she was on a ship headed towards Naples, Italy. Not near his hometown of Milan, a good ten hour drive she'd heard from the women at the Red Cross office when she asked them if they happened to know how far it was to Milan, where she had an old friend. She wanted to go there at some point to visit her friend. They gave her an estimate, eight or nine hours, or so. She didn't know how this would end with Alessandro. Maybe she'd find him. Maybe not. Maybe he still loved her. Maybe not. Maybe it wasn't too late for them. Maybe it was too late. It was all uncertain, that was all she knew, but Frances had hope that she would at least find him to deliver the fiddle, to tell him she was sorry for hurting him and that she was sure of only one thing in life these days, that she loved him.

Frances placed the violin back into the suitcase and found a spot for it under her bunk. A deep breath followed, as if she needed more oxygen while she took in her surroundings. Hands steady now, she leaned back against the metal wall behind her, shaking off the chaos of the busy morning. Her mom carried on during the four-hour drive to the Long Beach port, trying to get Frances to back out, which only made Frances more determined to go. It was time to get away from home to find her own way. She was ready.

The door opened and another Red Cross worker was shown the compartment by the cadet.

"Hi. I'm Christina from San Diego," the young woman said as she came in and placed her suitcase in the center of the space.

"Frances from Palm Springs," she answered, then the seaman informed Christina that Frances would show her around, then left.

"Anyone else in here yet?"

"No."

"Then I guess we got lucky and get the bottom bunks." Christina placed her suitcase on the opposite lower bunk.

"Guess so. You ready for that tour?"

"Sounds good."

"Don't get your expectations too high, it's not a luxury yacht," Frances warned and they stepped back into the narrow hall. "And I may get lost as I just got her 30 minutes ago."

"Oh well, I wouldn't worry about it. How lost can we get on a ship?"

"Are you stationed in Naples?" Frances asked.

"Yes."

"Me too."

They headed out. "What brings you here?" Frances asked.

"I'm a widow. I lost my husband in the war. Figured I'd do something crazy, so here I am."

Frances stopped and took her hand. "I'm sorry," she said with genuine care and pulled Christina into an embrace like she was a friend she'd known her whole life. "You got me now."

Christina pulled back and wiped away tears that had built in her eyes. "Thank you, Frances."

Frances gave her the same tour she got from the cadet while thinking that this could have been her had Nicholas been killed. So grateful, was all she kept thinking as they walked through the ship, commenting on this and that, that he returned safely. This outcome was always there when he was away, a possible future life where she was the grieving fiancée and his family would have to endure the loss of their son. It was one of three outcomes. He'd not return. He'd return injured. He'd return unhurt. Those three futures were possible every day when he was away fighting. What her life would look like with each path played in her mind over and over. The outcome was out of her control and in the hands of the time's randomness. It was maddening some days then, but now she lived in an outcome she'd never imagined. That her future was living with the faint hope that she'd one day be with the man she loved, while living with guilt for betraying the man who loved her. She thought of the person she'd become during all those years waiting for Nicholas to return home, changed in every way during that time so that she became a girl who would sleep with her lover out of wedlock, in a date palm orchard, behind her fiancé's back. She had no regrets about her night with Alessandro, but guilt for betraying Nicholas was another matter. It lingered still and she figured it would throughout her life.

Sometimes she'd remember back to Mary teasing her that Frances Clark always gets what she wants, like her best friend was bullying her while pretending she was joking. She wanted Alessandro and had him for a moment, but she wanted him forever. Time will tell, she'd remind herself and would think of her mother saying time heals all wounds. She knew that wasn't true now. Time didn't heal all wounds, it just altered them so one could see other sides of the wound, but the wound never healed completely. Time would tell all once it passed. That was true. Would Alessandro be in her life again? Time would tell. There was randomness too, where what she wanted may not be. She read somewhere in the paper a line that stuck with her. We make plans, but our hearts do not listen. She didn't want to love Alessandro like this. She tried to wipe away what she felt inside for him, planning to go forward with marrying Nicholas, following through with that plan until the last minute, hoping her heart would follow, but it didn't, proving that we make plans, but our hearts never listen.

The other women arrived in their "compartments" and not more than an hour later, they all stood on the deck as the ship moved away from port.

"Can you believe it! We're going!" Frances grabbed both of Christina's hands excited as the ships horns blew.

"Can't believe it. We're going to Italy!" Christina yelled out.

The women waved to strangers on the pier excitedly who waved back.

"They don't know who we are." Christina yelled over the bellow of the ships horns.

"It doesn't matter. We wave and they wave. It's just what you do."

"I've never been away from home."

"Me neither." Frances yelled back. Her parents had left to go back home already, which she insisted they do, yet now as the ship pulled away from the shore, she wished they were on the deck waving goodbye. Leaving them for the first time, she felt now what her mother felt on the drive to the port. A part of her pulling away and this is what she knew was called missing your loved ones and she was not even out to sea or even a day from leaving them.

A young woman she'd seen kissing a man goodbye on the pier stood a few feet away wiping tears as she waved goodbye to him. She remembered how horrible it felt when she said her last goodbye to Alessandro before he ran back to the barracks. How after she waited on the side of the road, throwing rocks into the desert, hoping for one more sight of him as the caravan drove past. And the desperation she felt when she showed up at Mary's house that morning, sure she would die from losing him. Nothing hurt worse, she knew now and felt bad for the young woman but knew the girl would survive as she had.

The wind created from the ship moving out whipped up more excitement for the departure, giving action to the air that was stale on the shore. *I feel so alive,* Frances thought and could not stop smiling. The ship's horn continued to blow. Seagulls followed the ship like it was a moveable island they could set down on. She watched them zip and zoom in the breeze.

"Those gulls remind me of doing ribbon on a stick in gymnastics." Christina yelled out as she grabbed her long hair again to keep it from flying in front of her face, then motioned her free arm in the air as if she held a ribbon on a stick.

"What's ribbon on a stick?"

"You know. It's a ribbon on a stick and you move it around as you dance. Didn't you do gymnastics in gym?"

"No, I played tennis," Frances answered, thinking what else don't I know about from never getting out of Palm Springs.

The ship's engine churned, moving faster as it left the port, increasing speed to get them further out to sea. Frances stayed on the deck after Christina went back to the room, watching the California coast recede. "Alessandro. Alessandro. Alessandro," she whispered out to the vast ocean, like a mantra she'd speak when needing to calm herself.

She was moving closer to him as the ship took her towards Europe yet she knew little of how to find him. She knew his father had a bakery on a street in Milan where in the midday the sun rose between two tall buildings so that its rays streamed between them and landed on the front window of the bakery, lighting up the pastries so that their crusts sparkled like 24-carat gold. She knew his mother Bella passed away when he was young. That his big sister Natalia looked after him. That he worked at the bakery in the early morning with his father before school. How he loved the smell of fresh baked bread better than the smell of roses. That he was a professional violinist. Would she find the bakery? Did it survive the war? Was he performing again? Would she find him standing on a stage playing for thousands of people? And if she found him, would she learn that he was in love with someone else? Or even that he was married now? She didn't know him well, only that his smile was magnificent. His face perfection. That she felt at home when she was with him. "I love you, Alessandro," she said out loud because she was alone. She trusted that truth despite all the uncertainty of their situation. Time apart had only made her love him more.

She stayed on deck until the California shore was no longer visible and she was out in the vast sea of flat, blue, endless water. *No turning back now*, she thought, as an announcement came over the loudspeaker, "First call. Safety training. Main deck." Frances left the corner of the deck she'd been hiding in and joined the others for safety training, which wound up making her feel more nervous than safe.

"Now I know all that can go wrong," she told Christina. "I wish I didn't."

"Me too. Rather be ignorant than have all this safety training."

"I don't wanna know where the lifeboats are in case the ship sinks because there are sharks in the ocean and those lifeboats can't stop a shark from eating us."

"A bit of looking on the dark side."

"It's important that I stay away from all sharks."

It was only a few hours in when Frances became queasy. Seasickness kicked in and she spent much of her time for the next day vomiting in the head and having to visit the sick bay. The medic prescribed water, saltines, fresh air and focusing on one direction in the horizon, but this would trigger a feeling of claustrophobia. Having never been at sea, not having land in sight as an anchor image on the horizon like a mountain or a tree, she felt too contained on the vessel.

"I'm ready to get off this ship." She lamented to the other women in her compartment who had all, except one, felt ill.

"Unless you can fly, you're here for two weeks," the older gal on the top bunk told her, which made them laugh.

"I wish I could fly," Frances moaned back as she lay on her bunk miserable.

"Me too," Christina added. "I'm taking a plane when I go back home. I'm never getting on one of these blasted tin cans again."

"If this is what morning sickness feels like, I'm not having kids."

Packed, the ship was cramped, a sardine can of military and civilian workers, which didn't help make those early travel days with sea sickness fun. There were four in their small compartment, so the only space Frances had was either on the deck or on her bunk, as she hoped to get better. She'd never been uncomfortable before, being an only child with well-to-do parents. She'd never had to share a room with a sibling or wait for her turn to use the head. It was a rude awakening that life wasn't as easy as she thought and she wished she were home in her comfortable room and bed.

"I miss having my own bathroom." She'd say after having someone repeatedly knock on the bathroom door when she was too nauseous to leave the toilet.

"I miss land. I'm sick of being on water." Christina would chime in.

"I miss my comfortable bed." She'd complain at night when her thin mattress felt like a rock.

. . .

Day three, the nausea subsided.

Healthy, Frances found her way to the mess and the deck with Christina to hang out with others on the ship. In the day, she read, wrote in a journal, played charades with the women in her compartment. Mostly, she'd be on the deck, talking to people and watching the wake left by their ship. She and Christina would help clean up in the mess to keep from having idle time and help out, but the ship ran like a machine without their help, every crew member knowing their job.

While anxious, she didn't miss home too much, except for the comforts of living at home. She'd been worried, having never left her family or Palm Springs, that she'd be homesick so bad that she'd be miserable, but she was fine despite a few pings of homesickness. The trapping of her past not as strong as she'd worried. Then at night, she lay in her bunk, thinking of the day, worried about what was to come and trying to keep her anxiety from taking over. She slept, but not well since she was not used to sharing a room with other women and woke up at any small sound they made. The older woman above her bunk coughed a lot during the night which she didn't like. She took to covering her ears every time she had a coughing fit until it stopped.

A few days in, she talked to an older sailor in the galley who said he was called Master Snipe, but she could call him Chuck. He'd been with the ship since it launched and was the head engineer. He talked in short sentences, like he'd forgotten how to do long conversations. His body seemed to have an oil slick here and there. His cuticles black, neck decorated with rings of dirt, tattooed arms. Yet his face was so clean that a red rash on the rise of his cheeks and nose stood out against the white skin, as if only those parts had been in the sun too long. He told her the SS Mormacdove was a cargo transport ship and one of those hastily made ships churned out quickly during the war called a C2 ship. Chuck said it was designed for function, not beauty. Frances told him so long as it gets them across the Atlantic and back to dry land, she didn't care how it looked, to which he assured her it would. This was his fourteenth time making this journey and he didn't worry a bit about the safety of the vessel. Frances told him this was nice to hear because she had no interest in being a shark meal. Sharks are ferocious beasts, he confirmed, then told her about his adventures deep sea diving where he swam with sharks and watched them attack shark bait.

Many days in, Frances became irritable without reason and feared she'd get back into the sullen mood she'd had when she stayed in her room. She got out of bed and made herself stay engaged with everyone, fearing going back to her solitary ways. At breakfast, she talked to a cook from outside Sacramento who grew up on a farm that raised cattle. He was missing home and his dog, Huntley, who was a chocolate Labrador retriever who used to meet him outside the high school every day and walk home with him. At lunch, she talked with another guy about his life back home. He was a rodeo circuit competitor from Montana. He was married and as soon as he got out of the Navy, they planned to start a family.

On day nine, there was a storm. It was announced for all non-crew to get into their rooms for safety. It was mandatory, not an option, as the storm was large and the concern for how they would fair was grave.

On the way to her cabin, Chuck yelled as he rushed past and down a staircase to the engine room. "Get to y'ur bunk Miss! Cover y'ur ears. Close y'ur eyes! Gonna be rough! We'll turn the corner!" Tension was heavy as men yelled from all parts of the ship. Rough seas ahead! Turn 2! Pounding coming! Pitch and roll! The yelling didn't end as she made her way. It was the first time since she'd walked onto the pier with her parents that she felt scared.

The storm was rough, waves lifting and dropping the vessel like it'd been something foreign it was trying to shake off its surface. Frances tried to sleep through it in her bunk with the other women, but she and Christina whispered to each other, keeping their voices low to not disturb the other two women in the upper racks. When the metal vessel creaked from the seas attempt to break it apart, reverberating metal that made a sound Frances though sounded like a moan, like the ship was in pain, they'd reach out and hold hands. The ocean tossed the ship around on its surface with its mountain sized waves. Their whispers stopped when Ms. Landon on the top bunk asked for quiet so she could get herself asleep and ride out this damn storm unconscious, which made them all laugh. Fortunately, Frances seemed to have moved past feeling seasick. *If I can keep it together during a storm, I'm in good shape.*

It was an hour later that Frances finally dozed off as the noise of the ship lessened. The storm was dying down as the ship had moved through it and was coming out the opposite edge. Hours later she opened her eyes and the stillness of the ship told her the storm was over. *Another storm, another ending, another beginning,* she thought, as she lay there listening to Mrs. Landon breathe heavily above her. Quietly, she snuck out of the cabin and up to the deck with a blanket wrapped around her shoulders. Hazy, dim light lifted in the horizon to the East, the West still cast as night. Only a few moved around as the crew, up all night through the storm, went down for shut eye. The hustle and tension yesterday before the storm was gone. Another storm weathered and a new day began. Life moved on. She closed her eyes, felt the breeze on her face rushing past her skin, leaving tiny specks of moisture on her face with a salty scent, until a crewman asked her if she was feeling ill, to which she said she wanted fresh air. She returned to her bunk and went to sleep again, knowing their lives were in danger throughout the storm, to which she thought if my life was never in danger, then I'm not really living.

The day before they were to arrive, rain came again. This time a light rain mixed with winds switching directions so that the droplets almost didn't know which way to fall out of the sky. It reminded Frances of a snow globe she had as a little girl of Santa's North Pole and wished the raindrops would turn to snowflakes so she could see them swirling around before falling into the ocean. *So much water,* she would think every day on the ship, *water, water and more water.* The ocean was massive, the world bigger and different than the world she left behind. Oklahoma, Nicholas, Alessandro, all the soldiers she'd worked with for years at Torney had all been out here, in the world, on the ocean, in far off lands like the Solomon Islands, Europe, North Africa before they came to Torney. Travelers walking through battles that tested them and made them question everything. She'd give them a harmonica to play, a book to read or a smile on a hard day. Some went home, some were shipped home in a casket, but each of them before they came to Torney had been out in the world, in storms, in battles, afraid to be killed or to kill.

She couldn't imagine being on a ship and knowing you had to storm a beach that was entrenched with the enemy who could see you, but you couldn't see them.

It was the night before they were to land in Naples. No war raged in Italy now, just the repairing of what the war had broken: food supplies, work opportunities, housing, displacement. She didn't approach the shore knowing she would be shot at and may end her life on beaches of Naples like they had in Normandy. It was unthinkable for her to try and imagine how the soldiers felt. Impossible unless you'd been there and absurd to even try. Torney patients knew what that was like and as she eagerly awaited being able to get to dry land and off the ship, she kept thinking how odd it was that most of the guys just wanted to get on with their lives. That was what she'd always seen in each guy that came through Torney, they all wanted to move on, just get on with living as best they could and they all talked about living a simple life, marrying their gal, having children, a house, a good job and that seemed to be more than enough after being out in the world.

She understood now. Well, as best she could.

Chapter Nineteen

F rances stood next to Christina on the ship deck as they neared land, taking in the sight as the ship slowly moved closer. The port was inside a half-moon curved shoreline, a natural inlet for the ship to glide into, like an open mouth on the edge of the land. How it is that I'm here, she asked herself, not yet knowing herself well enough that she could answer that she'd made it happen as the confidence she had grown still felt like shaky insecurity for as a woman in a time of men, this was hard to embrace about herself, like the magnitude of the universe, or the expanse of the human condition

Naples was old, with stone buildings created long ago like nothing Frances had seen before. The port was a mix of local fishermen boats and large vessels used for cargo and passengers so that it felt industrial and provincial. Their ship moved into the upper right side of its curved land and stationed itself parallel to a pier where American Navy men waited to secure its position for the unloading of cargo. All of this took longer than the women expected so that their excitement that had them nearly jumping up and down at the sight of land, had now turned to them sitting on the deck watching and waiting until they could disembark.

"I think the sky is a different color in Italy." Frances said to Christine as they waited with the group. "Look at that light blue." She pointed to the sky.

"It can't be different. I think it's the same sky 'cause the planet turns underneath it," Christine said, dead serious so that it made them both laugh.

"Wait, you think that's true or does the sky turn with us as the earth turns?"

"I don't know."

"I don't either," Frances added and they both started laughing. "We shouldn't ask anyone. They'll think we're dumb."

"It's our secret." Christina added.

Thirty minutes later, carrying their luggage, they departed the ship, walking down the large ramp to the pier where they were asked to step to the side by a Red Cross worker who was there to bring them to the facility. Once the eight Red Cross workers were gathered, they moved down the pier with their luggage. When they stepped onto land and the ground beneath them no longer rocked, all of them laughed at the sensation of getting their land legs back.

Frances was in awe of the city, though and took in its beauty despite the devastation from the war. She'd heard on the ship that Naples had been a center for the liberation of Italy as it was a major port for trading with Africa, so she expected damage, yet still it was surprising. She could see it on the face of the city in the marks the war left. Yet it was still beautiful.

The women were brought to a Red Cross truck and driven a few miles inland to an old apartment building the Red Cross had secured for their living space. Frances looked at the people there in the streets, some walking somewhere with intention, others going nowhere, kids playing in the street. She noticed the clothing was different than what they wore in the states. The men had pants on, but the tailoring was different. The women wore dresses, but more flowing and colorful. Another place where people lived their lives with so many similarities and with as many differences.

Their living space was an old apartment in the center of the town that the Red Cross secured. The building was a four-storied building with one two-bedroom apartment on each level. The Red Cross had the first through third floor. The top level unlivable. It had sustained so much damage that the top of the building didn't have a roof and was open to the elements. After getting herself settled in her room she shared with Christina and two other women, she took the stairs up to the top floor to look out at the city. The apartment looked as if the people who once lived there could step back into their lives in a kitchen that was unharmed by shelling. Frances walked around wondering about the family that lived there before. A kitchen rag still hung over the kitchen cabinet door. There were yellow stripes on the white towel, both now soiled from the dust so that the colors were muted. Stepping into their lost lives, looking at where they were, trying to imagine who they were, as if a historian looking through the ruins of a society that lived long ago, but war made it so that you could walk through devastation that happened so recently that the fibers on the hand towel hasn't had time to disintegrate. The soft parts of life hadn't withered, leaving only the bones to analyze.

Christina called up to her: "Frances, you up there?"

"Yeah!" she hollered back, then saw Christina's blonde hair rise from the staircase, no door or wall at the top to block her from view.

"Oh wow." She said, as she looked up at the sky.

"Such a shame." Frances said as she let go of the towel and opened a few kitchen cabinets, which were empty. "Someone took the food left."

"Hey, come on girl, some of us are going to go on a walk over to the warehouse. You wanna come?"

"Sure." Frances followed her down the stairs to the third floor where there was a wall and door that blocked them from being seen as they arrived on that level. They went down to the first level to the front door where two other young Red Cross women waited.

"Found her," Christina said.

"I was snooping on the top level," said Frances as they headed outside and down the street.

"We go up there at night to look at the stars and recover from the day."

"That tough?" Frances asked, a little nervous of what was to come.

"Not always. Depends on the day," one of them said.

They walked around the streets, showing the girls around. Frances took in the neighborhood faces, olive-skinned, darker hair. Alessandro fit here, she thought as she walked with the girls, taking in the smells and sights of Naples. Frances saw a young mother hugging her baby daughter she caught after tickling her sides and chasing her as a game. An older man sat on a chair against his apartment building, arms crossed over his lap, back straight against the chair, greeting those that walked by. All seeming to know each other.

"I like it here," Frances said to Christina.

"It's different than I imagined," Christina said as she kicked a rock down the road. Frances chased after it, to kick it next and Christina tried to beat her.

"Got it!" Frances said as the rock rolled down the road and out of sight.

"Don't go off on your own," One girl warned. "You've got to be with someone when you're not in the center. The place is safe in the day, but at night..."

"Don't worry, I'm not going out alone at night," Frances confirmed. "I'd be too scared."

The women reached the warehouse where they'd start work the next day, less than a mile walk from the apartment. They looked inside the warehouse, which had stacks of supplies just brought in from the ship they'd traveled over on, ready to be unwrapped, sorted and distributed. Afterwards, the women walked back to the apartment to eat and rest after their long journey on the ship.

. . .

Later that night, Frances and Christina went to the top floor to look out at the city. They looked out at the sky, lit with hills and lights across the view and sounds of animals and birds and city sounds she wasn't used to hearing in Palm Springs.

"You miss home yet?" Christina asked.

"Little here and there."

"I don't miss it. Is that wrong? You think I'm weird?"

"Nah, it's only your first day here. Everything's new and exciting still. Give it a few weeks."

"I don't know, Frances. I got cut off a little when Henry died?"

Frances looked at her. "What did you say?"

"When my husband died, I got sort of hard of heart. Afraid I'll stay this way."

"Your husband's name was Henry?"

"Yeah, Henry Charles Thomas. I am, or was, Mrs. Henry Charles Thomas."

"You still are and if you think of it, you're his one and only, forever. Sort of sweet."

"Never thought of it that way."

"I had a good friend named Henry who died. He was one of the first patients I worked with at the army hospital. That's why I reacted that way. I lost Henry and even though he was just my friend, it hurts bad. I can't imagine how you feel."

"That's what I'm worried about. I don't feel like I used to, you know. Got jaded from it."

"You're just protecting yourself. You'll come out of it. The way I look at it, time won't heal your broken heart, but it will show you different sides of who you are. This is just one of your sides."

"Yeah, guess so."

"So just go with it. How you are today?"

"I don't have a choice really," Christina answered and looked up above. "Even the stars look different here."

"Seem closer." Frances reached up and grabbed at one. "Got it."

Christina laughed.

Frances put her fist in her pocket, the pulled it out with an open palm. "See. It's in my pocket now." She smiled. "I'm tired," said with a yawn.

"Let's get inside."

"Goodnight stars."

It was only two days after arrival that the girls were at work distributing bundles of food to the hungry, food that was brought in on the ship and that they had to package up for handing out, machinists' keeping the engine going, tying the food inside rags one would use in a kitchen. Non-perishables like canned goods and pickled goods.

They spent their days organizing the food and then during the distribution hours every other day, they set up a table in front of the warehouse where people would line up to get their bundle. They also gave basic first aid help to those who needed it, wound bandaging, passing out Band-Aids and antiseptic cleaners. The first day on the food line, a young boy missing a leg and part of one arm below the elbow stood, leaning on a crutch made of sticks, the top softened with a rag. Frances tried not to react to his condition as she handed a bundle to him.

"Can you make it?" She asked.

"*Grazie*," he replied, then said in Italian something she couldn't understand with a smile on his face which he said repeatedly. The kid was barely twelve years old.

"How do you say, do you need help?" Frances asked another worker who spoke Italian.

"*Aiuto*."

Frances turned back, but the young boy had moved off. She went after him. "Wait..." She got in front of him. "*Aiuto?*" she said and pointed to the bundle under his arm.

He shook his head no and said with a big smile on his face. "*Grazie*."

Frances moved to the side and he moved on.

In the next week she saw him every day on food distribution day and each time she insisted on helping him carry the food home to which he said no.

One day, frustrated at his unwillingness to accept her help, Frances told Christina, "I'm going to follow him. See where he lives."

"Don't get in any trouble."

"I won't. I'll be right back."

Frances followed the boy, making sure to hide if he looked back. The longer he walked he slowed, rested, rubbed under his arm where his crudely made crutch hurt. In a building more than a mile away, she saw him go into a basement door. She debated following him inside, waited a moment, then looked around the building to see if there was a window. Around the side of the building she found one. She crouched down, wiped dust off the basement apartment window and looked inside to see the boy and an older woman going through the donated food, then the woman placed both hands on the boy's head and patted him lovingly.

"*Ehila! Ehila!*" an older man began yelling at her from down the alley, thinking she was up to no good, startling Frances so that she rushed off and back to the warehouse, making sure to mark the directions in her mind so she could return.

Getting back to the warehouse, Christina whispered. "You scared me. That was a long time. I worried that you got kidnapped."

"I know. He lives a long way from here."

"And he walks it on that stick, over and over?"

"He brought the food back to an old woman in a basement apartment. I saw them through a small window."

"Probably his nana."

"Yea." Frances told her. "He's not coming here again."

"Why."

"I'm bringing food to them." She looked back at the crates of supplies in the warehouse. "And there's gotta be crutches somewhere in this pile of stuff."

Christina placed her arm on Frances shoulder. "You're sweet."

"No, I'm mad."

Two days later, on food distribution day, Frances, Christine and another woman who was fluent in Italian headed out early to the boys home, carrying two bundles of food and a set of crutches. Frances remembered each mark she'd memorized. Left at the corner with the yellow store, straight when we hit the fork in the road until the clock store, then a sharp right and a left. Once there, Frances knocked on his basement apartment door. The old woman, frail, thin, answered and the Red Cross worker who spoke Italian told her they had food and crutches for the boy. The old woman called out to him and when he came to the door, Frances handed him the set of crutches.

"*Aiuto,*" she told him and he smiled.

"*Grazie,*" he said as he took the crutches from her.

"*Prego,*" Frances answered.

The Red Cross worker spoke to them in Italian then spoke to them both, keeping their attention in between the older woman moaning with gratitude to what was said to her. Then Christina handed the food bundle to old woman who reached out and hugged her unexpectedly. Christina was taken aback by it, uncomfortable by the show of emotion. They said *grazie* and closed the door.

On the walk back to the warehouse, the Italian-speaking Red Cross worker told their story to the women. "The boy's parents were killed when a bomb hit their apartment building. It's how he got his injuries. The older woman is his grandmother and can no longer walk at all due to her arthritis, so the boy goes out to get their food. Otherwise, they'd starve."

"I could see you didn't like getting hugged, Christina," Frances teased.

"I didn't not like getting hugged. I'm not that far gone yet," She joked.

"Nah, far from it," France said and smiled. "There's hope for you."

"Oh, jeez," Christina added. "Aren't you the clever one there being all happy I'm not an emotional jaded shell."

The boy never came to the food line again, because Frances and Christina delivered food to their apartment after this day and this became the beginning of a delivery program for those too sick or injured to make it to the warehouse. Frances was the coordinator and led the logistics of the deliveries and outreach to those who needed this added service after talking to her supervisor and explaining how she ran the library at Torney and created the instrument program.

Then one day, a young woman came to them carrying her daughter who'd cut her leg but it was getting infected. The girl was cleaned by the nurse, then Frances and Christine drove them home. They lived in a displaced persons camp on the edge of the city with hundreds of homeless or Jews freed from concentration camps or on a path to immigrate out of Europe. Young women, some with children, some without, some left without husbands who had died, or entire families, orphans, young and old men and women without anywhere else to go. Frances was shocked to see the place, a former school, where the people lived in classrooms and ate food in the auditorium. Frances was shocked by the camp, unable to speak as she and Christina walked around and explained they were from the Red Cross and heard some of their stories. How one day were living a good life in their neighborhood, in their own home and now it was all gone. Most had only what they wore and most had no family left alive, or if they did, they were all displaced. After that day, Frances added the camp to their distribution list and began visiting twice a week to deliver food and provide first aid.

Enduring rations and needing to grow victory gardens had seemed an unfair consequence to endure at home during the war. She'd think of how easier people in the states had it compared to what she was seeing in Europe and thought of how she got it as she'd read the articles in her father's newspaper. No words, once on paper, had given her the full story. It was a moment in time telling of facts, but these lives affected by all that happened, their stories were ongoing and just the beginning of years of change. Her mother did the best she could, leading efforts at home with the Woman's Club to get War Bonds purchased and making casseroles to avoid food waste, but it wasn't enough. It was so much bigger than anyone back home realized.

But she shook it off in the evenings, before the sun set, when she and Christina walked to the shore and scanned the beach surface for seashells, the ocean horizon for boats and the picturesque view under the dwindling sunlight. She'd think of Alessandro, their last moment together, his head leaning into hers, his hair, thick with waves falling over his forehead. That true and perfect moment. And when she stood in front of her mirror naked in the dim light the night, she'd risked it all just to have a moment with him, seeing herself clearly, of who she was, no disparateness, no confusion. Minutes of hyper-awareness of every part of life, being who she was without apology and these were the minutes she lived that had become more meaningful than years lived.

After they'd take their evening walk, they'd return to the apartment where they'd go to the top floor of their apartment building with the other women before turning in for the night for an even better view of the city lights, boats on the shore and those they could see in the distance, the stars and moon. And they'd discuss what went on in their day, or who got a letter from back home. Mostly they'd laugh about this or that that happened during the day, but every night before she left the roof to turn in, she'd look north, towards Milan, thinking about how she might find him.

Chapter Twenty

There was dust everywhere, on the seats, in the air, on her skin. She could smell it, taste it and feel it in her lungs. The microbes of it hiding in her pores like embedded soldiers in the dirt.

The windows on the bus were open and tires churned the dirt on the unpaved road they traveled so that it became part of the atmosphere. The cloth over the ripped seat she sat on was dirty from having absorbed it, its pattern a mash-up of small squares that reminded Frances of parquet floor in the lobby at Torney. She'd been on the bus for four or five hours now, watching countryside all around her and staying put as the bus stopped at its pickup and drop off spots. She'd only gotten off twice to relieve herself, then rushed back on, afraid the bus would leave without her and she'd be stranded.

"Wait for me please," she'd say to the driver as she stepped off, holding her bag and the violin, not trusting to leave it behind as it could be taken.

"*Andare! Andare!(Go. Go.)*" he'd say to her, being an ornery old man who'd lost his patience with life. But he waited for her both times, even when he'd been ready to leave and saw she wasn't back.

She had a hard time finding the bathroom he told her to use which was an out-house hundreds of feet behind an old, abandoned apartment building.

Frances was hard to forget as she sat behind him in the front row and asked him questions along the way. Where is this? What is that? How much longer? Over and over, she'd ask questions like a child. No map to refer to, she only had him to tell her where she was and how long until they arrived in Milan. His English was passable. Her Italian had improved a bit. As a stranger to the country, he'd give her talks about this place and that to help settle her. Ornery, he'd answer, but a softie for beautiful American girls too, he'd promised he'd get her there safe. He'd driven many Red Cross workers, young women like her, across the country since the war ended as his living and treated them like his daughters. He could tell she was getting scared the farther they drove away from Naples so as they spent hours together, he began telling her where and how long until Milan before she asked.

It was getting close to evening and Frances worried that she wouldn't be able to get there before dark and kept asking, "Will we get there before dark?" She was staying at an apartment of a woman he knew as he had a network of places to stay, was safe and inexpensive. She'd be getting there close to dark or soon after, even though they set out early in the day. The bus had a lot of stops where people got off and had to get their luggage down from the cargo rack on the top. Then people would hop on an need their luggage placed up top. The old man had a ladder he leaned against the bus and would have the suitcase handed to him as he teetered half the way up it.

She paid a good price to get the ride and afforded it by saving up her pay for a few months to have enough money. When she became eligible for time off, she was ready to make the near ten-hour trip.

Traveling to Milan, searching for a bakery she didn't know the name of and didn't know if it existed was her next adventure, one that promised to put closure on the uncertainty she'd been living with since she last saw Alessandro in the back of the military truck, being driven away. Maybe he was working as a violinist again and she'd find him performing somewhere in the city. Or maybe he never made it back to Milan after all. There was no guarantee Alessandro was even alive, as so much can happen in a year. She had clues to follow and a violin to return to him if she could find him and now she was going through with it. Maybe, kept popping into her head. Maybe I'll find him. Maybe I won't.

"Ah, the circle of it," she said as she rubbed her forehead for a second, then the bus hit a pothole and everyone inside stood.

"*Perche?*" the ornery old man asked. "*Perche cerchi?*"

"What?" She asked him.

"Why you talk of circles?"

"No. I meant my mind. It goes in circles, over and over things." She circled her finger around the side of her head. "It's maddening."

He laughed. "Young ones."

"What?"

"Brittle bones. You break too easily." He laughed again like she was so naïve due to her age.

"You don't know who you're talking to then?" she said arrogantly and with her chin up. No brittle bones in me so you can stop laughing."

"Ahhhh, have fighter here. That good. That good."

She smiled, then leaned forward and whispered to him. "I'm on a mission now. Can't tell you for what or else I'd have to kill you. Top secret US government mission. Very dangerous."

He looked at her in the rear-view mirror, now a little nervous of who he really was transporting north. She looked back at him and winked, which set him into a hooting holler of laughter which made her smile. They liked each other.

Between Naples and Milan, they drove past farmlands and forests and small villages, each place with its imprint of the war in some way there, but as they neared Milan, it seemed the bombing of the areas had been greater than in any other part of Italy they'd driven through. As the bus moved into the city, stopping in two other parts of the town that were not her stop according to the old man, she could see the beginning of the city in some parts where buildings stood strong and untouched next to buildings that were missing gaps from being hit and while still standing, no longer useable. The beauty of the architecture could still be seen despite the building being damaged and even seeing the old buildings and the history of the place from them, she felt she'd stepped into a rich, historic place.

Frances couldn't believe she was there at all, having learned about this place in the hospital room when Alessandro talked for the one and only time about missing home. Then on the third stop, the ornery man pulled over, shut off the engine and told her to get off the bus, that this was her place. She looked out at the battered old apartment building in the faint light that still hovered over them. He got off the bus and greeted a woman around forty years old with a big hug and she heard papa, papa, mi papa, being said by the woman. Frances grabbed the suitcase and the violin case and stepped off the bus.

"Frances, this is Ava, my daughter."

"*Benvenuto*, Frances."

"Back in three days," he said to her. "Good luck on your mission," he said with a wink to Frances, then got back on the bus and drove off.

Frances looked around the street that was dark now as the day was over.

"Come," Ava said to her.

"You speak English?"

"Some."

"Food?"

"No. Sleep," Frances answered as she followed Ava to her room inside her apartment, her candle lighting the way, pointing out the bathroom as they passed it. Ava said goodnight and left Frances in her room. So tired, she fell to sleep soon after arriving.

. . .

She woke early the next morning and was ready for the day as the sun rose. She looked out at the city from her apartment window, but the view was limited to a small view of the street in front of the building.

She heard Ava in the kitchen and headed out. *"Buiongiorno Ava."* Frances said as she walked into the room.

"Caffe?" Ava asked her.

"Si, grazie," Frances answered as she sat down at the kitchen table.

She served her coffee, then sat down at the table with her. "What will you do?"

"Excuse me."

"In Milan? *Missione?*"

"Oh, just here to see a friend."

"Your *missione?*"

"Si." She didn't want to tell Ava why she was there. She didn't know her and didn't trust blindly anymore.

"Is it your lover?" Ava asked.

Frances blushed. "No! Of course not."

"Why no?"

"Maybe," Frances said after and smiled.

"Buona fortuna," Ava said and smiled. *"Amore*—is a treasure."

"Si."

Ava took two hardboiled eggs from her cold box. *"Que. For missione."*

"Grazie." Frances took the eggs.

"Ava, *caffe pasteria?*"

Ava pointed north. "This way."

Shortly after, Frances began her search carrying the violin case inside a canvas bag since the handle was still broken, going half a mile away to the closest bakery Ava told her about. Once there, she asked if they knew Alessandro Reggio. They did not. She walked on, then asked people on the street the way to the nearest café Pasticceria, which led her to her next place.

She walked for hours, enjoying the beautiful city, it's destruction, it's resilience. The ornery man told her all about how British bombers hit the town and destroyed hundreds of buildings and destroyed his sewing factory where he created upholstery and drapes. The buildings so close together and many stories high with levels of brick after brick stacked tall and close. Lines of laundry between the buildings, up above the like kites stationed in the sky above the cobblestone streets.

Frances had found five cafés, knowing before walking in that they were not the bakery most likely as no tall buildings stood around them in a way that the sunlight would be narrowed and shine the light on the window. Yet she understood that this was how it was before the war and today that may not be. So, she entered and asked, *"Scusami, lo sai Alessandro Reggio?"* None of them did, so she'd leave and ask someone on the street. *"Scusami, dove si trova forno?"* And she'd be pointed this way or that by an Italian man or woman who didn't want to be bothered much. She didn't know how long she would do this ridiculous adventure. The wandering of a city she'd never been to find a man she hardly knew. It was closure at least. The final step she had to take for herself to be able to move on. She walked the city for hours thinking of Mary, who had a healthy baby girl and Nicholas who was engaged to the pretty girl she saw him walking with on the street that day. They'd all moved on with their lives. She was too, only in her unusual way, walking the streets of Milan, searching for Alessandro.

She came across a piazza with a fountain and watched birds flit around, hoping for food droppings from people eating in the square and enjoyed that nothing felt wrong. It'd been so long since nothing felt wrong that it stood out. She peeled a hardboiled egg and ate it, tossing the shells into a bush beside her. She'd already eaten a *sfogliatella* and *brioche* as she walked, enjoying the fresh pastries that tasted like nothing she'd had in Palm Springs.

A boy chased his dog across the square trying to catch the puppy who would stop, then run, stop, then run, making the boy his toy, until the boy caught him in his arms and carried him off. Two lovers leaned against the building on the right, touching each other without touching each other, she leaned close to him, he looked down at her, the curvature of his large frame taking on an umbrella form, covering her. She took off her shoe and took out a twig that had gotten inside, poking at her toe for the past mile. Across the piazza, a group of guys looking over at her, a young American girl alone in the city. She decided it was time to go.

A young woman carrying a bag of vegetables passed. *"Scusami, dove si trova formo?"* Frances asked. The girl unhappily pointed to a street to the east. She headed off, turning right on the street and found herself in the narrowest street she'd been on yet, with apartments on each side, maybe ten stories high. Laundry lines between them holding dresses and shirts and pants with few clips so it seemed ghost people were flying above. She walked a long way down the cobblestone street, counting them in her mind when her mind got bored. It was a condensed neighborhood of families who all seemed to know each other, perhaps generations having lived in the same apartments so that each had an extended family due to location not blood. Kids played stickball in the street. Women gathered to have coffee on doorsteps. Yet, no bakery in sight.

Getting tired and frustrated she leaned against a wall for a break. You are so ridiculous, she thought of herself. The feeling of peace she'd had in the piazza, gone now as she considered the ridiculousness of what she was doing, stumbling around Milan searching for Alessandro's family bakery. Tears welled up in her eyes and she couldn't keep them back, like pressure in a tire that needs to be released, she allowed herself to cry for a minute, before telling herself to knock it off.

She looked back from where she'd been and saw down at the other end of the street, at a fork in the road, was a bakery. If she'd turned left, she would have seen it. The sunlight focused between the tall buildings and landed on the front windows of the bakery. She knew, before taking one step, that she'd found it. She thought of running towards it, but was so shocked, she couldn't move. *I found him,* she thought, then picked up the bag with the violin, anxiety and excitement racing. She headed off, quickly, fast steps, yet it felt as if she were in a dream and would never get there as she passed back by the kids playing stickball and the women on the porch steps, their eyes following her, suspicious of the outsider walking on their street. She stumbled, her shoe clipping an uneven stone and almost fell, but caught herself and continued, nearly a mile, stopping in front of the bakery.

"Caffe Pasticceria Bella." She giggled and came to tears at the same time as she knew Bella was his mother's name. Frances closed her eyes, to squeeze out the tears so they could roll down her face and she could wipe them away. She filled her lungs with air, opened her eyes and let out the deep breath and pulled open the door and walked into the quaint bakery. It was smaller than she imagined based on Alessandro's description so long ago in the hospital room. Tables lined the wall with croissants, muffins, fresh baked bread, a little space of heaven in the middle of a bombed city. And yet, being there, taking in the scents, seeing the golden bread illuminated by the sun beaming into the room, the place felt like a fairy tale.

A man could be heard singing in a back room, "*Alla mattina appena alzata*

o bella ciao bella ciao bella ciao, ciao, ciao."

The bell on the door chimed as it closed behind her alerting him to a customer. Stephano came out from the back, his hair tucked under a bakers hat that was a white circle on his head that made her think of the chef afraid of knives in one of the picture books she read to the toddlers at the library.

"*Ciao,*" he said, wiping his hands with the dish rag.

She smiled, but did not speak, standing still and quiet.

He waited for her to speak, but she stared at him and did not speak. "*Brioche?*" he asked her while waving his hand over a plate of scrumptious croissants in front of her with caramel colored flaky skin.

"Yes," she answered and with that he knew how to proceed and he took tongs off an overhead hook, grabbed one and placed it on a small piece of paper and handed it to her. "*Grazie*," she said. "*Quanto?*" He waved his hands up as if to say, no payment needed to which she disagreed and took a coin out from her bag and placed it on the table. She didn't leave. He didn't know what to do with the young American girl who stood before him who didn't eat her croissant yet didn't leave the bakery.

"*Pardon*," she asked. "*La scusa...*" she said and then reverted to English in frustration. "I'm looking for Alessandro Reggio."

"Alessandro? *Siete?*"

"My name is Frances Clark. From America."

He looked stunned, as if she were a dead person who came back to life. "*Materre in guardia! Pericolo! Pericolo!*" He called out as he rushed to the back, leaving Frances alone, yet she knew he said danger which concerned her. She heard him talking heatedly with a woman and it sounded that they were fighting as they said her name repeatedly. Frances was uncomfortable and considered leaving. The woman could be his wife and that is why the old man yelled danger.

Frances backed up closer to the door, ready to flee when a young woman came out from behind the back, looking angry. The old man followed her. "You are Frances Clark?" she spoke English with a heavy Italian accent. Frances didn't answer. "Frances Clark? From America?" she asked again when Frances went speechless.

"*Si.*" Frances whispered, confused of how to take their anger.

"*Que?*" the woman said and moved close to Frances and looked her in her eyes.

"*Si.*" Frances answered.

The girl had another heated exchange with the old man, both using their hands and exaggerated expressions so that Frances worried what she'd uncovered.

The girl looked to her. "I will take you to Alessandro." The young woman took off her apron. "*Viene con me.*"

Frances followed her out of the bakery and they turned right and walked down the street. "Where are we going?"

"To Alessandro."

Frances stops walking. "*Aspettar!(wait)!*"

"No. *Viene con me. Importante.*"

"No. Who are you? His wife?" she had to know before going forward. Who was this woman to Alessandro?

"I'm Natalia."

Frances smiled. "His sister?"

"*Si.*"

"You look different."

"Different? *Come?*"

"Than how I imagined you. Alessandro told me about you."

"And he told us about you. There were many days we thought you were a girl he dreamed."

"I don't understand."

"He talks about you all the time. Heartbroken over Frances Clark."

"Alessandro?"

"Yes. My brother speaks of you often. How you helped him. "*Ora sbrigati! (now hurry)*" Frances followed her as she turned off the street, cutting down a few other alleys, walking quickly so that Frances barely could keep up. "*Ora sbrigati!*" she kept saying as they turned down many different streets until they came to a large building and stopped. "*Teatro Alla Scala,*" as if Frances should know what the building was, but she did not. Natalia entered. Frances stayed back. Natalia opened the door. "*Andiamo. Ora sbrigati!*"

Frances stepped inside the breathtaking marble foyer and stood still again. "Where are we?"

"*Teatro Alla Scala.*" Natalia grabbed her arm, "Frances Clark, *ora sbrigati!*" she said with a smile.

They passed through another set of doors to the theater with a magnificent chandelier in the center of its high ceiling. The seats were covered in red fabric that hit her eyes as a sea of vibrant red. The walls rose up from the floor with row after row of pockets for patrons to view the stage, so that not one place in the theater did not focus your eyes on the stage where an orchestra stood ready to begin as the conductor signaled begin. The orchestra began a piece she'd heard Alessandro play at Torney as she stood high in the El Mirador Tower. He was in front of the musicians as he played, the star of the group obviously. Frances placed the bag with the violin on a seat and leaned against it. There he was, on the stage. "Alessandro." She whispered. She watched as he commanded the performance.

The song ended and the conductor and Alessandro discussed something in Italian when Natalia called out, "Alessandro!" she yelled and waved her arms.

He looked out into the seating area; unable to see who was in the stands because of the lighting. "Natalia?" he yelled back, squinting and blocking the lights to see her in the back of the theater.

"*Si. Vieni qui. La fretta.*"

He rushed off the stage, worried something was wrong, then stopped when he saw Frances. "Frances?" he said, in shock.

"She came to the bakery." Natalia said, "Looking for you."

"I found you."

Overwhelmed, Alessandro asks, "You are married? No?"

"No. I didn't marry Nicholas.

"I brought you something." She held out the battered case.

"The... fiddle?"

"A violin is a fiddle. I couldn't marry Nicholas because I love you."

Natalia looked at her brother. "Alessandro?"

"Yes." He answered her.

"Did you hear her?" He looked at both like he couldn't believe what he'd heard. "She loves you."

Alessandro moved close to Frances and touched her face, gently wiping away a tear that flowed down her cheek. "Amore mio."

"Si." She answered.

And as he had so long ago, that night in the rain when she went looking for him in the laundry and went to find her, risking it all, he leaned down, placed his hand behind her neck and pulled her close and kissed her.

"*Ti amo*, Frances."

"For life."

"Alessandro?" The conductor called from the stage. The musicians were waiting for him to return to rehearsal.

"Will you wait for me?"

"Si?"

Alessandro headed back onto the stage as Frances sat down. The orchestra began again, playing that song she'd heard him practice so many nights on the old fiddle.

She closed her eyes for a second, ingesting the sounds like a meal, and thought of Oklahoma. She missed him, even more in that second than the day he died.

She opened her eyes, and the tears pooling in them trickled out.

"How ya doing Oklahoma?" she whispered to herself and wiped the tears away on her face, then answered for him. "Better, now that you're here."

END

Book Club Resources

For a free Chapter Book Club Discussion Guide, please visit www.lalalandpress.com

To request **author Rae Weiser** to visit your book club or for speaking engagement in person or virtual, please email lalaland-press@gmail.com.

Reading Group Discussion Topics:

1. What is your opinion about the **US using POWs for domestic labor**? How do you feel about the Italian Service Units receiving preferential treatment once Italy joined the allies? Did you know hundreds of thousands of POWs were in the US during WWII?

2. **Frances and Oklahoma** develop a close relationship as patient and volunteer. Discuss how the situation of being a young man never to have fallen in love and knowing he was going to pass away, and how that made their connection even more poignant. Discuss the lesson Oklahoma taught Frances, which was to be brave. Don't be a dog on a chain. Discuss the increased challenges

women of that time faced and how Frances had to challenge expectations to be her authentic self against societal pressure.

3. **Frances and Mary** are best friends until Frances wants to pursue Alessandro. Mary becomes the traitor, giving her up to Edith and pressures her to stay away from Alessandro and suppresses her communication about her true feelings by devaluing what is important to her, but claims she is trying to protect Frances. Discuss what the basis of a friendship is and the obligation one friends has over another to stand by each other? Do any of you feel Mary was genuinely doing what she thought was best for Frances? Do any of you feel Frances could have handled this situation with Mary differently?

4. **Frances and Alessandro** fall in love under uncommon circumstances. Do you believe her pursuit of him was right? How did you feel about her not letting him go? Was the relationship about him at the core, or was he the catalyst that made her understand her true self.

5. **Frances and Nicholas** are two strangers tied together by a commitment years before when they were high school sweethearts. Nicholas represents the life path Frances would have taken had she not been awakened by her work as a Gray Lady during the war and relationships she had with patients at Torney. Discuss the complexity of this relationship driven by the difficulty of obligation Frances felt towards Nicholas as a young man fighting for the country, and her own obligation to live her life authentically.

6. Through her mother and father and their guests at the dinner party, we see the underbelly of **opinions about the POWs.** Racism, name calling, even hatred towards them is expressed. We learn of the internment camps for

Japanese Americans. Discuss the layers of complexity inside the Palms Springs community during this time.

7. **Youth in America were influenced by WWII.** Discuss the challenges Frances and Mary faced, as young women and as Gray Ladies working for the Red Cross at Torney General Hospital? Such as sickness, death, depression, an uncertain future, food rationing, what is stolen from their young adult lives, as well as what might they have gained that they otherwise would not like empathy, love, service to others.

8. Frances struggled with the dropping of **nuclear bombs** by US, the mass casualties and that she felt she could not talk about this for fear of being labeled unpatriotic. Discuss how the nuclear bomb changed not only the outcome of WWII, and challenged humanity to consider that we now had the power for our own destruction.

Afterword

Thank you to my family and friends for your support. Special callout to Dylan, Cooper, Jason, Thompson, Brian, Hunter, Joyce, Mary, Skates, Rebecca.

Thank you to Robert Fisher for being the Word Engineer, offering superb guidance and confidence boosting conversations.

Thank you to Newspapers.com for saving the history of this time in Palm Springs and Southern California in your database.